I0762535

Delicious Praise for
THAT WHICH FEEDS US

"A creeping, bloody horror wrapped in sweet fruits and sugarcane; this astounding book is both a finger pointed directly at the rotting heart of colonial greed and a truly heart-pounding mystery."

—Andrew Joseph White, award-winning and *New York Times* bestselling author of *Compound Fracture*

"Set on a haunted planation, *That Which Feeds Us* is a fierce debut with vivid prose, where the lasting effects of colonialism almost suffocate you. The dreamy landscape and rich characters are lovingly rendered, and Kendall digs to the rotten core, making this the very best of YA horror. A must read."

—Jamison Shea, author of *Roar of the Lambs*

"With incisive prose that brings the plantation turned luxury resort of Kōpaʻa alive in all its excess and fruit-spoil, Kendall offers a striking Hawaiian gothic that is as terrifying as it is emotionally resonant. A deeply intimate tale of belonging, sisterhood, and intergenerational trauma bookended by larger inquiries of colonialism exploitation, *That Which Feeds Us* bites with real teeth and is sure to leave its mark."

—Jihyun Yun, author of *And the River Drags Her Down*

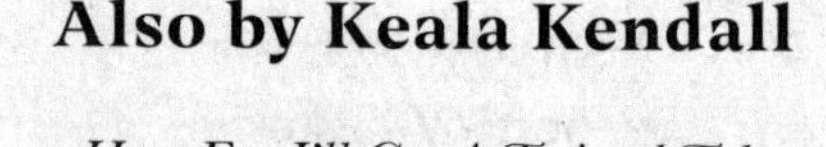

Also by Keala Kendall

How Far I'll Go: A Twisted Tale

Nobody Gets Left Behind: A Twisted Tale

THAT WHICH FEEDS US

A Hawaiian Gothic

KEALA KENDALL

RANDOM HOUSE NEW YORK

Random House Books for Young Readers
An imprint of Random House Children's Books
A division of Penguin Random House LLC
1745 Broadway, New York, NY 10019
penguinrandomhouse.com
getunderlined.com

Editor: Tiffany Liao
Cover Designer: Liz Dresner
Interior Designer: Michelle Canoni
Copy Editor: Clare Perret
Managing Editor: Rebecca Vitkus

Library of Congress Cataloging-in-Publication Data is available upon request.
ISBN 979-8-217-11796-3 (trade) — ISBN 979-8-217-11797-0 (ebook)

The text of this book is set in 11-point Baskerville.
Interior art used under license by Adobe Stock

Manufactured in the United States of America
1st Printing

The authorized representative in the EU for product safety and compliance is Penguin Random House Ireland, Morrison Chambers, 32 Nassau Street, Dublin D02 YH68, Ireland, https://eu-contact.penguin.ie.

Random House Children's Books supports the First Amendment and celebrates the right to read.

For my grandmother Joyce, a true kamaʻāina.

Hawaiʻi is this way.

LETTER FROM THE AUTHOR

When people learn I'm from Hawai'i, they tell me about their vacations. Their destination weddings. Their anniversaries and honeymoons. Their second homes. Our islands are used as a shorthand for paradise.

The "World's Enchanted Island Playground" is a vision of Hawai'i that has existed in the public consciousness since the early twentieth century. Our home was imagined into an idyllic island chain removed from modern complications—a "never-to-be-forgotten dream"—and our unique culture was romanticized to depict our islands as timeless and separated from modernity. When outsiders visit my homeland, they're looking for an escape. But that wasn't my experience when I lived in Hawai'i. To write about *my* Hawai'i was to learn about the mythmaking of paradise—a paradise I'd been priced out of—so I could uproot this myth.

I'm writing to you from Los Angeles, where I live as a part of the Native Hawaiian diaspora. We're a growing majority as more of us now live outside of Hawai'i than in it. I didn't plan to write a horror about my homeland. But as I researched this story, I realized there was no other genre that would fit this telling. As the most isolated population center on Earth, surrounded by ocean, Hawai'i is a natural fit for a gothic novel for the same reason so many come to my homeland seeking an escape—its remoteness and seclusion.

To reach the fictional resort of Kōpa'a, you'll visit the very real town of Lāhainā first. A location that no longer exists as I've depicted it. I finished the first draft of *That Which Feeds Us* in April 2023. A couple months later, when the devastating Lāhainā fire occurred, I found myself in the uncomfortable position of watching my novel become timelier due to tragedy. Ultimately, I chose not to change the pier featured in my story because of my own family memories of visiting Lāhainā, and because the same colonial history that contributed to the town's devastating wildfire is deeply entwined with the themes of this story: neocolonialism, tourism gentrification, the commodification of Indigenous culture, capitalism, settler colonialism, and the ongoing impact of the plantation era's racial and socioeconomic hierarchies and unrepentant resource exploitation on present day Hawai'i.

Once the capital of the Hawaiian Kingdom, Lāhainā used to be a flourishing wetland full of abundant forest streams. Until the 'ulu (breadfruit) groves were slashed and burned, turned into water-intensive plantations. The streams were diverted to water sugarcane, then pineapples, radically transforming the once-lush former capital's ecosystem into a dry tourist town and the site of 2023's devastation. The wildfire raced through the parched invasive grasses of those former plantations because the waters of Lāhainā are still being diverted by the same sugar oligarchs and their corporate successors: luxury real-estate developers and modern-day resorts.

As I write this, it's now been over a year since the deadly fire destroyed 2,200 structures, most residential, and Lāhainā families are still struggling to get by. By featuring Lāhainā, my hope is that the devastation and people affected will not fade from memory—forgotten in the next news cycle as they're evicted from their short-term housing to make room for incoming tourism and left to fend for themselves.

Because even paradise has ghosts.

Hawaiian hauntings and superstitions aside, *That Which Feeds Us* is inspired by real-world events and history. It is about home and legacy, family and grief, and the cost of paradise. To tell this story, I had to weed through the history of my homeland portrayed as a ripe fruit—as fantasy islands waiting to be plucked and enjoyed. As such, *That Which Feeds Us* contains discussions of death, colonialism, racism, family estrangement, abandonment, loss of home and displacement, mentions of blood, sexual harassment, and depictions of violence. Persimmons are bitter when they are harvested too soon. You have to let them ripen until they are almost rotten to enjoy them at their most flavorful. Remember, you can always choose a sweeter fruit if you find any of these topics triggering.

With all that in mind, are you ready to visit Kōpaʻa? The

resort's persimmons will soon be ripe. I can't guarantee their flesh will be sweet or that you'll enjoy your stay. Paradises are fragile. After all, the Garden of Eden was held up as the original vision of paradise—and that higher place was also felled by the taste of a forbidden fruit and another girl looking for answers.

For now, all I will say is e komo mai. Welcome.

Mahalo,
KEALA

He aliʻi ka ʻāina; he kauwā ke kanaka.

The land is chief; man is its servant.

—ʻŌlelo Noʻeau #531

1

ʻĀINA:

that which feeds; land

ONE

TWO WEEKS AGO

The week after she started at the mortuary, Lehua learned the dead didn't stay asleep.

The first time a deceased had woken up, she'd been assisting her new boss Avery in the embalming room. As the mortuary's newest initiate, Lehua had been tasked with disinfecting the man's body with a soapy sponge, working each stiff limb out of rigor mortis, readying him for Avery's scalpel and drain tube.

Lehua had been running the sponge down one of his arms when the hair along the back of her neck rose at the sudden feeling of eyes on her face.

His brown eyes. The dead man's open eyes had bored into her skull, his face etched sharp by the room's harsh fluorescent light strips. She had clamped down on her scream but dropped the sponge, splattering her newly bought scrubs with soap and water.

Avery had only glanced at Lehua. Above her respirator, her kohl-rimmed eyes had crinkled into a smile. "Sorry," she said, fitting a small plastic disk—an eye cap, she would later explain to a less shaken Lehua—beneath the man's eyelids one by one, sealing them shut once more. "Sometimes, they wake up."

Lehua suspected it had been a test from Avery. A rite for new recruits. When Lehua had handed Avery her scalpel and watched the man's skin break beneath the blade near his collarbone, she had apparently proven herself. But since that moment, the man's eyes had been scorched into Lehua's memory, their color haunting the darkness behind her own eyelids. Walnut brown, gold-veined, like the hardened sap of a tree.

Lehua remembered those amber eyes now as she looked down at the body bag on the gurney. Its zipper pulled like an open wound. Inside the tarp-like bag, the deceased—Sarah Brown—gazed ahead with glassy eyes.

Lehua had been at the Phoenix mortuary for half a year now and had seen plenty of open-eyed, slack-jawed corpses. Yet there was always a tight inhale, a squeeze in her chest, whenever the dead watched her work. She couldn't shake the eerie sense that she was moored to the dead's bedside in the hushed mortuary. But the quiet purpose centered her.

"Our work," Avery had explained when Lehua had first been hired, "requires precision."

Any mistakes, and she could ruin a family's goodbye.

Lehua rolled the gurney through the crematorium's double-wide doors. A row of steel cremators reflected the room's sterile light. Each machine was flanked by an adjoined observation room's glass window. Tonight those navy wainscoted rooms were empty.

Lehua pushed Sarah toward the nearest cremator. A wooden casket lay atop its conveyor belt. Using the body bag for leverage,

Lehua hauled Sarah into the bare pine box. She folded Sarah's stiff hands onto her stomach, noticing the delicate nail beds, the polish on their filed ends, the pale outline of a ring, now gone. Sarah had been in her apartment, sans air conditioning, for a week before a neighbor had noticed the smell. Even in November, the stubborn heat in Phoenix had only cooled so much and her pale skin had started to blister.

On a copy of Sarah's photo ID, her white bob framed a furrowed face, fringing eyes like tanzanite. Normally, Lehua would try to match the corpse in front of her to the photo. She would clean Sarah's body, plumping her cheeks with cotton before shuttering her eyes once more, and then she and Avery would give her family a chance to say goodbye. Except Sarah had no family left. Lehua would be her only send-off, a depressing party of one.

Lehua flicked on the cremator's touchscreen and started preheating the furnace for Sarah's exit. She didn't carry the same dark humor as her boss. The dead they prepared weren't asleep, their ghosts on the verge of waking up. No.

Growing up, she'd inherited a legacy of native Hawaiian superstitions from her grandparents. "We never kill night moths," her grandfather used to whisper, gently cupping the dusty-winged creatures that darted inside their home. "They're the spirits of our visiting loved ones."

She thought she had already uprooted those seeds of island superstition when her grandparents had died and no night moths came to visit her. But when she'd met the man's eyes that first week at the mortuary, what had surprised her was how blank they'd been. How empty.

That's what's next? she'd thought, her heart seizing in her chest like it'd been trapped in a vice, strangling the remaining roots of her grandparents' stories. Back then, she'd felt like a fortune teller gazing too far into the future, unable to unsee what they'd learned. Now, it was with finality that she met Sarah's dead eyes. *That's what's next.*

Lehua stepped away from the casket, unlocked her phone to clock the cremation time, and froze.

Six missed calls. All from her twin. Ohia.

Lehua considered ignoring her, but whatever peace the mortuary's night shift and its collection of dead had brought her was lost. Ohia hadn't called in three months. Not since their fight.

Since Lehua had dropped out of college, they repeated the same conversation about how Lehua was "letting her future drift away" every time they spoke. Only it had ended differently the last time they saw each other. Ohia had looked at her accusingly from beneath her dark lashes, her mouth had crushed into a disdainful line, and she'd said: "You're wasting your life away."

Lehua had been too shocked to say the words rising in her throat now: *Screw you, Ohia*. But six calls in the last half hour alone meant something bad had happened. Because Lehua wouldn't be her sister's first call in an emergency. She'd be Ohia's last.

Lehua retreated into the observation room. Through the viewing glass, she could still see Sarah in her casket, blue eyes staring up as Lehua dialed her sister. She rapped her knuckles against the glass, waiting.

Ohia picked up on the second ring.

"There you are," her twin said by way of greeting.

"What's wrong?" The words were out before Lehua could stop them, but she had no idea how else to start. Growing up, she and Ohia had been inseparable. But a rift had been growing between them, even before their fight. Lehua had wondered if there was an elusive shorthand she was missing, the way twins like them were supposed to communicate.

Now the silence that followed went long enough that Lehua was convinced Ohia had hung up on her.

"Jesus, Le. Nothing's wrong," her twin finally answered, laughing low. "I'm going home. I got a job on a small island farm near Maui—"

"Oh," said Lehua without meaning to, wondering if the cremation retort roaring in the other room had messed with her hearing. "Home like Hawai'i?"

"Yes, like Hawai'i," snorted Ohia.

"On a farm?" Lehua tried to keep the skepticism out of her voice.

"Yeah, it's like an internship."

That's why you're calling? Annoyance spiked through Lehua. *That's it?*

She tried to picture the homeland she'd only seen in photos. The islands their mom had abandoned them for shortly after their birth, leaving them in Arizona to be raised by their grandparents. Their grandparents had been nostalgic for their homeland, too, sharing its legends before they'd died, and their wistfulness had been contagious. Enough so that when Lehua imagined the islands, they were like a fairy tale long worn into memory, effervescent and hazy. But she could clearly imagine Ohia in Hawai'i, watching the tide ebb and flow, her umbra eyes shining like the blown-out end of a smoldering match.

The mortuary's viewing glass reflected Lehua's own smudged silhouette. Her short curls fell like a crow's bent wing over her shaved undercut, and her eyes were two inkblots. The mortuary was the one place where Lehua fit and Ohia didn't, which had been a large part of its appeal. When she had told Ohia about her job, her sunny sister had reliably shuddered. "Never touch me again."

Lehua knew she should be glad for Ohia. A better sister might've pried for details, gushing about how *lucky* her twin was, exclaiming at all the right moments. And she wanted to be. But all Lehua heard was *You're wasting your life away.*

Even living outside her sister's orbit, Lehua scrolled past enough of Ohia's interviews to know she was a top favorite among college runners nationwide. It was the type of fame they had dreamed about together, until six months ago when Lehua abandoned that dream. At least that's how Ohia interpreted her dropping out. Because her twin had never considered how it felt for Lehua to always be chasing her, and always coming second.

Lehua didn't know how farming factored into her sister's bright future as a track superstar—and she didn't care enough to ask, either.

"Well, I get off in the morning," Lehua offered, more generously than she felt. "I can pick you up for breakfast or—"

"I can't."

"You can't," Lehua repeated, hoping Ohia heard the annoyance lacing her voice. *Can't or won't?*

Ohia swallowed, a sharp break before she sighed, letting Lehua know her not-so-subtle message had been received.

"No, Le. I *can't*," she said tightly. "I'm on the boat now."

Then the words that cut deeper than Avery's scalpel, breaking skin: "I'm already gone."

TWO

NOW, FRIDAY

Please call me.

Lehua cradled her phone on the inn's veranda, her back turned toward the ocean and the saltwater wind clawing into her hoodie. The text stayed delivered—but unread.

Rain puddled along Canal Street, reflecting Lāhainā Harbor in ripples of purple, blue, and pale yellow, shining like a healing bruise.

That evening, she shared the Maui veranda with a pair of disappointed vacationers in formless kaftans. The middle-aged women leaned against the inn's wall, waiting out the rain. Fliers and posters were taped behind them, the largest of which read *Charter a Romantic Maui Dinner Boat Today.* Underneath that ad, a poster of a smiling woman with brown skin.

MISSING read a painfully familiar word above her head, the letters long and red like scratches, and Lehua thought of Ohia leaving for a small island farm. She hadn't suspected anything was wrong until two days ago when Ohia's coach had shown up at the mortuary, and cold dread had washed over her like the sea.

"Lehua?" Coach Ulrich had called, half running to keep up with her long-legged retreat to her car. "Where's Ohia?"

That had stopped her in her tracks.

Lehua hadn't spoken to him since she had dropped out and turned in her uniform. Of course his first words to her in six months had been about Ohia. Old Uzzy hadn't changed.

"Wouldn't you know? She's doing some internship on a farm."

"What internship?" he had snapped. "Ohia's on academic suspension for her failing grades. She left the team." He had frowned, implying well enough what he hadn't said. *Like you.*

Lehua had gotten in her car and rushed to Ohia's apartment. Her sister couldn't have been suspended. Uzzy had to have been mistaken. During their freshman year, Ohia had averaged a 4.0 with ease while Lehua had limped into class after practice, struggling to keep up. But when she'd gotten to Ohia's apartment, her room had been cleared out, and her roommate's girlfriend was already moving in.

"She's taking a year off," her roommate had said blithely. Lehua had left, confused and angry, reeling from the strangeness of it all. Had they been talking about the same Ohia?

Lehua turned her back to the missing-person flier stuck to the hotel. *Ohia's not missing*, she thought obstinately, scrolling through her unanswered texts.

uzzy came to see me

is everything ok

what's going on

where are you

call me

please call me

She dialed Ohia, and her twin's photo—smiling out of the corner of her mouth, her hair falling in dark waves—filled her screen. The two-second tone rang, and Lehua imagined Ohia on a nearby shoreline with a brand-new trail of freckles, answering with a scowl. *You were worried?*

That image dissipated as Ohia's phone went straight to voicemail.

She redialed. The same trill answered her. "Hi. Sorry I missed you. Leave a message and I'll get back to you—"

No. Lehua hit the End Call button. *You won't.*

That made thirty-five unanswered calls, ten voicemails, six text messages, and not a single word from her sister.

Where are you, Ohia? she thought for the tenth time that day. She'd been looking for two days now. The only certainty Lehua had that Ohia was even in Hawaiʻi was her bank charges.

After leaving Ohia's apartment, Lehua had phoned her sister's bank, claiming she'd lost her card, and had learned Ohia's last two transactions occurred on Maui two weeks ago. She had withdrawn three hundred dollars and bought something at a Lāhainā convenience store, exactly twenty-five minutes before their phone call. Lehua had immediately called out of work and booked a flight to Maui.

Yesterday, she had landed in Kahului Airport with a single bag, alone in a homeland she had never been to. She'd caught a bus to the west side of Maui and shown Ohia's photo to everyone, asking if they had seen her or heard about a small island farm, only to reserve a hotel room hours later, two paychecks poorer, red-faced and defeated.

Today had to end differently.

Lehua glanced at the time. *Almost six.* She left the veranda's shelter, departing the Maui hotel she had checked out of, and headed to the pier to continue her search. That morning, none of the local fishermen she had talked to had recognized Ohia. But they recommended coming back in the evening to ask the private charters. "She looks like a yacht girl," one of the men had said under his breath.

Tourists formed queues along the docks. In the rain, they looked like shadows behind the ocean's mist and fog. Lehua felt like a stranger walking past them. Lehua showed Ohia's photo to everyone she passed and checked the signs for the tour boats—*Maui Whale Watch. Dolphin Encounter. Sub Boat Expedition*—until she saw a pretty brown girl.

She stood separate from the tourists, wearing a green crop top and denim cutoffs that brushed her knees. The highlighted ends of her hair twisted toward her waist like an unfurled garter snake.

The girl with her crammed duffel bag didn't look like she was there for any of the cruises. She was the same age as Lehua but a full head shorter, staring at an anchored trawler boat until she noticed Lehua.

"Hi," Lehua said, caught. "Sorry."

"Can I help you?"

There was no irritation in the girl's voice, but her expression had gone from wistful to bemused. Lehua ignored the heat growing in her cheeks and offered her phone with the picture of Ohia, the false version of herself coming to life.

"I'm Lehua," she said, flashing her most winning smile, a poor facsimile of the one Ohia wore in her picture. "I'm looking for my sister, Ohia."

Her sister was the charismatic and charming twin. At least, that's what everyone said, and Lehua would be hard-pressed to disagree. In college, their teammates and friends had gathered around Ohia, pulled by a gravity Lehua had never learned to wield. On her own, some people liked Lehua all right—if they met her before Ohia.

"I'm Melia." The girl looked at Lehua's phone. "Oh, your twin," she said in a low voice, more pitying. "Sorry, I haven't seen her."

Lehua's shoulders slumped. She didn't know why she'd been so hopeful that this girl would recognize Ohia. Beyond the fact that Melia was also Pacific Islander and alone—as alone as Lehua imagined Ohia had been two weeks ago. If just one person had stopped to ask Ohia where she was heading moments before sundown, maybe Lehua wouldn't be scouring the pier now.

Melia noticed her disappointment. "How long have you been looking?"

"A day and a half."

"She disappeared around here?"

"She called me from a boat leaving Maui two weeks ago." Lehua joined Melia by the ocean's dusk-stained edge. "That's all I know."

Why was she admitting this to a stranger? She was getting

sidetracked, talking to this pretty girl. But Melia's voice was warm and vibrant, a deep alto that pulled Lehua closer, like the tide ebbing beneath the pier—and when Lehua looked at Melia and her lashes streaked with rain, she felt a strange swell of familiarity.

"So it wasn't a sunset cruise," Melia said, and the word *runaway* hung between them, unspoken but implied.

The fear of Ohia being dismissed as some runaway was exactly why Lehua hadn't called the police. After their grandparents died, she and Ohia had spent their teenage years in the Arizona foster system, and most of those years had been spent trying to stay together despite the system. She knew how things looked. Ohia was an adult. She had been suspended, left her team, and seemingly lied to everyone before disappearing. The police would file a missing person's report for Ohia, but that didn't mean they'd actually look for her. They'd assume she ran off with some guy from a frat party.

Except something else was going on. This behavior wasn't like Ohia. But whenever Lehua asked about a remote island farm, she got blank stares. A part of her was starting to believe the farm didn't exist—that Ohia had disappeared, just like their mother.

Lehua masked her unease with a smile. "Ohia was going to work on some island farm near Maui. She said it was like an internship."

Melia blinked. "I dunno about any internship, but I'm heading to some island farm near Maui," she said, jabbing a thumb toward the trawler. "It's a work–stay opportunity on a private island called Kōpaʻa. You work six days a week and they give you a weekly stipend and a place to sleep."

She tugged a battered brochure from her bag. *KŌPAʻA ISLAND RESORT, FARM, AND ORCHARD* read the creased, glossy front. A picture of black-limbed trees heavy with bright persimmons: *Start your life anew.*

The paper unfolded into a three-page pamphlet full of sleek photos, depicting white-and-walnut resort rooms, a misty Hawaiian loch surrounded by palm trees, and a horizon line of sugarcane. *Become a part of Kōpaʻa today.*

A resort? Lehua's throat tightened as she read. Melia must've noticed her souring expression because her voice softened. "I mean, it might not be the same place. But I can ask the guy onboard if he's seen your sister." She checked her phone. "We're supposed to leave in three minutes. At six."

When Ohia had called two weeks ago, it'd been a little after nine p.m. in Arizona, six in Hawaiʻi. The boat's schedule matched.

"That would be great. Thank you," Lehua said, offering Ohia's picture.

But Melia was already on the boat, her smile framed by two dimples. "I'll just point you out to him."

While she waited, Lehua typed the resort's URL into her phone. The website was frustratingly minimalist, the type that spoke of luxury and money. Lots of money. No phone number, email, or physical address, just the same photos from the pamphlet with an invitation to would-be guests: *Reap the benefits, rest in Kōpaʻa, become a planter today.*

She searched *Kopaa island.* In 1893, the twelve-thousand-acre island, originally called Pala, was purchased and renamed Kōpaʻa by a sugarcane farmer, Horace Jacobs. His father had first settled the island as a missionary. Apparently, Horace established a plantation town that thrived until the plantation closed in the 1950s. The island was rebranded into a wellness resort, which now farmed and sold persimmons, all while hosting the very rich.

Could this high-end resort really be the same place Ohia had been talking about? If so, Ohia calling it a *small island farm* seemed like a major—and intentional—understatement.

Lehua was zooming in on a newspaper article about the exclusive resort when Melia returned.

Ohia's not here, she thought, and maybe she wanted Melia to say that. *Your sister isn't on a private island resort, picking persimmons for wellness, ignoring you and your calls. She's on a* different *island farm.* But the other girl's expression wasn't optimistic. *Something is wrong.*

Melia's eyes were dark. "His boat isn't the only one they charter."

Then Lehua had no other choice. She had to go. The only way to know whether Ohia had gone to the resort was to visit the island and search for her twin herself.

KŌPAʻA ISLAND RESORT, FARM, AND ORCHARD

Start your life anew
Become a part of Kōpaʻa today

ROOTED DEEPLY IN HISTORY, HERITAGE, AND PRESERVATION

E komo mai. Kōpaʻa Resort, Farm, and Orchard welcomes you into the privacy of Horace Ira Jacobs's historic estate. As one of our workers, you will . . .

Harvest our world-famous persimmons, taking part in our proud agricultural legacy.

Unwind on your personal days, exploring our island's rich history.

Help our exclusive planters enjoy the Aloha spirit and our island, creating a connection with the land that goes beyond the surface.

Through the generations, our resort has preserved Kōpaʻa's original character and heritage. We offer an intimate retreat into old Hawaiʻi's way of rejuvenation, and invite you and our esteemed planters to join our history.

THREE

Lehua was a hundred dollars poorer, soaked, and seasick. She hung her head between her knees on the boat to Kōpaʻa.

When they had left Lāhainā Harbor, Lehua had texted an update to Avery, letting her boss know she might have found a lead, as if a gut feeling about an island farm counted. But she'd quickly lost signal, her text undelivered. In minutes, the water had turned choppy, and Lehua had sunk into a wet chair, mouth dry. A spot she hadn't moved from since.

From the plane, the ocean had looked small, reduced to a cut of chalcedony, its waves static and flat. Now it roared at Lehua's back, rattling her bones, throwing cold salt and spray onto her skin. The mortuary's silent rooms with their formaldehyde and antiseptic perfume felt like a faraway refuge. A reward awaiting her once she found Ohia.

She saw her sad reflection in the trawler's many puddles. Her shorn hair was dyed black by the damp and plastered to her head.

Lehua still couldn't believe she was actually there. In Hawaiʻi.

She hadn't expected her ancestral homeland, the fantasyland of her grandparents' stories and superstitions, to be like this. Her grandmother had always told them that Hawai'i was beautiful because of their people's connection to their islands. "If you took care of the land, it would take care of you, like it has our ancestors." She saw her grandma's eyes silvering with tears. "You'll see it one day, then you'll understand."

Her grandma had been wrong about that, too.

How did Ohia manage this? Had her twin been as wobbly and seasick as she was now? *No,* a low voice answered. *Ohia wouldn't have struggled at all.*

Unlike Lehua, who hadn't known she could get seasick until now.

She had gone in the water only once in the last five years, when a track teammate had dragged her to their high school's swim tryouts, and she'd been laughed out of the lap pool. "You looked like you were trying to run *on* the water. You sure you're Hawaiian?" the girl had snickered.

That taunt replayed in Lehua's mind as she watched Melia lean into the sea, her hair rising with the wind, while every lurch of the boat sliced through Lehua's stomach, leaving her sweaty and cold. She didn't even notice Melia sitting beside her until Melia's arm brushed hers.

"First time in Hawai'i?"

Lehua forced a weak laugh. "Is it that obvious?"

Melia smiled. "Nah, I thought you and your sister might be local. Where are you from?"

"Phoenix." Lehua felt a strange surge of shame, as if getting seasick and being from Arizona were both personal failures. "Our grandparents were from O'ahu, though. They moved when our mom was still in high school." *And pregnant.*

"But you're Kanaka, right?" When Lehua didn't answer, Melia clarified, "Hawaiian."

"Oh, yeah, but we—I mean, I don't speak it," Lehua said with another pang of shame.

"A lot of us don't," Melia said softly, as if she'd sensed Lehua's embarrassment. "Where is the rest of your family? Are they looking for your sister in Arizona?"

"No." Lehua turned away. She hated answering questions about their family, hated being caught between the *normal* expectation that there was someone—anyone—waiting at home for her and Ohia. She had to pry the words out every time. "Ohia and I . . . we're the only ones left."

Of course, Lehua didn't know if that was true. But it was the simplest answer. For all she knew, their mom could be alive and well, living happily in Hawai'i. Hell, she could've been reading a book under the inn's veranda that afternoon and Lehua wouldn't have recognized her. The last photograph they'd had of her had long faded, worn into shreds like torn gossamer.

Melia's eyes warmed. Despite herself, Lehua leaned closer, angling her body toward the other girl. Melia was beautiful, the kind of girl Lehua would tangle with, had they met anywhere else—or at any other time.

"I'm sorry to hear that," Melia said. "I bet your sister's happy she has you."

Lehua swallowed thickly, not knowing how to answer. The words fell like a heavy mantle. Ohia had never apologized after their fight and the wounds hadn't scabbed over. How would Melia react to the truth—that Lehua was glad Ohia might need her?

During her flight, Lehua had envisioned finding her sister. Ohia would palm her forehead with embarrassment as she apologized. She'd assure Lehua that she was, in fact, doing an internship on an island farm. The college's system must've glitched out, and both her roommate and coach had heard her wrong. *Somehow.* Ohia would be grateful Lehua had cared enough to clear up this mess before it got any bigger.

A part of Lehua knew how implausible that sounded, but it seemed more likely than her star sister staging a disappearing act. Ohia wasn't the kind of girl whose face adorned lampposts, junk mail, and newspaper ads reading *Have you seen me?* until the paper was recycled and reprinted with the next lost girl's face.

Ohia wasn't their mom.

"What about you?" Lehua asked, pulling away from Melia, eager to change the subject. "Any family?"

"No," Melia answered, that earlier softness vanishing. She rose to her feet, scattering a lace of rain from her hair. "Look."

The sea's churning had quelled, and the rain had stopped. The sky was a heavy quilt of indigo and sooty twilight. Melia returned to the boat's edge, her raised hand smudging against the descending night.

Lehua swayed to her feet, reluctant to follow. Melia had a way of distractedly peering over the rail's edge that upset Lehua's stomach.

"Wow." Melia's finger pointed toward the lambent horizon.

Curtains of rain swept over the ocean, but seemed to shy away from the island, as if Kōpaʻa had bargained with the rain. Instead, the island was a streak against the sky and sea, shrouded by the surf's mist. "We're here."

From the trawler deck, Kōpaʻa had been hidden, wreathed in fog. But when Lehua stepped onto the island, a silent town waited, untouched by rain.

Wood-framed houses loomed over a wide dirt road, carpeted with wild sea purslane. Red dirt clung to their foundations in a cascade of rust to brown, dyeing the wood like poured cider. Thick vines had overtaken the windows, growing over the white walls and a bulletin board full of yellowed fliers whose letters had long faded. The town seemed preserved in time. Static and eerily beautiful, it reminded Lehua of a postcard—an idyllic souvenir of a town preserved in ivy rather than paper.

"Looks abandoned," Lehua said. Despite the faraway lights they'd spied from the ocean, there were no streetlamps and no movement in the houses. They'd have to rely on their phones and the moonlight to find their way.

"Nah, I don't think it is," Melia said, tilting her head toward one of the town's second-floor windows. "I'm pretty sure I saw someone up there."

The window's darkened glass revealed nothing but rotten lace curtains, glistening like spiderwebs. Unease trickled down Lehua's back. "Is someone from the resort supposed to meet us?"

"No," Melia answered, peering into a window with her phone's flashlight. The window was painted black and swallowed up the light, reflecting back nothing. "According to the email I got, the resort shouldn't be far, we just need to follow 'the road.' "

Lehua nodded. When she'd left the trawler, she had passed by the captain, a white man in an anorak, and pressed another hundred dollars into his hands, promising she'd return in an hour. The island had looked small from the boat. If her sister was here, that would be enough time to find Ohia, demand she answer her goddamn phone next time, then leave.

But the town had the same abandoned feeling the mortuary had during her night shifts. It was hard to imagine anyone sleeping here, let alone living here. The air tamped down on her chest—thick with humidity, reminding her of Phoenix's monsoon season when the pressure changed, bruising the city's skyline purple with ozone and storm clouds.

Lehua resisted wrapping her arms around herself. She pointed down the town's lone dirt road. "I'm guessing the resort is that way."

She turned to Melia, finding the girl slack-jawed, gripping a wooden beam. Lehua followed her gaze, then froze.

A dead bird was splayed under the house's awning. Half *eaten.* It was as big as a falcon and its black plumage was pulled out in wet tufts. Its bright red bill was cracked open and full of dried brown blood. All that was left of its stomach was a pit of rotten pink gore.

"Looks like a cat got carried away. Is that a duck?"

Melia met her queasy look, then shook her head. "No, it's an 'alae 'ula. They're a wetland bird. Endangered, too." She turned her back to the dead bird with a tight smile. "I read about the old plantation town. For such a fancy resort, I'm surprised they didn't tear it down. It reminds me of where I grew up."

"Where's that?"

"Pāʻia," she answered. Together, they climbed the red slope running like a vein through the island's verdant hills, kicking up dust plumes in their wake. "When the sugar plantation there closed, it became a massive surf town, so it's full of tourists now. But the houses and stores look the same as here. Except for the old mill. After it closed they put a fence around it, but that doesn't keep anyone out." Her voice grew low, wistful. "I used to climb the funnel loader alone and watch the porch lights extinguish at night."

The way Melia talked about Pāʻia reminded Lehua of her grandparents, how they had ached for their homeland every day until they died. Lehua didn't feel nostalgia for Phoenix, and its red rock and intersecting city roads. Only rank familiarity.

"Sounds dangerous."

"A couple of rusted buildings?" Melia cast her a sideways look, that wistfulness returned to a brittle edge. "There are worse things."

There was more going on with Melia than she let on, that much was clear. A girl didn't island-hop in the night when her life was going *great.* Lehua had staged enough disappearing acts of her own to recognize that same resolute look in Melia's eyes. But Lehua didn't want to think about worse things. Not when her twin was missing.

Her twin who was okay, she reminded herself, and who'd always continue being okay, because Ohia wasn't the type to run away. When they found Ohia at the end of this walk, she would toss her hair over her shoulder and pierce Lehua with that look of hers—the one that both soothed and unnerved her, that confident half-hooded look her sister had mastered at fifteen. *Everything's fine, Le.*

Lehua's throat tightened. Maybe her sister wouldn't be glad to see her at all. She shook the thought away. "How'd you hear about this place, anyway?"

Melia glanced at her, then at the path ahead of them where a field of sugarcane swayed, leaves glinting like silver beneath the moon. Lehua hadn't meant to pry. She could tell Melia hadn't liked the question from her long sigh.

"A case worker at the Maui unemployment office told me about it," Melia said, and Lehua thought she'd leave it at that until she added, "No need to look surprised. I needed a job, and the caseworker told me this place is always hiring. She went on and on about the people she had sent here and how their lives had changed, saying it was exactly what I needed. The usual crap. I think she wanted me to stop showing up every two weeks." She snorted. "Well, I sent an email. Here I am."

That didn't explain how Ohia, if she was here, had heard about the opportunity. Maybe she'd found the resort online or one of her teammates had mentioned it.

"It seems this resort demands a lot, making their employees move all the way out here," Lehua said.

"That's life in Hawai'i. You don't have a lot of options unless you're here on vacation."

Lehua felt a pinprick of shame. Melia was her age. At nineteen, they were technically adults, but she couldn't shake the feeling that Melia had been pushed into adulthood suddenly. With her guard down, Melia looked ropy and small next to her—lost and, if Lehua wasn't wrong, alone. At least she'd had Ohia after their grandparents died.

In silence, they climbed inland until they were surrounded on all sides by tall grass shoots of sugarcane and another plant Lehua didn't recognize. Variegated green leaves spiraled out from its thick wooden stem, like flames from a lit match. The tall leaves hedged the road, standing like a botanical barricade between them and the cane fields.

"That's ti leaf," Melia said, pulling out a water bottle and taking a long sip. "It brings good luck and wards off evil spirits." She wiped her mouth with the back of her hand, leaving a carmine streak of dust.

Lehua looked at the long line of ti leaf. It ran all the way up the hill, continuing over its summit. "They must be really superstitious."

"What about you? Do you believe?"

Lehua resisted a snort. "Not really, no."

"What? Why not?"

I work with dead people.

"I work in a mortuary," Lehua said, yanking off her hoodie. With the gathering dark and nearby sea, she had expected a chill. But the air was hot and soaked her neck. She was used to the heat in Phoenix, where it was a stifling, dry thing. Here it left sweat tracks down her tattooed arms like a second skin. "If there was something beyond this world, I'm pretty sure I'd know about it."

Lehua tied her hoodie around her waist as Melia took in her tattoos. She had started adding to the inky garden on her arms when she quit college six months ago and met an apprentice tattoo artist willing to work for cheap. But Lehua still wasn't used to the attention, and her skin burned under the scrutiny.

What does that one mean? people would ask, brazenly brushing their fingers over the shapes on her arms, lingering near her neck. *Is that for your parents? Your sister? Your dead grandparents? Are there more?*

She'd started with pink mallows and white blooms of asphodel climbing up her triceps, their unopened flower buds, dark anthers, and filaments inked black. Now there were night moths tucked behind the leaves and petals, the edges of their wings feathered and gray; and yellow fruit with freckled skin.

But Melia didn't ask to see more. Her eyes traced the lilies veining Lehua's forearms, following the stems that curled into shrubs and ferns cinching her wrists like bracelets. "You haven't seen anything?" Melia's searching gaze met hers.

Lehua thought of her grandparents and the superstitions she'd buried after their deaths—and the man's sightless stare that had confronted her that first week at the mortuary. "No." A flicker of judgment lit Melia's eyes. "Do you believe?"

"Yes. I've seen too many things on these islands to dismiss the possibility."

Lehua had no reply to that. It felt like the same sort of explanation her grandma would have offered, so she pointed to the upcoming light burning through the dark. "Look. We're almost there."

Melia's shoulders hunched together. She looked like she'd

rather be anywhere else. Before Lehua could ask why Melia had taken this job when she so clearly did not want it, they had already departed the cane's thick canopy. Together, they stopped on the red road, their eyes widening.

Horace Jacobs's estate rose against the night sky, a bright blot blurring the horizon.

The ivory resort towered over them and the rest of the island from atop its hill. Light streamed from a veranda full of large French windows flanked by matching shutters, ornate railings, and massive white pillars. A wooden bridge arched over the wide loch in front of the house, leading to a floating gazebo. The loch's breeze spun around them, heavy with the scent of ripe fruit. Ti leaf fronds dipped into the pond's hazy surface, which reflected the house's lights like fireflies in the night.

Lehua had never seen a place so grand except in movies. It looked like something out of a fairy tale, summoning the stories her grandparents would tell of old Hawai'i, green and lush—so unlike Phoenix, with its red rock borders and resilient desert life. She remembered little of those interred stories except for the spark of connection she'd felt as her grandparents had told them. Their passing had pruned her and Ohia from that connection, unmooring them from any real past or home.

That same unmoored feeling grew stronger the closer Lehua got to the grand house and its fairy-tale loch. The fantasy felt tentative. Fragile. One wrong step and the house would disappear like some verdant vision.

The two girls approached the resort's covered entrance, trading red dirt for gravel. The tall entryway was patterned with thin shadows like cobwebs. Beneath the long archway, a woman stood so still, Lehua almost mistook her for a statue.

She was pale like marble, wearing a floral white aloha shirt that was near luminescent in the dark. Her black hair was pulled into a low chignon and a small smile toyed with the corner of her mouth.

"Melia, good evening. My, you're even prettier in person. I'm Chiyo Amaya, Kōpaʻa's manager," she greeted in a soft lilt. A green braid wreathed the manager's arms, matching the leaves Lehua and Melia had passed on their way to the resort. A ti leaf lei. She draped the adornment over Melia's shoulders. "Welcome."

Chiyo could be any age south of forty. Her dewy skin flushed a delicate pink near her cheekbones. Her crescent eyes flickered between the two girls before stopping decidedly on Lehua with a flash of familiarity, then confusion at Lehua's hair and tattoos. Like Lehua was a puzzle she couldn't work out, the funhouse version of another girl—her twin, Ohia.

Except that wasn't the name Chiyo said.

"Alana?"

FOUR

Who the hell is Alana?

A dozen questions burned in Lehua's mind. It was hard not to feel that Ohia was somehow watching from the resort's bright doorway. But when she passed Ohia's photo to Chiyo, her twin's haunting presence ebbed into the night, the feeling no more than a wisp.

Because her sister wasn't here.

The manager's recognition had been unmistakable, and the only reason Chiyo could mistake Lehua for "Alana" was if Alana was not there. Not anymore.

Still, she felt a sharp stab of disappointment when Chiyo handed her phone back.

"Yes, that's Alana Holt. She quit after her first week here." Chiyo shook her head. "Her decision was so sudden—we were reeling. I can only assume she is your twin. The resemblance is uncanny. Is something wrong?"

"She's missing."

"Missing? Have you gone to the police?"

"Not yet." Lehua exchanged a sideways glance with Melia. *Runaway* shone plainly in her eyes now, that unspoken word seeming more and more likely. "I thought she was doing some kind of internship here."

Chiyo frowned. "Kōpaʻa does not offer any internships, but our employees do live on-site. Alana—"

"Ohia. Her real name is Ohia Sayers," Lehua corrected in a waspish voice she instantly regretted. It wasn't this woman's fault Ohia had left. "I'm sorry. It's been a long couple of days, and I thought I would find her here."

"Please, I understand completely and wish I could offer more assistance." Chiyo offered a sympathetic smile. It was probably the same smile she gave resort guests when they ran out of scented towels. "Which is why I am sorry to be the one to say this, but Alana—well, Ohia clearly stated she was an orphan and had no family. Do you have identification? I want to sort this misunderstanding out right away. To protect our guests' privacy, we carefully register and vet everyone who visits our island without exception. I hope you understand."

What the hell, Ohia? Stunned by her sister's lies, Lehua handed over her ID. *First a fake name, now this?*

"Hey. Are you okay?" Melia asked after Chiyo disappeared into the resort, promising to return shortly.

No. Her throat was too thick to speak. She'd always wondered what Ohia told her friends about her dropout sister when she wasn't around. What did her perfect twin say about her, the screwup?

Now she knew. Ohia pretended she didn't exist.

"I'm okay." Lehua gave a small nod. She doubted Melia bought it, but she was desperate to hide how much it stung. How could her sister have changed this much since their fight? Everything she'd heard in the last couple of days didn't sound like the Ohia she knew at all.

Lehua was the one always slipping out the back like their mom, not Ohia. But Lehua had been wrong and their coach had been right. Ohia had quit the team.

Must run in the family, she imagined Uzzy gloating.

Ohia had said as much before she hung up two weeks ago. After Lehua learned her twin had already left Phoenix, their call had exploded into another fight. "You don't understand," Ohia had hissed, a whisper snarled over the ocean's tossing waves: "I *need* to do this, Le."

Chiyo reappeared, leaving the resort door open. Another woman followed her, warily tucking a strand of hair behind her ear. She was fair, blond, and pretty, wearing an ivory-stitched shirtdress with a faded black pinafore. Her name tag read *Daisy.*

"I apologize for the wait," Chiyo said, returning Lehua's ID stacked atop a printout.

Lehua scanned the paper. *Alana Marie Holt* read the copied Hawaii state ID, next to an address she'd never heard of and her sister's face. Apparently, Ohia had felt attached enough to keep her middle name and birthday—just not her flesh and blood.

Chiyo saw her chagrined look. "I figured you'd want to see our records as well. I also grabbed one of our staff, Daisy," she said, and Daisy bobbed her head with the same rigidness ROTC cadets displayed. "She will get Melia settled in while you and I talk about Ohia."

"What else is there to talk about? She's not here," Lehua muttered, and Chiyo gave her an assessing look, saying nothing. Lehua wondered if Chiyo's silence was out of pity. What sister—what twin—left the other with nothing more than a trail of lies? Daisy led Melia away from the resort's half circle of light, while Lehua's throat tightened.

"Did my sister say why she quit?"

"No." The resort manager didn't elaborate.

So helpful. "Did she say where she was heading next?"

Chiyo shook her head. "Not to me."

"She just quit and . . . left?"

Chiyo smiled apologetically. "I can't even imagine how distressing this must be. Believe me, I wish there was more I could tell you."

Except Lehua wasn't anxious. She was angry. For once, Ohia wasn't perfect, and it was falling on Lehua's shoulders to bear. Her star sister had run away.

It wasn't like Kōpaʻa was some giant tourist hub her sister had happened across. There was one boat in or out—that was it. How had she even heard about this island? Why would she get a fake ID only to leave a week later? Where was she now? She was a week ahead of Lehua and out of reach, gone on another boat. If finding her twin meant catching up . . .

Lehua never would.

No one could catch Ohia when she was running.

As far as "Alana" was concerned, she had no family. Fine. It was time Lehua returned to Phoenix and let the police handle finding her sister.

Will they? There was a reason she hadn't gone to the police in the first place. People were buried and forgotten in case files all the time. Her, Ohia, their grandparents, their mom. But Lehua had no leads and limited options.

"I'm gonna go," she said. "I left the boat captain waiting. Thanks for your help—I mean it—and sorry for all this trouble."

I'll figure out what to do next in Phoenix. She turned her back on Chiyo and the grand resort. After she returned to Maui, she'd update Avery, then convince someone to buy her an entire bottle of the cheapest whiskey in Lāhainā. Tomorrow, she'd bake under the sun, sipping until she got deliriously dehydrated. She wanted to be more than drunk when reality pulled her back to Arizona, three paychecks and a sister poorer.

"Unfortunately, the captain has already departed," Chiyo said. "I radioed him inside. You didn't show, so he assumed you were staying."

"He left?" Lehua checked the time on her phone and swore. Fifteen minutes early. "Can't you tell him to come back? I'll pay extra."

Chiyo shook her head. "I already offered to pay. A storm is heading for Lāhainā this weekend. He can't risk returning until Monday evening."

Monday? It was Friday night. What was she supposed to do for three whole days? *This can't be happening.* "Uh, okay," Lehua said, trying to sound calm, as if she wasn't completely stranded. "I'll find a place to stay in town."

Maybe she could bunk up with Melia for the weekend. She began to walk away, her gut tightening with heady anticipation at seeing the pretty Hawaiian girl.

Chiyo grabbed her hand. "No, Lehua. You'll stay here. There's nowhere else to stay on the island and you have traveled so far." Chiyo steered her toward the resort's honeyed light.

"Here?" Lehua gave her a flat look. "I can't afford it." Her remaining thousand dollars wouldn't cover a closet in the resort for one night.

"We have a room you can use, so it's no trouble at all. Be reasonable."

Be reasonable, and then what? What was she supposed to do while she was stranded? Sip virgin coladas? Three days in a resort she could never afford even if she saved every paycheck until the day she died.

A resort her twin had needed to visit so badly, she became Alana for a week.

Lehua swallowed her unease. She'd been prepared to return to Phoenix, but she was stuck now—and her sister had come here for a reason.

Ohia had stayed for a week. She must have talked to someone. If Lehua asked around, she might discover why Ohia had come here and where she was heading next. Then she'd have a lead the police couldn't ignore. Because unlike in their mom's case, Lehua wanted a real answer about her twin and whether she was okay. *She has to be.*

"Fine."

Chiyo beamed. "Excellent. Please follow me."

FIVE

The resort reminded Lehua of a wake.

Glowing brass sconces pearled the lobby's white walls and walnut paneling, dripping honeycomb light. Three archways revealed a sitting room on either side of the lobby and a hallway with half a dozen closed doors. On the other side of the lobby, a grand staircase curved along the far wall, its dark wood twisting away from view like a serpent's tail.

"Welcome to the historic home of Horace Ira Jacobs, Kōpaʻa's founder," Chiyo said, resuming her role of hotelier. She gestured Lehua forward, inviting her to look around and enjoy the resort's splendor. "The ground floor holds our lobby and sitting rooms in the front, and our main suites, kitchen, dining room, and lounge in the rear."

Chiyo called the resort historic. More like a capsule from another century. Everything was beautiful but decades old. An ornate grandfather clock ticked in the sitting room. Thick curtains draped the wooden shutters, hanging from gilt fixtures.

Sun-bleached pillows were nestled into deep rattan couches, framing the house's two bay windows. The wooden floors whined, protesting her welcome.

It feels like a monument, not a home, Lehua thought, awed by its sheer size. The word *home* sent her back to a cracked sidewalk in Phoenix. At twelve years old, she and Ohia had watched as their social worker locked their grandparents' house for the last time.

"Don't cry, you're going to a new home," he'd promised, assuming the state would track down their mom and reunite them in no time. But their mother's missing person's report had become just another buried page in their file as they were shuffled between fosters.

Lehua felt the same emptiness walking into the resort's lobby. By the front door was a carved plaque made from a darker wood than the rest of the house. The words, wreathed by ornate carvings of bundled sugarcane, read *The harvest is plenteous, but the laborers are few.*

Lehua bit her lip. *Not exactly live, laugh, love.*

Chiyo saw her look and laughed. "You'll find many scriptures during your stay. Horace's father was one of the first missionaries to come to Hawaiʻi. Although he chose a different path, Horace never forgot his roots." She caressed the staircase's carved sugarcane motif, a stalk of cane grass cut into the stair's newel post like a waving flame. "Much of what you see is original, of course. Horace asked that all of Kōpaʻa be preserved in perpetuum to preserve the island's history." So that explained why the resort felt like a museum and the plantation town hadn't been torn down.

As Lehua took in the resort's many framed photographs, paintings, and wall adornments, her eyes were drawn to a hooked, machete-like blade tucked neatly behind a case. A gold plaque beneath it read *Jacobs & Pacific's First Cane Knife.* Lehua got the feeling she wasn't rich enough to appreciate the décor.

"A few additions have been made to accommodate our needs as a retreat, like our wellness spa. If you're interested in yoga or lei-making, I can set you up with an appointment with Daisy. She's our new residential jack-of-all-trades." Chiyo slanted Lehua another smile, like she was simply another guest, and an uneasy feeling prickled her neck. Why was Chiyo being so kind?

"Since we already have a full group staying with us, all our first-floor guest rooms are occupied, so you'll be on our second floor. But your room has a lovely lanai that overlooks the cane fields," she went on as if Lehua would turn down a free room because, god forbid, the view wasn't nice enough.

"Thanks again for letting me stay here," Lehua said, scanning the lobby, keeping an eye out for more of the resort's staff and guests. "You must have a massive staff to run this place."

"Quite the opposite. We intentionally keep a skeletal resort staff due to our usual clientele," Chiyo said, and Lehua tried to hide her disappointment. A smaller staff meant fewer people to ask about Ohia. "Our guests are extremely private individuals who come to Kōpaʻa for a secluded escape—and we protect their privacy. We mostly employ field-workers, but our persimmons are late this season, so we haven't brought back our full work crew. Instead, we're training our new hires until our harvest is ready." Chiyo nodded toward the doors. "Like the young woman you met tonight."

At the mention of Melia, Lehua offered, "If your field-workers aren't around right now, I'd be happy to use one of their rooms."

Chiyo waved her off. "Our workers stay in a co-ed longhouse. You'll be much more comfortable here. Besides, we would be remiss to not offer our full hospitality. Your sister may not have stayed with us for long, but she was one of our workers. I hate to use such a cliché statement, but we consider all our staff family." She handed Lehua an ivory business card. "I know you're only here for the weekend, but when you return to Maui, please stay in touch. We have some resources. Past guests we can reach out to. If there is any way I can assist you in your search, I'd like to."

"I dunno what to say." Lehua pocketed the card, surprised. The manager's offer was unexpectedly generous and . . . seemed genuine. After spending years in foster care and adapting to multiple home placements, Lehua had learned to trust her gut feeling for people. Perhaps Chiyo meant it when she called her staff *family*. "That would honestly help a lot."

Maybe the police would actually look into it, pressured by the type of wealth that demanded results. A call from Chiyo could help guarantee her sister wasn't left in the same bureaucratic sinkhole that had claimed their mom. With Chiyo's help, someone would have to find Ohia, then Lehua could know her sister was fine and, more importantly, safe.

"You must be tired. You've had a difficult night." Chiyo slid Lehua a look. "Has Ohia run away like this before?"

"Never."

"Strange. The people we take in are often desperate for the opportunity to work here. So many have been displaced from their homes," Chiyo said. Lehua thought of her grandparents, priced out of paradise, and looked away. "We try to provide a haven for our workers, and in return, we simply ask for their help maintaining our historical roots as a working farm and orchard. When I met Ohia, she seemed kind of lost. I thought we could help her here. But some people don't want to be found."

Lehua ran her nails over her palms, scratching at the red dirt hidden there, the phantom touch of her sister's twelve-year-old hand encircling hers.

"That doesn't sound like Ohia," Lehua returned quietly. Not the Ohia she knew. The girl who'd knotted her hand in Lehua's as they left their grandparents' home, determined to never be separated.

"Remember the story of our names, Le," Ohia had whispered into her hair each time their social worker introduced them to a new house and guardian. "'Ōhi'a lehua. We're *meant* to stay together."

"She's lucky to have a sister like you." Chiyo smiled.

"Well, it's just Ohia and me."

"No other family? Friends? A boyfriend?" She laughed at Lehua's suddenly flushed face. "Sorry, I'm not trying to interrogate you. We don't have another spare room, and we wouldn't want another person to become stranded if they came looking for you."

"No," Lehua answered quickly, checking her phone. No bars. "But I need to call my boss and let her know I'll be here until Monday. I don't have any service. Can I use your phone?"

Chiyo sighed as they climbed the stairs, the aged wood groaning beneath their footfalls. "Sorry, we don't have a phone, and you won't find any reception or Wi-Fi on the island, either. Kōpaʻa is an off-the-grid retreat—we're tech-free," she clarified. "We have a radio for emergencies, of course. But our guests expect a true digital detox when they're here."

No landline and no reception because a bunch of rich people didn't know how to log off without help. Lehua drummed her nails against her phone until she remembered the resort's contact form on their website. Chiyo had printed a copy of her sister's fake ID, too. "What about a computer? Melia said you emailed her."

Chiyo's guest service smile pulled taut. "We have a staff computer to handle reservations, employee applications, and resort paperwork—nothing more. To use it otherwise, I would need to file a request with Mr. Jacobs—"

"Mr. Jacobs? The plantation owner? I thought this place was a resort now."

"Yes, the resort is run by Ira Jacobs, the current head of the Jacobs family."

At the top of the stairs, they entered a tall corridor. Portraits ran the full length of the wallpapered hall. Silver tintypes were interspersed with faded paintings, a collection of black-and-white photographs of the island, sepia-toned canvases, and sleek, glossy photos of glittering parties. Everywhere, there were snapshots of the resort and its glamorous guests—grinning, laughing, drinking from sugar-rimmed glasses and cocktail flutes with speared pineapple. But at the top of the expansive gallery, one impassive face stood above the rest.

George Jacobs read the plate beneath the tintype portrait. The photo was starched by age, the whites of the man's eyes indistinct from the rest of his gaunt face. A scripture adorned the portrait's frame like a crown: *Take my yoke upon you, and learn of me.*

"You see, Kōpaʻa is still a family enterprise," Chiyo said. "Ever since its dedication to Horace's father, George, this estate has remained the Jacobs family home, housing each generation."

Under the old man's portrait were other photos, spread along the hallway like the roots of a tree, interspersed with the resort's glittering guests. *Charles Jacobs, O. Orin Jacobs, Sylvan Jacobs, Margaret Jacobs, Willamina Jacobs.* Even without their names, Lehua would've known they were family. All their faces had the same shade of milky white skin and striking eyes, blue like varicose veins, framed by gently curling blond hair. Even their plain smiles were grooved with the same lines. But for all his esteemed achievements, she couldn't find Horace on the wall.

Lehua's eyes lingered on a patch of faded wallpaper. Where a portrait had once hung, now there was empty space. Maybe Horace's portrait was getting polished.

"Mr. Jacobs is, well, a benevolent man," said Chiyo. "I'm sure he'll understand your need when I file your computer request tomorrow."

Should I write a formal petition? Lehua certainly hoped the elusive Mr. Jacobs would feel benevolent enough to grant her request to send an email. Maybe she'd be lucky and he'd permit an hour's use of the internet, too. *Wouldn't that be a treat.* Avery needed an update about how long she'd be gone. "Why tomorrow?"

"I'm afraid Mr. Jacobs has already retired for the night. In fact . . ." Chiyo paused, her words turning hushed. "He keeps a room farther down this hall, same as me. But you are under no circumstances to bother him. To tell you the truth, he is quite sick. It would be best if you did not speak to him at all," she said with a meaningful look. "If you need anything, please remember *I* am Kōpaʻa's manager."

Lehua nodded, but she had detected an undercurrent of bitterness in Chiyo's voice. There was obviously some ire between the resort manager and the island's owner.

"Beyond that, Kōpaʻa has some rules that we'll need to quickly go over."

"Rules?" Lehua repeated. "Isn't the point of a vacation to get away?"

Chiyo's smile thinned. "We are a world-renowned resort, but Kōpaʻa is still a home and a preserved historical site—which is why we have our rules. Don't worry. Nothing extravagant." Chiyo offered a folded paper to Lehua.

Prohibited Conduct read the thick paper.

You may not interfere with any other guest or their wellness journey.
You may not attempt to access any information about Kōpaʻa's guests.
You may not interrupt the island's workers or disrupt our farm's operations.
You must remain inside the resort's immediate premises after sundown.
You may not pick any of Kōpaʻa's crops without express permission.
You may not wander off the property's marked path.

Lehua's eyes widened. Chiyo had said the rules were nothing extravagant, but they sure seemed strict. She and the resort had differing views on relaxation.

"Marked path?" Lehua asked since there wasn't a map on the resort's fancy flier.

"Our island's ti leaf. It encircles the entire resort, clearly denoting safe paths for our guests to follow," Chiyo said. "Kōpaʻa is small, but it is easy to get turned around here. Believe me, you don't want to get hurt exploring on your own."

"Is that all?" Lehua slid the flier into her pocket alongside Chiyo's business card. She hoped the resort's rules wouldn't get in the way of finding answers about Ohia. But if she had to bend the rules, it wouldn't be the first time. She just couldn't get caught.

Chiyo nodded. "Please don't take these rules harshly. We hold the same expectations for each of our guests."

"And your workers? Do they follow the same rules?"

"Outside of their duties, their rules are similar." Chiyo raised a brow. "Do you think it was our policies that influenced Ohia to quit?"

No. When Lehua used to complain about Uzzy, Ohia had never joined in. Her twin was the compliant one. "Did she mention them?"

Chiyo shook her head. "Not to me."

Lehua hesitated. She was starting to wonder how many words Chiyo and her sister had actually exchanged. The resort manager liked to ask questions. It was hard to believe Chiyo hadn't interrogated Ohia about her reasons for leaving.

As they walked farther down the burgundy hallway, Lehua could see why most of the guest rooms were on the bottom floor. Up here, the house was still beautiful, but it was cold and the old wall sconces barely flickered. Condensation ghosted the windows.

The hallway's chill mapped the clammy trail of sweat drying on her tattooed arms.

But worst of all was the saccharine perfume in the air.

Sour musk, browned sugar, and something astringent like antiseptic clung to the air, nauseatingly so. The entire floor needed to be aired out. Yet there was something familiar about the resort's strange odor—

"Here's your room," Chiyo said in front of an intricate wooden door, marked number seven. Like the staircase, the door's inlaid pattern resembled a stalk of sugarcane, a fanned frond with a tangle of roots taking seed. Chiyo unclipped a key from her heavy key ring, then unlocked the door.

A teak canopy bed with an ivory quilt took up most of the room. Sheer curtains clung to the French windows and moonlight peered through the slotted lanai door like fingers. The orchard wallpaper burgeoned with gems of golden fruit, painted in blooms of orange, indigo, and green. A bright contrast to the spartan room.

"I apologize for the cold. Mr. Jacobs thinks it helps with his recovery." Chiyo opened a louvered door, revealing a jade bathroom. Exposed copper pipes glinted alongside a claw-foot tub, scalloped marble sink, and foliate wallpapered paneling. "No expense was spared in the building of Horace's estate, so you have your own private bathroom. You've missed dinner, so I'll have Daisy bring you some tea and leftovers. Do you have any food sensitivities?"

Lehua shook her head, wide-eyed. *This is my room?* It was a far cry from the quaint Lāhainā inn she had left, the once-white walls yellowed like jaundice.

"Daisy will be up soon," Chiyo said. "After you eat, you may join our other guests in the lounge for an after-dinner reflection period. Unless you'd rather rest."

Lehua shrugged off her bag. She'd much rather sleep than attend what sounded like rich people's evening therapy. But meeting the other guests would give her a chance to ask them about Ohia. Her sister, with her cheery personality and easy smile, would've made an impression. "I'll come."

"Then I'll have Daisy deliver a set of clothes with your dinner as well. We've had so many guests over the years. Things inevitably get left behind. I'm certain we can find something appropriate." Chiyo offered another five-star service smile, and Lehua realized then that the resort had a dress code.

Chiyo's generosity, coupled with her persistent offers of assistance, felt a little excessive. Lehua couldn't shake the suspicion that there was something behind her eagerness. The complimentary room, food, and now clothes were offered without hesitation, almost eagerly. Then again, this was a pricey resort. Maybe the service was supposed to be over-the-top.

"Welcome to Kōpaʻa, Lehua. You're our guest now—and it's my pleasure to assist you." Chiyo bowed quickly, lowering her head, but not before Lehua caught the way her eyes darkened. "Please enjoy your stay."

SIX

Lehua dipped her head under the bathroom's faucet, lathering the resort's persimmon and cedar body wash. The island's dirt rinsed down the marble drain. Back in their high school locker rooms, Ohia would always finish showering first and scrawl drippy messages on the mirror: *Gone to class, had a meeting, see you at home. O.*

Lehua switched the faucet off, her reflection blurred in the iron mirror. I RAN AWAY, she wrote, streaking her finger through the steam's wet trail. O.

She read the message over and over as if that would make the words any easier to believe. They bled down the mirror, revealing Lehua and the soapy rivulets running down her collarbone. Ohia's last words whispered like a specter in her ears: *I* need *to do this, Le.*

Do what? Lehua ripped a plush towel free. If her sister had planned on running away, why had she even bothered calling?

Had that been some crappy goodbye? Well, Lehua deserved better. An apology, for one.

An image of Ohia holding their dorm room door open flashed through her mind. "You just started college, Le. You can't quit during your first year. That's like forfeiting a race before you've heard the bell," she had said, laughing, after Lehua "joked" about taking a break.

The final lap of a track race was called a bell lap because a bell was rung to alert all the runners when the race's leader started it. Why Ohia had thought a sports metaphor would motivate Lehua was beyond her, but that was the sister Lehua remembered. If she had quit after a week . . .

What had made her leave? *Something had to have happened.*

Lehua turned away from the mirror. She didn't want to keep looking at her eyes dilated despite the bathroom lights, to see the fear widening them, the uncertainty surrounding her sister's whereabouts.

The resort's sour odor singed her nose again. Lehua went to unlock the lanai door and stepped outside onto the balcony. A warm wind skated over her, scattering the fetid smell from her nose and some of the tension from her shoulders.

Her room was on the west side of the resort, facing the island's edge. The ocean blurred black on the horizon, clotted with thick clouds. She never would've guessed the sea was that close. The resort's heavy silence swallowed the crash of the waves, the wind, and even the cries of the insects that must have lived in the tall cane grass surrounding her room. At least it smelled better.

Beyond the beach was the outline of the town, fields of sugarcane, a couple of weathered buildings so pitted and corroded by time they were indistinguishable from the island's dirt, and a dark smokestack looming against the sky. All part of the old plantation. Toward the right was the resort's persimmon orchard. Skeletal trees and spindly overgrown roots waited beyond a chain-link fence's tarp-covered wire.

The sugarcane seemed to trap the resort. Lehua tried to envision Ohia cutting their stalks, shoving her way through that dense thicket. Her lean body, trained to run a hundred meters in under eleven seconds, pushing a cart ladened with fruit instead. Lehua couldn't imagine it.

Her phone buzzed. Lehua expected a low battery reminder. But her heart kicked with alarm when she read the notification graying out her screen, blanching Ohia's face in the background.

Nearby Personal Hotspot, the box read. *Do you want to join "Ohia Sayers's iPhone"?*

SEVEN

Their phones didn't connect.

Lehua's heart rabbited in her chest, kicking against her ribs, as she opened her phone's Wi-Fi options, scrolling down to where her sister's phone should've been listed. But there were no available networks or devices nearby. She tried refreshing the list, but it didn't change. She even checked her sister's location on her contact, ignoring the app's server error telling her she wasn't connected to the internet. Her sister's location was the same as when Lehua had checked it two days ago: *No location found. Last seen 2 wks ago.*

Lehua forced herself to take several deep breaths. She could hear her blood pounding in her ears, roaring like a freeway. Was her sister's phone somehow on the island? Or had the notification been a strange technical error caused by the resort's ridiculous dead zone? She turned toward her room.

Daisy stared at her from her balcony's doorway.

Lehua leaped backward, swearing, and hit the railing. How long had Daisy been standing there?

"Jesus," Lehua said as an oily feeling swept down her back. Hadn't she locked the door behind Chiyo? Seeing how Daisy was *inside* her room with a silver dinner tray, she must have forgotten.

"Welcome to Kōpaʻa, Miss Sayers," Daisy said with an overly friendly smile, her pale eyes flashing from Lehua to her clenched phone. "I'm sorry, I didn't mean to startle you. I've brought you your dinner and some fresh clothes."

Lehua exhaled brusquely. "A warning knock would've helped."

If Daisy was offended, she didn't show it. Her smile remained unchanged, and Lehua couldn't resist rolling her eyes.

Daisy's dated outfit and demure gaze had to be a part of the resort's weird historic experience. She looked a year or two older than Lehua and her starched pinafore clashed with her bleached blond hair. She looked like she belonged on a spring break beach, not role-playing as a maid in a bad historical drama. "You'll find your new clothes in the washroom."

The washroom. Lehua cringed. "You know I'm not really a guest here. You don't have to do this whole performance for me."

Daisy's eyes rose, and Lehua's spine stiffened as she took a sudden step back. Under the dim shine of her room's lamp, Daisy's face looked a bilious green. Her wide-eyed gaze skittered along the resort's walls and windows as if the girl was . . . afraid.

Of what? Lehua glanced around. The hair on the back of her neck rose. The acres of sugarcane loomed outside the balcony, the island wind whistling through like dissonant voices. Was there something out there? Was that why Daisy's attention kept darting toward the windows, then back to her feet?

Turning toward the blond girl, Lehua slowly pulled the lanai door shut behind her. "Are you okay?"

Daisy's lips disappeared with a sudden laugh, revealing perfect white teeth. "Of course," she said, pointing toward the bathroom again. "You'll find your new clothes in the washroom."

"Right, you said that," Lehua said, confused. She was slow to enter the bathroom. Once inside, she leaned on the sink's still-wet basin and shook her head. Palming her phone onto the sink's marble, she shut her eyes and took a low, shuddering breath.

The resort's second-floor lighting was weak and thin. Even in here, the fluted glass softened the honeycomb light trying to seep through. Had the bad lighting darkened Daisy's features, casting that strange look onto her face? *I'm just on edge.* Daisy had surprised her after she'd gotten that notification about Ohia's phone, after all.

She saw the grayed-out text box in her mind. She considered asking Daisy about the island's weird cellular dead zone and the notification, but it seemed more likely the girl would commit further to the resort's historical role if Lehua used the words *Wi-Fi* and *worker rights* in her vicinity. She had a better shot at getting information from the guests tonight.

Lehua tugged the cream dress Daisy had provided over her head. The heavy dress was plain and hung short on her. Its hem collided with her calves and its sleeves were snug over her forearms. It was nicer than the faded shirts and cutoff shorts she'd packed, but she still winced when she peered into the mirror.

Her slick curls looked tangled, casting a wreath of shadow

over her thin cheeks and eyes circled with exhaustion. She hadn't packed any makeup. The thought hadn't occurred to her in her rush to get to Hawai'i.

Looking at her clean face, Lehua wished she had something to hide the dark look in her eyes, to paint a glossy smile on, to be anyone else. But Daisy was outside. It was time to go.

When she opened the door, Daisy had uncovered the silver tray. Bleeding cuts of rare meat, seared vegetables, and a thick slice of sourdough bread lay next to a metal pan of creamed butter whipped like icing.

Lehua accepted the tea saucer Daisy offered and stuck her pinky out like she'd seen in a movie. "Thank you."

Daisy's eyes darted to the floor, and Lehua wondered if the other guests didn't say thank you until the bitter tea hit her tongue—she resisted gagging. No wonder Daisy had looked away. Her tea was acrid with a strange metallic taste like ash, reminding her of the crematorium. "What kind of tea is this?"

"Black tea made from the sugarcane harvested on our island."

"It's not very . . . sugary."

"It's from unrefined sugar cane, Miss Sayers," Daisy said, beaming.

"Oh." Lehua carefully set the saucer down. She ate the rest of the dinner quickly, chasing away the tea's burnt flavor. By the time she finished, the resort's strong astringent scent had returned. It coated her tongue, mingling with the tea's aftertaste.

"What's that smell?"

"Smell?" Daisy's smile faltered. "What do you mean?"

"You don't smell it?"

Daisy gave her a dull, searching look. Maybe the other girl had grown used to the strange sweetness. *But how?* The putrid odor knotted Lehua's stomach.

"You mean our persimmons!" Daisy exclaimed. "Our guests can them in the basement. They relish the opportunity to create their own souvenir from the persimmons they harvest, a part of the island they can take home. It's our most famous offering." Daisy's lips bloomed into another overly enthusiastic grin. "Would you like to try one? He won't notice if one goes missing."

He? Lehua could only assume she meant Mr. Jacobs. She shook her head, leaning away. Daisy's eyes were glassy and huge, and seriously weirding her out.

"Why not?" Daisy asked.

Lehua hated to imagine the employee handbook Daisy had been indoctrinated by. "I don't think I'd like the taste, but thanks," she said, forcing a smile to end the conversation. No wonder the fetid smell had seemed so familiar.

The neighbors of one of their foster homes had owned a grapefruit tree, and its fruit always rotted in the summer heat. The rank grapefruits had drawn flies and led to Lehua pushing away anything that reminded her of the spoiled citrus. Her stubbornness had annoyed their guardians. Until Ohia chastised her for being difficult. "Do what they say. Things could be worse."

Warning had flashed in her eyes, and Lehua relented. *Worse* meant separation.

Lehua shoved the memory away. Thanks to Ohia, that *worse* had happened. She reached for her shoes, a pair of black Nikes, and her phone.

"Apologies, Miss Sayers. Cellular phones are not allowed in common areas."

"Why? It's not like there's any service." Lehua tacked on a laugh. Daisy's expression only tightened. "Well, I can't leave my phone. It has my sister's photo on it, and I need to ask the other guests about her."

"Unfortunately, our guests value their privacy, and your cellular phone would make them uncomfortable." Her tone left no room for complaint, and Lehua resisted making a face.

Somehow the walk back to the stairs seemed longer than before. They passed through the hallway like two haunting shades, their white dresses stained red by the resort's antique sconces. Daisy never looked back, and Lehua couldn't shake the feeling that Daisy would vanish if she fell behind. No more than a wraith devoured by the resort's drowsing darkness.

"Is it normally this dark in here?"

"It is nighttime," Daisy answered.

Once they cleared the staircase, the resort brightened. Sibilant voices echoed from another wing of the house, interrupting their own creaking footsteps.

"Is that wise?" a man's voice carried—unable to match the soft whispered words coming from deeper inside the resort.

Before Lehua could hear more, Daisy led her into the first-floor hallway. Mini chandeliers with brass chains hung from a coffered ceiling. The wallpaper had a ti leaf motif, leaves of dark green and rich magenta crawling over a navy backdrop like thick brocade. Lehua counted six doors as they passed, all closed except for one. A wall of security monitors was barely visible through the open door—a slit in the hallway that hadn't been there during her tour with Chiyo.

That's a lot of cameras, Lehua thought, eyeing Daisy, then the screens with a pinprick of unease. *For a* tech-free *resort.*

The resort's white façade and still loch played on one screen. Another showed the jagged tops of a cane field and a faraway silo. But when Lehua saw the back of her head and Daisy's quickly disappearing figure on another screen, she hurried to catch up.

Daisy waited for her in front of two large double doors at the end of the hallway.

"You'll find the lounge that way, Miss Sayers. Miss Amaya will be in there, should you require anything else." She pointed her chin toward the closed doors meaningfully. "We're here to make your stay as rejuvenating as possible."

Daisy's stare moved past her. Lehua looked from her to the doors. She had the uncanny feeling Daisy had seen someone else standing in front of them. But there was no one there. Only the ebony doors and a large doorknob made of cut crystal fitted with brass fruit. What was making Daisy so nervous? While they'd been walking, the other girl had definitely been distracted, warily checking the resort's darkened windows.

"Thank you," Lehua said. But the blond girl had already vanished, deserting her.

Voices evanesced from beyond the door. Years of eavesdropping on foster parents had Lehua curling instinctively toward the conversation.

"I still don't understand," a man said, struggling to keep his voice down. "And I am not entirely convinced it's the truth—"

“Of course you don’t understand, Leigh—” said a dry voice, high and feminine.

“What’s that supposed to mean?” the first voice retorted, a peevish whine. “Why should she stay here? She should be kept outside like the workers.”

“How hospitable,” returned the second voice, brimming with sarcasm.

There was a tense pause before a new voice answered, flat and full of familiarity for Lehua. *Chiyo.* “Unfortunately, that is not your decision to make, Charles. She’s a guest of our resort now and you will treat her as such.”

And then, from the door, a rattle as someone tried the knob.

EIGHT

Lehua ran.

It was old habit. A hard lesson learned from the many guardians she and Ohia had lived with. You stayed quiet, you didn't disobey, and you especially didn't get caught if you were misbehaving. That was how they had stayed together in the Arizona Department of Child Safety—and it was how Lehua found herself hidden inside the security room.

She held her breath while Chiyo pushed apart the lounge's doors. Thankfully the security room had been empty when she rushed in. She watched Chiyo disappear on the monitor—the same one she and Daisy had been on—and appear on another feed seconds later. *Kitchen.*

The screen was one of a dozen camera feeds. There were other monitors labeled in handwritten cursive: *Dining Room*, *Cannery/ Basement*, and *Lounge*—all of which were switched off; while another, *Upstairs Hallway*, showed her room's door and the resort's gallery of photographs and portraits in a long gloomy loop. *What the hell?*

Lehua shook her head. There were cameras placed all over the island—not just the resort. *Sugar Warehouse*, *Machine Shop*, and *Camp House* were turned off. But she recognized the resort's pixelated gravel entrance. The resort couldn't be worried about break-ins, right? So what was with the over-the-top surveillance?

She eyed the monitors. Chiyo's back was still turned toward the camera in the kitchen. A metal office desk was tucked in the security room's corner with a printer, some sort of radio, two storage drawers, and a built-in file cabinet. All of the drawers were locked.

Lehua wished she had a pin or a paper clip to unfurl. She could've tried picking the locks. She'd learned the basics while sneaking out of their foster homes. There'd been a couple of times Ohia hadn't woken up to unlock the front door for her—and Lehua had to get creative. But the office was immaculate and the space was free of personal touches except for the perfect cursive penmanship on the drawer labels. Chiyo's desk, no doubt.

Based on the proximity of the printer, Lehua was willing to bet the resort's computer was stored in one of the drawers. *Employee Applications*, *Reservations*, and *Guest Profiles* were written on some of them.

Lehua shot one glance at Chiyo's screen. The manager had a new drink tray fully assembled. Lehua knew she should leave before Chiyo returned, but . . .

The conversation she overheard curdled her stomach. *She should be kept outside like the workers.* It was obvious the other guests were upset someone like her was getting a free stay that they had paid for. She knew what clientele the resort served. At their track competitions, she and Ohia had met plenty of rich kids with vacation homes in St. Bart's and whose parents hired charter planes. When she and Ohia won their races, those kids always took their losses the hardest.

A part of Lehua wanted to storm into the lounge and defiantly meet the guests' eyes. Except no one would tell her anything about Ohia if she did that. They had been loud enough that if Lehua joined them straightaway, it wouldn't have been a question of whether she had heard but *how much*.

There was clearly more going on at this supposedly tech-free resort than Chiyo had let on. The extensive surveillance system reeked of paranoia—and it unnerved Lehua. She didn't know what situation she'd gotten mired in, but she needed to move smarter with the guests if she was going to find out anything about why Ohia left.

She closed her eyes, took a deep breath, and calmed her shaking hands. Then she slid out of the security room and pushed the lounge doors open. A musky scent ebbed free, carrying the overripe smell of persimmon rot.

The lounge was cavernous, painted in hues of navy. A crystal chandelier cast prisms from the peaked ceiling, dramatically crowning a long bank of gabled windows revealing the island's dusky landscape and faraway sea. Near the four-sided bar, a fireplace burned, filling the balmy room with woodsmoke.

Bracketed by overfilled bookcases, two white men appraised her from their plush wingback chairs in front of a grated fire. One man was older, Lehua guessed he was hovering around his early fifties. But it was hard to tell. His smooth face was puffy, almost swollen atop his neck, and he was soft-bellied and graying in his crisp black suit. There was a furtive look in his sunken eyes, full of undisguised scorn; and his gaze followed her over the rim of his glass topped with a twisted fruit peel. She thought of the peevish voice she'd heard, suggesting she be placed outside. *Bingo.*

The other man slouched in his chair, stretching his crossed ankles toward the fire. She was surprised at how casual he looked. He wore dark jeans, a camel button-up, and shiny penny loafers. The glow of the fire lit up his handsome face, turning his golden hair red.

She forced a smile as she shuffled across the lounge's herringbone floor toward the small library, pretending to be absorbed by the rows of medical journals and frayed leather-bound books crowding the shelves. Above the books were two framed displays. One held chains of pinned insects—butterflies, night moths, and beetles. The other case caged colorful taxidermied birds on ebony branches. A dark ʻalae bird sat in a pile of decayed leaves, its glass eyes unblinking. THE FAUNA OF KŌPAʻA read the plate next to the display.

Lehua cut a path toward the empty bar. A scripture verse was emblazoned on another plaque behind the counter. *God took the man, and put him into the garden of Eden to dress it and to keep it.*

She felt the old man's stare as she pulled out a barstool. "So that's the girl . . ." he whispered, the rest of his words indecipherable as the lounge doors swung open.

Lehua expected to see Chiyo, but instead found a dead ringer for Lady Elaine Fairchilde from *Mr. Rogers' Neighborhood*. Her hair was cut into a dirty blond pixie, her pale face was sunburned red, and she was making a beeline straight for Lehua.

"Figures," the woman muttered, and Lehua thought she might

be famous. Her face and voice were familiar, though Lehua couldn't place her. "I've been looking for Chiyo everywhere, but I guess one of you ghouls will have to do—"

"What the hell?" The word *ghoul* seared like a slap. Lehua's nails dug half-moons into her palms. But before she could say anything more, another voice cut in.

"Lehua's not one of our staff, Jennifer."

Jennifer's neck twisted. Behind her stood Chiyo.

Chiyo was pouring liquid from a treacle-colored bottle into a cordial glass. Then she handed the glass to Lehua. Perfectly composed. "I can't offer our famous persimmon wine to someone underage, but here is a lovely lime and elderberry tonic with cardamom and hibiscus bitters, Lehua."

Realization dawned on Lehua at the woman's name. It'd been a year since she'd sat down in her college sociology class and seen one of her recorded talks. *The Disillusioned Binary: Men and Women and the Fight for Equality* by Jennifer Lynn Ibsen.

"I thought . . ." Jennifer's eyes whipped between Lehua and Chiyo, saying far more than her words did about her assumptions. A quick look around the room made it clear why Jennifer had assumed Lehua was staff. She and Chiyo weren't white like the resort's other guests.

"No, Miss Jennifer. I think the words you're looking for are, *I'm sorry I was racist*," someone called out, and Lehua stilled.

She hadn't noticed the girl sashaying her way toward them in her gown, but now Lehua couldn't help but gawk. She wore opal earrings, strappy silver heels, and a high-neck ivory dress with a slit revealing her bare white thighs. *Sacha Tasse.*

She was a renowned trendsetter who had grown up dodging paparazzi cameras at the back of her mom's fashion shows, alongside her famous mother with her trademark oversized sunglasses. Now Sacha had a beauty brand of her own and four hundred million people following her.

Lehua couldn't believe it was her. Sacha regularly adorned billboards in Paris, Milan, and Tokyo, and magazine covers at the grocery store. Enough so that Lehua had seen the girl's hair dyed every shade between black, brown, lavender, and red. Tonight, it was bleached blond. Crimped waves hung around her pale face, pert mouth, and azure eyes, floating like windblown dandelion seeds.

Jennifer's sunburned face reddened further. She mumbled something far too low for Lehua to hear, practically diving for the lounge's exit.

Chiyo followed the woman out, leaving Lehua with one of the most famous people in the world.

"What a shitty thing to say," Sacha mused, her mulberry-stained lips forming an apologetic grin. "Well, I for one am sorry for Miss Jennifer's behavior."

"Nothing I haven't experienced before." Lehua sipped her drink and almost sputtered. It was aromatic and sour, sliding down her throat like black currant jelly.

She held out her hand. "Sacha."

"I know."

"There's a name I've never heard before." Sacha's eyes glittered, glowing bright blue even in the firelight of the lounge.

"Sorry, I'm Lehua."

Sacha laughed. "It's okay. Miss Jennifer makes people forget their manners all the time," she said, clicking her nails against her amber glass.

"Why do you call her that?" Lehua asked brazenly, but Sacha didn't seem to care.

"Hmm. You caught that?" she smiled thinly. "Miss Jennifer Lynn likes to put me and every other woman on blast for how we make our money. She forgets she married into wealth. She's a widow now but acts like her husband never existed." Sacha downed the rest of her drink, and liquor beaded her lips like resin. She winked—a Sacha Tasse trademark. "Everyone has secrets here, but hers are the most fun to laugh at."

Everyone has secrets here. What kind of secrets could Sacha be alluding to? The usual run-of-the-mill gossip? Or something worse? As she'd been talking, Lehua had noticed the coy way the influencer's eyes had settled on her lips. Maybe she could convince Sacha to share what she knew. The secret lives of the guests might not have much to do with Ohia's departure, but Lehua wasn't going to rule anything out yet.

"What's your story? Chiyo mentioned you're here because of the storm?"

"Something like that. I came here to find my sister. My twin." They headed toward the lounge's bank of windows and Lehua's reflection shone next to Sacha's. "I got stranded instead." She forced a laugh like Ohia would—it rang hollow.

Gazing at their reflections side by side, Lehua thought Sacha looked different in person. Dark circles laced the underside of her blue eyes, giving her a doe-eyed look. Maybe it was her smudged, winged eyeliner. Or perpetual jet lag. In her last post from ten days ago, the influencer had been posed in front of the Eiffel Tower, lounging against a thick stone balustrade in a vintage fur coat.

"She's missing?"

"Maybe?" Adding a heavy note of uncertainty to her voice wasn't hard. Lehua could count on one hand how much she knew about Ohia's disappearance. Predictably, Sacha's eyebrows drew together.

"That sounds like a story. For how long?"

"Two weeks. Chiyo said she left the resort a week ago. Did you meet her?"

Sacha offered her a one-shoulder shrug. "I'm sorry. All I heard was a field-worker left."

A field-worker? "Do you know why she might have left?"

"Wait." Sacha glanced at her. "You're asking me why your sister quit? You don't know what happened?"

"That's what I'm trying to figure out. So far, all I know is she came here to work, then left." Lehua was glad to have the window as a distraction. She didn't have to look at Sacha's surprised expression. *Some sister you are.* Even this close to midnight, the relentless island heat pressed against the resort, weeping condensation over an empty pool filled with dead leaves, and Lehua realized the lounge's windows were a large glass sliding door leading out to the pool. The pool didn't look used much. *Probably because it's over a cliff.*

The resort crowned the island, overlooking its postcard-like town and sea of sugarcane. But there was no barrier between the deck's edge and that treacherous drop into the ocean. The view was beautiful. But it was the same type of menacing beauty she associated with desert thunderstorms in Phoenix, igniting monsoon clouds with licks of white flame.

"That's not much to go on," Sacha said.

Right? "Chiyo said—"

"Chiyo?" Sacha leaned forward, her voice a covert whisper. "Please, the woman's a walking help desk. She wouldn't say anything that'd rock the boat. If she'd been on the *Titanic*, she would've been sitting with the orchestra until the boat sank, still pouring drinks. This is your twin, right? What do you think happened?"

Lehua winced. That was always the expectation, wasn't it? Because they shared a womb, Lehua had to know her sister better than anyone. But . . .

"I don't think Ohia would quit without a reason," Lehua confessed, and Sacha's eyes widened.

"Do you think Chiyo's lying, then?"

Lehua shook her head. She couldn't say for sure. It wasn't Chiyo's fault if Ohia hadn't been forthcoming with her. But thanks to that phone notification and the resort's extensive security, she couldn't shake her suspicions that there was more going on than she'd been told. "I don't think my sister would've told Chiyo anything. When she called me, it was the first time I'd heard from her in months."

At Lehua's forlorn look, Sacha softened. "Here, let's get some air." She opened the lounge's back door, then beckoned like a gracious host for Lehua to follow her. Once outside, Sacha sighed. "I'm sorry, I didn't mean to pry. I'm a true crime nut—I listen to *Graveyard Gossip* at the gym. I'm sure everything's fine. Nothing ever happens here." Sacha patted her arm. "This island is the most boring in all of Hawaii—that's why I'm here this time. I'm *indulging in the land* to heal from a broken heart. But I need some excitement."

Lehua hesitated, remembering that notification from Ohia's phone. She wasn't sure she agreed Kōpaʻa was the most boring island. Something felt off about this resort and the island's heavy atmosphere. But she gave Sacha a huff of sympathy. "For an island resort, it doesn't sound like there's much to do. Chiyo said it's a digital detox. Is there really no service?"

The influencer didn't seem like the type to disconnect. If there was service on the island, Sacha would know.

Sacha wavered, then gave her hand an understanding squeeze. "Yeah, unfortunately this place is stuck in the past. There's no reception anywhere—I know," she sighed. "I feel like I need to don a bonnet every time I visit."

Lehua feigned a laugh, but that heavy feeling that had haunted her since arriving still weighed on her. *Then how did that notification come through?*

As they sat on the pool bench outside, Sacha whispered conspiratorially to Lehua, holding her arm like they were good friends. It was easy to be swept up by the influencer like a bit of debris caught in her planet's orbit. Sacha quizzed her about everything from dropping out of college to her past relationships to Phoenix—to what it was like to have a twin.

"I'm an only child. Besides my mom, I have some cousins that I see once a year," Sacha said, before pointing to the resort guests inside by the fireplace. The older man was Leigh, who was in government but not *in government* as Sacha so helpfully explained to her. "And that's Oliver sitting next to him. He's a big film producer."

Sacha fanned her fingers out, picking at her perfect manicure. Her nails were painted a light yellow ombre, like lemonade that had settled at the bottom of a glass.

Lehua kept her own hands hidden. Her nails were short and ragged, cut below her nail groove and dried out from mortuary-grade hand sanitizer.

"He's like a hundred years old, but he wants me to star in one of his movies. I told him I'd have to check my schedule." Sacha grinned, and Lehua glanced at the men, surprised. Oliver didn't look older than thirty-five. Then again, the influencer worked in beauty and fashion. Turning forty probably felt like having one foot in the grave.

"They were going on and on about zoning permits. Can you imagine a worse topic?" She exhaled dramatically. "All they ever do is talk business." Sacha looked at her like she might understand, so Lehua smiled back in a way she hoped was just as knowing.

Oliver sauntered over then as if he'd been summoned, while Leigh stayed behind, shaking his head disapprovingly, muttering something. Lehua imagined *You're going to talk to a commoner?* wasn't too far off the mark.

"Hello, Oliver," Sacha chimed. "Meet Kōpaʻa's newest guest, Lehua."

"You're the stranded girl Chiyo mentioned." Oliver gave her a lazy perusal, and Lehua bristled. It wasn't like she'd been rescued from a shipwrecked yacht. Had Chiyo not shared the real reason she was there?

She knew the resort manager was likely doing damage control. Her missing sister couldn't be good PR for their high-end clients.

A private island getaway sounded like a luxurious experience until you learned someone had disappeared there. You couldn't charge top-dollar rates if your guests were worried about *Dateline.* That could also explain Chiyo's excessive charity and offer to help Lehua find Ohia on Maui. It had been an economic decision. But . . . the guests could know something and potentially provide a clue to Ohia's whereabouts. Chiyo could've at least asked.

"I'm trying to find my twin," Lehua explained. "She quit working here last week. Did you meet her?"

"Of course not," Leigh interrupted, coming up behind them. *Look who's talking to the commoner now.* Maybe he felt left out. "She wasn't a guest. She was a field-worker. And a likely runaway, as I heard it."

He sent her a contemptuous look. So Chiyo had shared some information with the guests, even though Sacha hadn't mentioned anything earlier. Had the resort manager really called Ohia a runaway?

Sacha rolled her eyes. "It's her first day here, Leigh. You can't expect her to know all of the rules. Let Oliver answer her."

"Sorry. Leigh's a longtime member of Kōpaʻa, and the rules prohibit us from talking to the workers." Oliver shifted and his skin grazed hers. "Chiyo told you about the rules, right?"

Lehua hesitated. She didn't like how close Oliver was. Silver feathered the scruff around his jaw and narrow face, but he was still handsome in that subtle Botox-and-night-cream-daily kind of way. "She mentioned some rules. They seemed strict for a resort."

Leigh narrowed his eyes. "I'd familiarize yourself with those rules during your stay."

"Are you trying to compete with Jennifer for worst first impression?" Sacha asked.

"Don't compare me to her," Leigh said, surprising Lehua. Given Jennifer's disdain for her, she would've guessed they were best pals.

"Don't make it so easy, then," Sacha returned, and looked pointedly away from Leigh. "Oliver, I was telling Lehua about your work."

"Oh yeah?" He smiled, pleased. "I always try to film in Hawaii because of its natural beauty. I actually started my career with *Aloha Lagoon*, *Pacific Pearls*, *Tears of Hawaii*, and *Resort Girls*. You know Rhys Warrick? I found his audition tape—a VHS—in a pile of cast-offs. I made him the star he is today."

Lehua had heard of the actor, a forty-year-old Hollywood heartthrob. She had watched one of his movies with her grandparents and Ohia. On the cover, Warrick had been posed on a beach with dark-skinned girls in dainty swimsuits draped over him like living leis.

The O'ahu military bases her grandpa spoke of never appeared in the film, only a sparkling beach resort. Nameless Hawaiians dutifully served the film's white tourists, moving like set dressing. Just another part of the film's palm-tree backdrop. Until a fat Hawaiian man started bumbling around. Lehua remembered feeling queasy when he spoke pidgin like her grandfather and looked like her grandfather, too. She understood the Hawaiian man was supposed to be a joke. When Warrick called him *lazy*, *stupid*, and *ugly*, he agreed, saying he would never find a woman without Warrick's help. Later, she had looked up the Hawaiian actor, only to discover he wasn't Hawaiian at all. He was a rail-thin comedian, spray-tanned and put in a fat suit for the movie.

Lehua's stomach churned. *Pacific Pearls.* So this was the man who had produced it. "Have the three of you been on Kōpaʻa long?" she asked, smiling with as much civility as she could muster. She just needed to play nice until she could get some information from them.

"Nine days," Sacha answered. "We leave Monday—thank god. The company has been lackluster."

"I wish your mother was here to rein you in," Leigh muttered.

Sacha's pretty smile tensed. "That's exactly why she isn't here—I'm on vacation," she returned archly. "Let's head inside, Lehua. We've exhausted the air out here."

Once inside, Sacha settled onto a teak loveseat and tapped the cushions next to her, a clear invitation for Lehua to join her. But Lehua was squinting at the empty lounge.

"That was everyone?" Considering the resort's size, Lehua had expected more people. Not four guests. That didn't leave a lot of people for her to ask about Ohia. In fact, Jennifer was the only guest left, and Lehua doubted the red-faced woman would be opening up to her—the ghoul—any time soon.

"Yeah, Kōpaʻa is big on exclusivity and *the experience*." Sacha put up air quotes. "They only schedule a handful of guests at a time. My friend Resi—Therese Ma, you know the famous nineties model?" Sacha's lips pressed into a satisfied smirk, reminding Lehua of a cat with a canary. "She's been trying to come here forever, but she can't get a booking. You have to be a member—a planter—and openings are rare. She's been waiting five years. But I've heard some guests can wait decades. Of course, I haven't seen the waitlist because Chiyo values her guests' privacy, but it has to be thousands of names long."

Our exclusive planters, the employee brochure had christened the resort guests. Lehua glanced at Oliver and Leigh outside, then at Sacha. The influencer was easily the youngest. She must not have been on Kōpaʻa's waitlist that long. "How did you get a spot?"

"Do you have to ask?" Sacha breezed out a laugh and winked. "They couldn't keep me out if they tried."

Lehua laughed like she knew she was supposed to, but she couldn't shake the feeling there was something that Sacha wasn't sharing. Why *couldn't* Sacha's celebrity friends get a reservation? The manager said they already had a full group. But when Lehua had shown up, Chiyo had a spare room ready, and the second floor was packed with extra rooms. Could all of them be empty?

She thought Ohia might have learned about the island getaway through one of her well-off track teammates. But it was clear now Kōpaʻa wasn't just for the rich, it was a resort for the one percent. Had her sister known how high-class and private the resort was? Had its exclusivity drawn her here? When they last spoke, Ohia's voice had been threaded through with such need. *Then why would she quit?*

Lehua glanced at the guests in the lounge. What if her sister hadn't chosen to quit at all? Maybe Ohia had been *made* to leave.

NINE

When Lehua parted with Sacha outside the lounge, the influencer pulled her into an embrace, holding on far longer than Lehua thought she would.

"I am sorry about your missing sister, but I am so glad you're here. I was starting to get bored," she whispered. Even though Lehua still didn't trust Sacha, the way she brushed her lips against Lehua's cheek as she departed left her with a heady buzz.

There had been boys and girls in Arizona—people Lehua had snuck out the window of whatever guardian's house they were living in to see—when she wanted her veins to burn with something other than anger. But she had stopped going out after she started at the mortuary, turning her nights over to the dead.

Lehua didn't think she'd imagined the desire in Sacha's eyes tonight, barely obscured by her thick dandelion hair. If it were any other night or place, Lehua would've closed the distance, Sacha's cloying perfume leading them to her room, their mouths melting together. But the longer Lehua lingered in the hallway alone, the clearer her head became.

I am sorry about your missing sister, Sacha had said lightly, and the words were like a well of icy water, floating Ohia's phantom face to the surface, a terrible reminder. She was here to find out what happened to her sister and make sure she was okay.

Lehua wound up the staircase alone. The second floor's cold chased her steps, emptying her of any remaining warmth. In her room, she went over everything Sacha and the other guests had said, writing every detail on her phone. By the time she brushed her teeth, it was past midnight, her mind already drowsing before her head hit the pillow. The resort stairs creaked outside—a haunting metronome that wouldn't stop.

Thud. Thud. Thud.

Lehua squeezed the bed's ivory quilt into a fist. "Hello?"

Thud.

Someone's outside. Except she could feel the presence *inside* her room, lurking somewhere in the dark corners. *Watching her.*

It wasn't until Lehua sat up—and looked behind her—that she saw the blur of pale faces.

They peered at her from the orchard wallpaper like Venetian masks with thick, heavy brows, long cheeks, and stitched mouths. Their eyes were blooms of indigo blue that spilled down the wall, sliding into her hair.

The wallpaper dissolved as the orchard pattern flowed down in ribbons, as if the room itself was weeping. She covered her head in horror, but the inky white and blue dripped onto her bare arms, bleeding into her tattoos and causing the flowers on her arms to wilt, then rot. She rubbed her arms onto the sheets, trying to remove the stains from her skin. But the new ink clung, burrowing beneath her flesh like a swarm of ticks.

Lehua tried to scramble out of bed, but the ink in her blood cured into concrete, her limbs becoming too heavy to move. Her eyes froze forward.

Without the wallpaper, there was nothing to hide the wooden people peering through the gaps of the ebony wall's planks. They gouged their fingers into the wood, tearing an opening. Then they hooked their elbows through the resort's broken wall, the sound like an axe chopping into wet wood—a damp *thunk*. The same noise the deceased made when they were dropped onto the metal slab in the embalming room.

Lehua was rooted to the spot like the taxidermied animals in the lounge. She could only watch as the people climbed out of the wall and reached for her with their clawed hands. White larvae burrowed into their wooden limbs, devouring the infested wood. Their fingers were long and bent with dusty moths clinging to them. As they smiled, their empty eyes glistened and their upturned lips contorted the maggot-ridden wood, revealing jagged teeth interspersed with beetles.

You shouldn't be here, a voice reverberated from their wooden mouths, washing over Lehua. She opened her mouth to scream, but her jaw was sealed shut.

Thud.

Lehua opened her eyes. She was standing over her bed with her hands raised, frantically batting the dreamed ink away from her skin. She'd never sleepwalked before and wondered if she was still dreaming. But the room was all too vivid. Moonlight dusted the furniture in silver.

Someone was talking in the hall, an unrelenting rasp. Until—

Thud. A knock on her lanai door.

Déjà vu, Lehua thought. A bead of cold sweat ran down her back as more knocks pounded the door. Peering outside onto the balcony, Lehua could just make out a shadow outlined by moonlight.

"Hello?" Lehua said. Goose bumps ran down her arms and legs. How long had she been standing, swaying on her feet? "Who's there?"

Could it be Ohia? A sharp pang of heartache and hope skewered her.

"It's me." The shadow laughed quietly. "Melia."

Lehua wound the quilt around her, then opened the back door. Her face softened when she saw Melia. "Hey," she said, taking a deep breath to slow the pounding in her chest. "What are you doing here?"

Melia pushed off the lanai's railing with a smile, "Sorry," she said, her eyes flitting from the heavy quilt to Lehua's face with concern. "Did I scare you? I didn't mean to wake you up."

"You didn't," Lehua said quickly, her nightmare's grip loosening at the sight of the other girl.

"I wanted to see how you were doing. I heard you missed your boat back?"

"The boat left without me," Lehua said, holding the patio door for Melia.

"Oh." Melia strolled inside, taking in the room, restlessly spinning a bit of ti leaf around her wrist. A fragment of the lei Chiyo had given her fastened into a loose cord.

"How is it over there?" Lehua nodded to the old plantation.

"Fine, I guess." Melia flicked on the bathroom's lights. Amber silhouetted her curls as she laughed. "Well, you're living in luxury. Do they run the bath, or do you have to pour your own bubbles? Oh, wait! I bet each bubble is *handcrafted* on the island and blown through a silver hoop for you."

"Ha ha," Lehua muttered. "Sadly, there have been no bubble baths."

"That's disappointing." Melia exhaled. "I thought I was working at a high-class resort. I'd address your complaint myself, but according to Chiyo, I'll be helping with the farm only. No guest interactions allowed." She rolled her eyes and Lehua caught herself smiling.

"You'll be working in the fields?" *Like Ohia.*

Melia nodded, illuminated by gold light. Lehua wished she was immune to the warmth flooding her at the sight of Melia's bright brown eyes. But it was as if Lehua were caught in a fierce undertow.

"So? Any leads on your sister?" Melia asked, breaking the spell. She sat on the floor, legs crossed.

"You heard Chiyo." Lehua sat next to her with her knees drawn up, letting the quilt fall off her suddenly too-warm shoulders. "Ohia used a fake name and quit after a week." *Supposedly.* Lehua still wasn't convinced Ohia had quit willingly. "What I can't figure out is why she'd come here."

"You said you used to have family in Hawai'i," Melia said. "Did any of them work here? Back when it was a plantation?"

Lehua hesitated. She didn't think so. Their dad had never been in the picture—she doubted he even knew they existed—and the only clue the police had unearthed about their mom's whereabouts was the phone number of an O'ahu shelter she had departed a decade ago. It'd been clear from their caseworker's downturned eyes what he thought: *She's probably dead.* Closing their mom's case had just been the bureaucratic way to tell them.

Six years later, Lehua was content to keep their mom's ending blank. But was Ohia looking for answers?

"If we had family out here, Ohia wouldn't have kept that from me." Lehua knew that much.

Melia frowned. "Did Chiyo say why Ohia quit, or where she was heading next?"

You'd think, Lehua thought, almost reaching for her phone. What would Melia say if she told her about that strange notification? *Would she think I'm crazy? Strung out?* Finally, Lehua confessed, "I think there's something else going on and that Ohia was forced to leave."

Melia straightened. "Forced? You don't think she quit?"

"That's the thing. Ohia wouldn't quit after a week," Lehua said, shaking her head. "She's one of those"—*annoying*, she almost said—"people who can pick up anything and make it look effortless. If she quit . . ."

Melia's dark expression matched hers. "Something must have happened."

Lehua nodded. "That's what my gut says. And—" She inhaled through her teeth, then recounted their fight, Ohia's phone call, the creepy notification she'd gotten, and how a strange dread had been tamping down on her ever since they disembarked.

It was the fearful way Daisy looked toward the resort's windows and the whispering sugarcane, the resort's insistence on being tech-free despite the massive security room and cameras strung up everywhere, and the leaves littering the unused pool outside the lounge.

"There's clearly something strange going on here," Lehua finished. "Nothing's adding up. But I think Ohia left in a hurry and that notification came from her phone."

"You think she forgot her phone?"

Lehua shrugged. "I mean, that's the only explanation that makes any sense. There's no service on the island, so that notification had to have come from somewhere nearby." She was flat out guessing now. But what other explanation could there be, given everything she'd been told?

Melia was quiet, picking at her nails, bitten down to the skin. Lehua wondered if she sounded more confident than she felt. Maybe her composure had given way—she certainly felt like she wore her misery and fear plain on her face.

Then Melia rose to her feet, smiling one of her loose, easy grins that pulled at Lehua's stomach. She extended her hand. "Hey, we'll figure it out."

Lehua stared at Melia's offered hand, not because she didn't like Melia. She did—probably more than she should. But why would the other girl want to help her?

I'm a stranger, Lehua almost said. *You don't know me or my sister.* But Melia's pretty eyes were open and expectant—and lonely, shining with the same unmoored feeling that had plagued Lehua since she'd arrived in Hawai'i searching for Ohia.

Lehua accepted her hand, letting herself be pulled to her feet. *We.* It felt like a commitment, an agreement between the two young Hawaiian girls—*we're doing this*—and there was a strange intimacy burrowed beneath the gesture. In the way they'd whispered to each other like they were sharing a secret, and the night filling the room, the rumpled sheets on her bed, and the honeyed light staining half of Melia's face.

It would be too easy for Lehua to shut her eyes and give in to her exhaustion and the illusion that Melia was in her room for a different reason than her missing sister—that her concern meant anything more—and that Ohia hadn't disappeared at all. But Lehua recognized herself enough to know when she was running headlong into trouble.

Lehua forced herself to let go of Melia's hand and moved toward the patio. The heavy scent of sap wafted through the open doors, overpowering the ripe fruit perfuming her room. "How do you know we'll figure it out?" In the dark, the sugarcane fields looked impenetrable.

Melia came up next to her. She silently rotated her ti leaf bracelet, her arm skimming Lehua's. "I did some research on this place—on Kōpaʻa—before coming here. Their brochure sells a pretty story about Horace Jacobs. But his plantation wasn't the benevolent paradise that cared for the land like they claim."

"What do you mean?" Unease snaked through Lehua from her heart to her legs. She was suddenly in her grandma's arms next to Ohia, flipping through her grandparents' photos of Hawaiʻi. *If you take care of the land, it will take care of you.*

A story for children, Lehua thought. Still, the dread weighing her down didn't lessen. "That was a long time ago. What does the plantation's history have to do with my sister?"

"Well, the brochure got one thing right." Melia swallowed. "This island has a history. One of my uncles was a fisherman, and he told me a story about this place years ago. He was leaving Lāhainā Harbor when he saw a man furiously swimming for the pier. It was close to three a.m. and my uncle thought his boat must've crashed. He threw him a life jacket, then helped him toward the shore. My uncle offered the man water and tried to find out what had happened. But all the man said over and over again was *Don't send me back.* When my uncle asked what he meant, the man said *Kōpaʻa.* It was the last thing he said."

"Wait. He died?"

Melia nodded. "My uncle said once they reached Lāhainā, the man closed his eyes and never opened them again."

"That can't be the whole story."

Melia's lip curled. "Unfortunately, it is. The Coast Guard came here to investigate, but they didn't find anything—there was no evidence the guy had even come from here. They closed the case, but my uncle never got over it. He said, *There was no lie in his fear,* and when the man died, he had a strange smile on his face." She shook her head. "The Coast Guard didn't believe he had been strong enough to swim through the Pailolo Channel, but my uncle did."

They closed the case. Lehua knew the feeling. She thought about the terrified look in Daisy's eyes and how she had avoided the resort's windows. "You said you did research. Are there other stories like that? About this place?"

Melia nodded. "I didn't mention it before because you said you didn't believe."

"In what?"

"Island superstitions," Melia answered, watching Lehua in the dark. "Kōpaʻa is ʻeʻepa. *Unexplainable.* History like that stains a place—it leaves its mark on the present."

It was clear from the resolute set to Melia's jaw that she believed the island's past could explain why Ohia had run away so quickly. And yet . . .

"Then why did *you* take the job?" Lehua asked.

"It's a job. I needed it," Melia said in a cool voice that allowed no further discussion. Then: "Why don't we meet up tomorrow morning? I have an employee orientation around eleven. If we meet up early, we can look through the barracks for anything your sister might have left behind. We can search the island together." She threw Lehua a winning grin. "What do you say, Lehua?"

Lehua hesitated, taking in Melia and her disarming ease. Melia knew the island and its history, and it wouldn't hurt to have her help searching the island for her sister. She could feel that same pull she'd encountered when they'd first met, like the tide drawing her in. But there was an undercurrent beneath Melia's pretty allure—in the terse way she refused to talk about herself—and her veiled bitterness. *It's a job. I needed it.* Yet her name in Melia's mouth sparked through her, sharp and electric. *We*, Melia had said, and the word buoyed Lehua.

"Let's do it—and let's meet there," Lehua said, pointing toward the silent town they'd arrived in. "If someone saw us arrive tonight, maybe they saw Ohia leave, too, and they can tell us what happened. After that, we can search the barracks for her phone."

Melia matched Lehua's smile. "It's a date."

TEN

Lehua watched Melia slide back down the balcony to the ground, landing beside a hedge of ti leaf. She waved as she left, then disappeared into the cane. Lehua couldn't help but wonder if Melia had actually winked, or if that had been a trick of the light. *It's a date.*

The words loosened the taut knot that had formed since she'd arrived. But Lehua's relief was short-lived.

Once she turned toward her room and the wallpaper above her bed, the memory of her nightmare constricted her stomach. The way the ink had rotted the tattooed garden on her arms. Now there were no peering white faces staring from the wallpaper—only a pattern of golden persimmons, glistening on indigo branches.

It was just a dream, she told herself. *A nightmare.* But Melia's stories about the island clung to the room. *Don't send me back.* The dying man's words kept playing in Lehua's head, melding with her nightmare. *You shouldn't be here.*

She shivered, gripping the edge of her quilt, avoiding looking at the wallpaper. With Melia's words fresh in her mind, she didn't want to get back into the bed where she'd been trapped. She took a shallow breath that did nothing to ease her anxiety and grabbed her phone. Lehua saw the time, 1:37 a.m., then swiped through her apps out of habit until she saw her open mobile browser. A search prompt was already typed in.

How long do u have to find a missing person

Lehua swallowed tight.

She didn't remember typing those words or her request timing out, leaving a gray web page. *Safari cannot open the page because your iPhone is not connected to the internet.* She threw her phone back onto the bed. She had to have typed that before falling asleep. *Why don't I remember?*

Her mind returned to the way she'd awakened from her nightmare, standing over her bed. She had no memory of climbing to her feet then, either. Was it possible she'd typed it then?

She heard Melia's resolute words. *Kōpaʻa is ʻeʻepa.* Unexplainable.

Don't be ridiculous. Lehua worked her forehead with her hands. Her eyes burned with exhaustion and her body was wrung dry from the long day she'd had. *That's all.*

She staggered to the bathroom and flicked off the light, shrouding her room in darkness again. She didn't know why she bothered. Rest wouldn't come—not with her nightmare or that internet search running on a loop through her mind.

The best thing she could do to find Ohia was sleep, but her fear had thickened into dread. She'd told Melia about the monster hiding in her closet, her fear that *something happened*—and instead of assuring her that there were no monsters in her room, telling Melia had been like opening the door, proving her right. *It's not your imagination. There* is *a monster living here.*

Her fear for Ohia had been a small parasite before—a pale worm feeding on her since she'd learned of her disappearance. But now it was growing, and Kōpa'a with its unshakable dread was the perfect habitat for it to thrive in.

As Lehua's mind raced, she saw lantern light streaking the fields outside.

Perhaps she and Melia weren't the only ones awake on the island. But why would someone be up after midnight, wandering the fields? The thought left her uneasy, unsure whether she was dreaming again.

Lehua unlocked her balcony door and padded outside, surprised to see the lights were coming from the old plantation. Light spilled from the windows, pouring across the sugarcane fields.

I thought the plantation was closed. Yet the mill hummed across the field, releasing a grinding moan that raised the hair on Lehua's arms. She jumped as she caught the silhouette of a person walking past one of the upper windows. She was leaning forward, trying to get a better look, when she saw the bodies spearing apart the cane.

Lehua backed into her room. At least fifty people were moving through the field, going toward the plantation's rusted smokestack, which exhaled exhaust like a mottled metal snake shedding its skin.

When Chiyo said Kōpa'a was a working farm and orchard,

Lehua had assumed the resort manager meant a handful of workers. Not this many. *Chiyo said they hadn't brought back their work crew.* The field-workers and their lanterns pierced the night, trailing as far as the persimmon orchard's chain-link fence. Who were all these people then, and why were they harvesting at night?

We don't cut plants after dark, my Lehua. A memory, a superstition her grandma had warned her about came back to Lehua.

They'd been in her grandma's garden pruning sage and chuparosa, gathering the loose flowers into a pile, when her grandma had suddenly guided Lehua to her feet.

"That's enough for today," she'd said, squeezing Lehua's hand. The deepening dusk had turned the strands of her grandmother's hair into charcoal.

"But it's finally cooled down," Lehua had protested. "Why don't we—"

Her grandma had sunk low to meet her gaze. Lehua remembered her hair raising at the pointed look in her grandma's eyes. "We don't cut plants after dark, my Lehua."

We. Even then, Lehua had known the word meant more than she and her grandmother and more than her grandfather and Ohia. It was the same *we* Melia had used when she'd extended her hand, offering her help to Lehua although they were strangers. *We'll figure it out.*

Because *we* meant Hawai'i.

"Why not?" Lehua had asked, wading back through the garden, hand in hand with her grandma.

"It attracts spirits," she'd said, and Lehua had melted into the comforting warmth of her grandma's arms. Even after all these years, her grandmother's passing felt fresh, a raw feeling spearing her chest at the memory.

Back then, Lehua had believed her. Now she eyed the field-workers and their knives, the blades transmuted into gold by lantern light. There was no way all fifty of them could be brand-new hires like Melia. They harvested row after row of sugarcane and maneuvered around the fields with a practiced ease.

Lehua considered the field-workers. One of them *had* to have met Ohia before she quit. She glanced over the balcony's edge, hovering only a couple of feet above the ti leaf stalks planted at the base of the resort.

The resort rules had been clear. Interrupting the island's field-workers and leaving the resort's immediate premises after dark were not allowed. But the need to figure out what happened to Ohia had Lehua scooping up her Nikes and phone. Hurriedly, she tossed one leg over the balcony's rim and leaped down.

She'd broken stricter rules in their foster homes for far less.

Tall stalks of ti leaf and sugarcane encircled the resort where she landed. The sugarcane field was bigger and more spread out than Lehua had expected. The cane was too tall to see over. Their leaves swelled with the wind, blotting out the sky. Could she find a shortcut through the field? She reached into the cane to begin walking through the field, then pulled her hand back with a hiss.

Blood darkened her knuckles.

"Dammit," Lehua swore, sucking the cut the sharp sugarcane had left. She'd have to use the resort path. At least the moon was bright enough that she wouldn't need her phone's flashlight.

A warm breeze carried the voices of the workers and the mill's drifting smoke as she started to circle the field.

Kaikamahine.

Lehua whirled to look over her shoulder. The faint whisper could have been the sway of the sugarcane field, twisting with the wind. Until she caught movement from the corner of her eye.

"Hello?" Lehua called, shifting her weight nervously. Was it possible she'd found a worker already?

She listened. The mill's electrical hum droned in the distance. But her eyes kept flickering over the tall shoots each time the sugarcane sighed, sawing apart the plush silence of the night. Because in the unsettling quiet of the thick field, Lehua heard someone *breathing.*

She muffled a scream as a blade's edge hacked through the grass.

An East Asian woman was carving her way through the nearby field, carrying a lantern and cane knife.

"Sorry," Lehua said, embarrassed, her heart pounding so damn loud she couldn't think. "You surprised me."

The woman didn't answer. She drifted through the cane on the other side of the ti leaf, her back facing Lehua, singing too low for her to hear the words.

"Hello?" Lehua said, moving slowly toward the woman. Still, she didn't turn. She just swung rhythmically, sliding the hooked blade of her cane knife through the stalks, singing sotto voce: "Isogu pau hana / Mibi no ha ga karamu / Korobya mi o sasu / Kibi no iga."

Lehua hesitated, her skin prickling with unease. The blade

sliced through the cane jerkily with a wet, tearing noise that echoed over the song, spreading the sweet scent of crushed sugarcane. Was the woman injured? Why was she moving like that?

Mibi no ha ga karamu . . . The song hung in the air, low and husky. But the sound of the sugarcane being severed was like the snapping of a bone, each stalk falling like a skeletal limb in the hushed field, making Lehua's heart leap in her chest.

Lehua shielded her eyes as the lantern light spilled over her. She could see the side of the woman's face, the lifted corner of her lips, spread into a smile. The woman wore long sleeves, a white apron, and a full-length skirt with a kerchief wrapped around her black hair.

Something rustled the cane grass near the woman. Another woman broke through the cane, wearing the same kerchief, long sleeves, apron, and floor-length skirt. A uniform.

"Excuse me," Lehua said, raising her voice. But neither of them acknowledged her. She stepped over the ti leaf and entered the cane. The razor leaves grasped at her knees and legs. The women continued their singing. *Can't they hear me?*

She was close enough now that she could see the sleeves of their blouses were bound up to their elbows with strips of stained white fabric—the same white muslin as the kerchiefs draped over their shoulders that were matted with . . . dark red.

Lehua froze. A familiar metallic tang filled her nose, sending her mind spinning. She was suddenly in Avery's embalming room, smelling the blood of the deceased as it was drained out of their femoral artery.

Are those bloodstains? Lehua drew in a sharp breath. As she retreated from the women, a cane stalk snapped loudly underfoot, interrupting their singing with a chilling echo.

Their scythes twitched in the air as their heads twisted toward the sound. Toward Lehua.

ELEVEN

As the women faced Lehua with their flat rictal grins, time seemed to slow.

What the hell?

Lehua's heart kicked with fear as she tried to form the words—*I'm sorry, please, I'm looking for my missing twin*—but nothing came out.

The women's pupils were dilated, black consuming the brown of their irises. Their unblinking gazes gleamed like greased coins placed on the eyelids of the dead. The women moved toward Lehua in a terrible shambling walk. Their shining eyes, perfect for nocturnal hunters, adhered to her, and their uncanny smiles widened as if she were prey.

What's wrong with them?

Lehua didn't intend to find out. She dove for the thick sugar-cane behind her, using it for cover as she ran. She shoved her way through the cane grass, throwing her arms protectively over her face. *Too slow*, she heard Coach Uzzy laugh, a mocking phantom she shut out. She didn't need to be faster than Ohia right now. She just had to get away.

With relief, she spotted the lights of the resort—and the shape of a person walking on the other side of the ti leaf. She kept running, not daring to look back at the singing women with their bloodstained kerchiefs and their sweeping scythes. She leaped toward the resort path, crashing through the cane stalks and ti leaf. A flash of fluorescent light struck Lehua's face, sending her stumbling onto the gravel.

Lehua rubbed her eyes, seeing inverted stars. Someone choked in surprise but she couldn't make out a face. She was kneeling on the ti leaf path, crouching under the resort's countless windows and ivory façade, her heart pounding against the bolts of her rib cage. She waited for the women to emerge with their glittering eyes and bared smiles, caught somewhere between pain and pleasure. But there was only the howl of the cane leaves pushed apart by the wind.

"What are you doing out here?" A shadow loomed over her. Lehua looked up to see a man cradling a massive camera. Oliver.

"Sorry, Oliver. It's me, Lehua. We met in the lounge earlier," she explained, scrambling to her feet. "I was taking a walk when I saw . . ."

She turned, waiting, she realized, for the women to crash out of the cane.

"I remember meeting you. Leigh gave you a big speech about following the resort's rules." Oliver chuckled, looking toward the cane she'd run out of. "How's that going for you?"

Lehua didn't answer as she peered into the silent field. A chill raced down her back. The leaves were crowded too tightly for her to see anything. But she didn't hear anyone coming. "Did you see them?"

"Who?"

"The workers," Lehua said, playing it over and over in her head—the two women chasing her through the cane before she fell. "I ran into some workers, but they were acting strange."

"Strange?" Oliver lowered his camera and offered her a wry smile. "You mean working?"

"No," Lehua insisted, her brow furrowing with confusion. "They chased me."

Oliver raised his camera, shaking his head. "You're the only runner I've seen tonight. You're probably just stressed."

Lehua ran her tongue over her bottom lip, remembering the unnatural way the women had jerkily moved. She couldn't shake the way the workers had leered at her, their lips stretched like they were held open by unseen hands. Their eyes had glowed, shining in the dark like an animal's. But that wasn't possible.

Lehua watched Oliver as he snapped pictures of the now-empty field. Had he really not seen anything?

"Never mind," she muttered. Her entire body ached with a familiar soreness, her legs throbbing like they used to after track practice. Her draining adrenaline left her shivering despite the warm air.

"Why are you out here, anyway?" she asked. She didn't care, but the alternative was returning to her dark room, and she still felt uneasy. She wasn't a photographer but two a.m. seemed like the worst time to photograph anything. She remembered his jab about the rules. "What about the curfew?"

Oliver's gaze swept toward her, then back to his camera's viewfinder. "I consider this island my second home. I find it fascinating. This place celebrates over a century of tradition and heritage, and this island feels . . ." He paused, lifting his camera again. This time, its lens was focused on Lehua. "Untouched by the deprivation of the Western world. A fantasy I can step into and explore."

The camera's flash flared, illuminating the skin covering Lehua's eyes as she blinked. When she could finally see again, Oliver had taken another step toward her. The film producer showed her his camera's mini display. She was a shadow against the plantation's blurry smokestack rising like a black steeple. Her lips were slightly parted—her appearance mussed, grass grazing her hair.

"Like a living photograph," he whispered.

Lehua didn't know what to say. There was something provocative about the photo, what Oliver was saying, and how close he was. Her heart pounded, a frantic drumbeat, as he didn't move away.

"Sorry, I interrupted your photography session," Lehua said abruptly. But as she moved to leave, the film producer followed her, closing in so tightly his chest bumped hers.

"You weren't interrupting anything," he said, his gaze snagging hers—trying to hold on. Lehua turned, looking for an escape. It was the dead of night, which meant she was alone in the dark with him.

They both knew where she stood in the resort's hierarchy. She wasn't a real guest. She was a poor girl being given a free room while he was a member. A *planter.*

"I have to go." Lehua tried to maintain her neutral expression as she shrank away, attempting to put some distance between them.

"Wait," Oliver said, drawing closer. "You said you're looking for your sister. Your twin."

"You met her?" Lehua paused, even as caution dug into her back like thorns at the film producer's lazily spreading grin. Oliver was giving her the once-over, a crude examination. Her throat tightened. Did he give her sister the same assessment?

"No, but maybe I can help you find her." Oliver reached for her face, gripping her cheek with his cold fingers. "Are you identical twins?"

"Back off." Lehua shoved him away, his nails dragging across her lower lip. She debated her next move as the sugarcane's sharp leaves pressed into her, giving her nowhere to run.

Oliver's hand stilled. His eyes drew tight, staring into the cane field behind her.

"Miss Sayers should be asleep."

Lehua and Oliver jumped at the clipped voice. Daisy stood on the gravel path behind him, wearing her ridiculous pinafore and carrying a heavy lantern that threw shadows over her.

"I will lead Miss Sayers to her room."

Oliver finally withdrew from her, making Lehua shudder. "I was only trying to help." He gave a contemptuous shrug. "But she didn't want it."

Lehua silently followed Daisy, pushing her hands into her pockets to hide their trembling.

"You know it's against the rules to leave the path," Daisy said disapprovingly, already starting for the resort entrance. "And you shouldn't be out here after dark."

"I'm sorry," Lehua said. She wasn't going to complain now. She preferred Daisy's scolding to Oliver's reaching hands, and Daisy's disapproval was softened by the smile she still wore. She didn't know if it was for her benefit—or a pretense for Oliver. She could feel his gaze tracing her fleeing back. Until the resort robbed him of his view. Relief flushed Lehua's skin. "Thank you."

Daisy said nothing as she led Lehua to the resort's long terrace. Cardinal creeper clustered around the porch, the red flowers flaring like starbursts on a garden trellis overlooking a plot of buffelgrass. Clutching a heavy key ring, Daisy reached for the branching crimson vines. A lock clicked. She stepped back and the lattice screen came with her, revealing a hidden entrance into the resort.

"After you, Miss Sayers."

Lehua paused in the doorway, trying to meet Daisy's averted eyes. "Thanks, Daisy. I mean it," she said. "You rescued me."

"I try my best to anticipate all of our guests' needs."

Once again, Lehua didn't know what to make of the girl and her careful, poised answers. Daisy was watching the fields closely, her pale gaze lost in the swaying cane. "You should watch out for him. You're his type."

"Young?"

"Hawaiian."

Lehua thought about the daintily dressed Hawaiian girls cloaking Warrick, Oliver's big star, and shivered. Oliver said he hadn't met Ohia, but Lehua wasn't sure she believed him. A handsy guest like him might have driven Ohia to quit—or someone else at the resort might have witnessed their interaction and *made* Ohia leave. Oliver was one of the resort's planters, after all, and Ohia had been a worker. The thought of Oliver trying anything with her sister made her skin crawl.

Daisy caught her shudder. "Good. Now don't forget it," she said with something like approval. "I can't always anticipate what our guests need."

Lehua understood the other girl's warning: *I can't promise I'll always be there.* She nodded, then entered the hidden alcove. Moonlight illuminated a corkscrew staircase inside, the spiral steps snaking up the space and disappearing into a dust-scattered gloom overhead.

Daisy shut the terrace's door behind them and locked it with the key. Lehua sniffed. Faint rot mingled with the dust in her throat. The resort's famous persimmons. Their fetid perfume wafted down the spiraling steps with a sickening sweetness. The fruit they kept in the basement had to be overripe. She imagined the flesh infested with flies, buzzing beneath the floorboards as they devoured the fruit—and her bile rose in disgust.

Lehua had tilted her head back, trying to ease the sour taste coating her throat, when she saw a figure on the spiral staircase, limned in darkness. She jumped.

"Who is that?" she whispered.

"Who?"

Lehua pointed toward the curved landing. But it was empty, lying in downy darkness. *Where did he go?*

Daisy blinked. "I don't see anyone."

How? Even though she'd just seen him for a moment, the man's appearance was burned into her mind, haunting the darkness. His intense blue eyes, the same color as the mortuary's body bags, set against a powdery white face lined with wrinkles. His flesh had looked like the rind of a fruit left on the branch for too long, tunneled with mold.

Am I losing my mind? First the workers, then this man. The thought capsized her stomach. Daisy was watching her with that darting look of hers. "Are you feeling well, Miss Sayers?"

Lehua shook herself. She was tired and anxious. That was the awful truth. She'd been on her feet, looking for Ohia since sunrise, and she'd left her room in the resort close to two a.m.—five a.m. in Arizona. Who knew how late it was now? She felt like she'd circled the bell lap on the longest day of her life.

But when a board creaked overhead, Lehua couldn't stop herself from quickly looking up for the man again. *You're acting ridiculous.*

"Sorry," Lehua told the other girl forcefully. "I'm just tired." It didn't matter if they were true, saying the words chafed Lehua. "What's up there, anyway?"

"That staircase leads to the cupola and Mr. Jacobs's room." Daisy slid her hand atop the aged cloth walls until a click sounded; then she was tugging open another hidden door for her and Lehua. "This is the only hallway in the resort that doesn't have cameras, as it used to be the service wing for his servants. They'd use the stairs to travel quickly between his room, the dining room—" Daisy pointed at an empty wall space. Undoubtedly another secret door was veiled beneath it, hidden within the resort's walls. Then she flourished a hand toward the wide passage she held open. "And what was once Horace's library."

Lehua hesitated, unsure if she should ask Daisy about the resort's security measures. Something in Daisy's tight smile made her think twice. She stepped into the hidden passageway and emerged on the other side, entering the lounge. With the room's lights extinguished, it looked like a playhouse's empty stage. Daisy closed the door behind them, sealing it into the paneling so tightly Lehua couldn't see the seam where the opening had been. "What happened to all of them? All of the staff."

A strange look flitted through Daisy's pale eyes. "After his fields spoiled for the first time, Horace stopped hiring servants for the house to save money and retrenched his staff."

The first time? Lehua blinked. But Daisy had already moved on, leading her back through the lounge to her room. Daisy paused, her hand on the glass doorknob carved in the shape of a persimmon.

"I'll have to tell Chiyo you were out there."

Lehua raised a brow. Chiyo. Not Miss Amaya. Was Daisy breaking character for her? "Am I grounded?"

She had meant it as a joke, a way to saw through the night's buzzing tension. But when Daisy's eyes cut to hers, they were wide with fear, her white teeth sinking into her bottom lip.

"You must remember the rules, Miss Sayers," she said, releasing her lip, and Lehua almost expected blood to wet the girl's mouth like lipstick. "They exist for a reason."

2

MAKAʻĀINANA:

eyes and face of the land; people of the land

TWELVE

SATURDAY

A faraway whistle woke Lehua. She stared at her room's unfamiliar ceiling, striped with dusky blue light. Kōpa'a. Hawai'i. Her homeland. The thought rattled in her chest.

Lehua stole a look at the time on her phone. A little after six. Thanks to her nightmares, she'd barely slept at all. She pushed herself up and winced. Her legs throbbed.

There was a time she would have rolled dutifully out of bed to run drills with Ohia, their heartbeats ticking out the seconds until sunrise. She didn't miss their track routine, but she hated how hard it was to peel herself off the bed every morning without that discipline. Now her body protested each step toward her balcony.

The farmworkers were cresting a hill, turning away from the rusted mill and silos. She glimpsed a row of kerchief-wrapped heads and remembered fleeing the two field-workers last night, the sugarcane's living labyrinth closing in on her.

Lehua swallowed. She had slept curled in a tight ball, the

night's eerie events following her into her dreams. But under the morning light, the terror and fear that had chased her through the field was hard to hold on to—and harder to believe.

Except for Oliver. She shuddered, remembering his leering. At least now she had a lead as to why Ohia might have left.

When she and Melia met up, she'd share what happened with the film producer while they searched the town for her sister's phone, passing on Daisy's warning about Oliver's type.

Hawaiian.

Lehua threw on a clean shirt and denim cutoffs; then she slipped her phone and rechargeable battery into her pocket. The cold enveloped her arms as she drifted toward the stairs. She saw Daisy disappear into one of the rooms near the end, abandoning a housekeeping cart piled with linens outside. She doubted the girl had gone to bed at all, which meant Chiyo had likely heard about her late-night rule-breaking. Lehua hoped Daisy had mentioned Oliver, too.

Once Lehua stepped outside the resort, the island stretched out before her, offering a stunning view of the ocean and Kōpaʻa's sugarcane fields. Lehua walked toward the town, brushing her fingers against the path's ti leaf. The farther she got from the resort, the more the island's strange claustrophobia eased, carried away by the wind, the air no longer thick with the scent of overripe persimmons.

By the time Lehua reached the edge of town, the morning sky was brightening to a lighter blue, softening the town's stark black-and-white paint. Before her, the plantation town rose, silent as a mausoleum—and just as devoid of people.

As Lehua walked by the empty stores, she noted the browned fliers adorning the shop walls. *Jacobs & Pacific: Good Wages and Better Living Conditions than California* read one of the less-tattered pages in big blocky letters.

Despite what Melia had said about seeing someone in a window, the town looked as abandoned as it had last night. Maybe they'd be better off tracking down some of the field-workers instead of investigating the town.

Since she was early, Lehua walked to the jetty, then checked her phone. A bar appeared in the corner of her screen. It disappeared as she paced. No matter what she did, there was only one bar—and no new notifications from her sister's phone. She knew getting a signal or another notification was a long shot, but she sighed anyway. *Where'd you go, Ohia?*

The tide came in and the salt spray chased away the persimmon smell lingering in her nose.

"Our ancestors were voyagers." The memory of her grandpa's voice rose with the tide. "And even though it's been years, I can still feel our home. That way."

He'd pointed, and Lehua and Ohia had checked the map on his phone, astounded he had been right. It became a game. They'd ask him which way Hawai'i was, and their grandpa had never been wrong.

When she and Ohia went to a track meet in Santa Monica in high school, it'd been both the farthest from Arizona and the closest to their ancestral homeland the twins had ever gotten—and the first time they'd seen the ocean their ancestors had sailed. Lehua had waded into the sea, waiting to feel that tether pulling her home beneath the brine itching her skin. But she had felt nothing. Lehua remembered pushing her wet feet back into her socks and sneakers, her eyes misting—and shook the memory away.

She was circling the hill around the plantation town when she saw the first gravestone, leaning sideways. It was twelve feet away, old and cracked like a broken tooth. Crouched behind the sugarcane, the gravestone was planted in an open plot leading to a larger graveyard beyond.

The air was thick and silent. The only sound was Lehua's footsteps in the mulch, softened by the tangle of weeds carpeting the graveyard, overrunning the neglected graves. Faded headstones were arranged in a row, trailing toward a granite mausoleum that overlooked the town. Though it was impossible to make out the name carved on the ancient stone, she suspected it was the Jacobs family crypt, standing vigil. Horace's legacy.

It was the opposite of the burial her grandparents had gotten from the state. Until they turned eighteen, she and Ohia hadn't known where their remains were. Now they knew.

Their ashes lay in a mass grave, marked only by the year they died. A plot for the unclaimed. It hadn't been meant maliciously or cruelly—the handling of their deaths had just been logistics. The county had no recorded next of kin except their mother, who had been officially declared missing, while she and Ohia had been forgotten in an online database, another type of bureaucratic sinkhole. But it had felt like another pointless injustice, a grievance she and Ohia would be expected to bear, on top of all the others.

It was hard not to feel that her grandparents were somehow

looking over her shoulder, staring at that crypt on Hawaiian land. The burial Lehua wished she'd been able to give them.

Hawaiʻi's this way, she could've told her grandfather, surrendering his ashes to the land.

She was about to return to the town to wait for Melia when she stopped in her tracks. An unmistakable trail of fresh footprints was pressed atop the graves. The footprints cut across the graveyard, leading into the cane field.

Lehua's skin prickled as the morning's heat grew heavier. She glanced over her shoulder. She felt as if she were being observed. The island's lone road stretched, empty except for her own footprints.

"Lehua?"

She jumped, a mixture of surprise and relief sweeping over her.

Melia emerged from the cane fields, wearing denim jeans, a tucked-in long-sleeved shirt, and tall boots. A mauve bandana held back her curly hair, but a few loose strands haloed her warm eyes.

"You're early," she said, fidgeting with the ti leaf wrapped around her wrist. "Couldn't wait to see me, eh?"

"No, I . . . I couldn't sleep." Lehua saw the divot above Melia's smiling lips and hoped the other girl would assume the red staining her face was from the sun.

"What are you doing up here, anyway?" Melia looked at the graveyard. "Are you clocking into work?"

"I was just looking around," Lehua said lamely, feeling embarrassed. "I don't work at a graveyard."

"Right." Melia smiled. "You work at a morgue? In Phoenix?"

"A mortuary. A morgue's different," Lehua said, descending the graveyard's sloped hill with Melia. Lehua was surprised to see her listening intently.

"Well, what's different about them?" Melia asked. "I definitely skipped the morgue and mortuary booth at our high school job fair."

"A morgue is usually in a hospital or a coroner's office. They have coolers for the deceased to stay in temporarily, but they don't handle funeral services," Lehua said, and she heard Avery's voice: *Saying goodbye is our job.* "A coroner will do examinations to figure out how they died—"

"Right, an autopsy."

"Yeah, so when they're done, they call someone to make the final arrangements."

"You."

Lehua nodded. "We pick up the deceased, then bring them back to the mortuary where we prepare them for their funeral."

"Is it hard? Witnessing all those goodbyes?" Melia asked.

Lehua swallowed. "The goodbyes aren't hard. Burying the dead who have no one to say goodbye to them is harder."

"Except you're there." Melia smiled. "For them."

Lehua remembered the funeral rites her grandparents had received. If someone had double-checked their file, she would've had a graveside to visit. An urn to say goodbye to when she left for work. A silver one with painted night moths on the exterior.

When they reached the town, Lehua noticed how the skin beneath Melia's eyes was furrowed like tilled soil, as if she hadn't slept at all. "Are you feeling all right?"

"I'm fine," Melia said. "It's hotter than I thought it'd be, that's all. It usually rains nonstop this time of year. Just not here, I guess. At least Daisy and Chiyo seem nice enough. But it's . . . quiet."

Quiet wasn't the word Lehua would have used, remembering the plantation siren echoing like a faraway scream in her bedroom that morning and the workers' voices filling her sleep with a droning hum. Yet the sugarcane fields around the town cloaked everything inside their bounds with a strange claustrophobic silence.

Melia was worrying her lip with her teeth now, as if she was thinking the same thing as Lehua.

"I am guessing you have to be a big fan of cane grass to live here alone," Lehua said, and Melia bubbled out a laugh, her eyes brightening.

"And dirt," Melia returned.

Lehua looked pointedly down at her own clothes, covered in field dust and red clay dirt. "You don't say."

Lehua resisted closing the distance between them. Why did she feel such a strong pull toward Melia? Was it the fact that Melia was the only other Hawaiian she'd met aside from her own family?

"Come on." Melia nudged her shoulder playfully. "Let's see if anyone's home."

As they walked up to each door, they left shoe prints on the terraces. Theirs were the only prints dirtying the porches, bloodying the white paint with the island's red dust. The surest sign that the houses were abandoned.

Melia knocked on the doors while Lehua checked her phone for any new notifications suggesting her sister's phone might be nearby, while periodically scanning the windows. There wasn't much to see inside, only impressions of the dark rooms hidden beneath the black painted glass. The blacked-out windows stared like empty eye sockets. Still, Lehua couldn't shake the nagging feeling that someone *was* watching them.

"Which house did you see someone inside again?" Lehua asked.

"That one." Melia pointed at the same house they'd found the dead bird lying outside, except . . .

The ʻalae ʻula had disappeared. There wasn't even an outline where its stomach had been unfurled, pooling blood. No flies circled where its picked-over insides had been, either.

Melia knelt, her face pale and strained. "I thought about burying it last night. Before we left," she said, and Lehua shivered. The air carried the faint smell of decay. "Maybe I should've . . ."

"Another animal probably found it," Lehua said, even though she didn't think a scavenger had devoured the bird. Unless it had licked the white porch clean like a dinner plate. There was no trace the bird had been there. As Lehua began to guide Melia away from the house, the front door slammed shut behind them.

Lehua whirled toward the sound, releasing Melia's elbow. But there was no one else outside. The doorstep was empty. How was that possible? She'd felt the slam reverberate through the wooden porch. It had shaken her feet.

"Lehua? Is something wrong?" Melia's wide eyes watched her with caution.

"You didn't hear the door slam?" Lehua asked. Her voice was

steady, but when Melia shook her head, confused, Lehua's chest squeezed. "Never mind. Nothing's wrong." Had she really imagined it?

Something wet dripped down her lip. She touched her face, dotting her fingertips with blood. Her nose was bleeding.

"Must be the heat," Lehua said quickly, wiping the blood away before Melia could see. "We should get out of the sun."

Lehua stepped toward the ʻalae house's front door, ignoring the goose bumps down her neck. She reached for the doorknob, her breath catching as she hesitated. *It might be locked.* But the door opened.

With a shaky hand, Lehua swung the door wide, peering inside to see if anyone was hiding. A stinking odor of charcoal, sweet decay, and dried ink wafted out of the house. Lehua saw a giant mahogany printing press and a dirty glass cabinet stretching toward the ceiling. Some of the glass doors had fallen off their hinges and lay scattered atop the stored woodcuts and metal letters.

"Lehua, what are you doing?" Melia asked.

"I was checking if anyone was inside," Lehua confessed. The house's undisturbed dust said more than enough. No one lived here. But she didn't want to go back outside, wondering whether she was losing her mind.

She could've sworn the door had slammed. But Melia hadn't reacted at all.

"Right, well, we knocked, and no one answered," Melia said, stepping inside. She picked up a bit of metal under her foot, the letter *J*, then suddenly coughed. "This looks like a tomb for literacy."

Melia was right. Framed newspaper prints shrouded walls darkened with dust, while a clothesline bearing abandoned newspaper prints was tethered across the room, dividing the long printing room almost in half. But they hadn't found anything outside. At least this was *something.*

Lehua drew closer to the clothesline. *Jacobs & Pacific Welcomes Families*, one newsprint read, and a woodcut image was printed alongside the blocky headline. A group of workers with withdrawn and weathered gazes were depicted in front of a sugarcane field. In front of the men was a handful of gaunt kneeling children, wearing aprons and woven sun hats.

Lehua peered inside the broken cabinets. A rolled-up sleeve of papers hung out of a smashed window. She flattened the paper's creases, unrolling a handful of sepia-toned photographs and balled newspaper clippings.

Crisscrossing white serration marks indented the pictures. In one, a warehouse filled with canning machines, so new they shone white. Rows of workers in bonnets and aprons were crammed inside, all the way to the end of the warehouse. *Jacobs & Pacific's New Cannery* was written in tight cursive on the back.

Lehua turned the photo over. She hadn't seen a cannery on the island. What happened to it? She flipped the next photo, a flimsy black-and-white tintype of the resort.

A group of five children stood in front of the house's pillars. They were all stern-faced, flaxen-haired, the girls wearing frilly dresses. At the edge of the photo was an old man in a crisp white shirt, cravat, and suspenders. His wrinkled face was gaunt and solemn, his light-colored eyes shockingly white against the photograph's backdrop, and his mouth was like a wizened fruit peel.

Lehua's throat bobbed. Unease chased through her, a chilling wave of déjà vu. He looked like a younger version of the man she'd seen—or *thought* she'd seen—shrouded in the service wing last night. Except that man's face had been decayed and white, like a corpse left out of storage.

Horace and His Children read the back of the photo. The man posed next to the children had to be the famous Horace Jacobs.

"Are those photographs?" Melia asked.

"Yeah." Lehua reached back inside the gaping glass to pull out one of the woodcuts. She blew the glass chips away from the intricate engraving, then held it up to the light. The woodcut had been hand-carved to resemble the photograph of Horace's family. "Looks like they made copies to print in the company newspaper."

"So the man had his own tabloid press," Melia said with a snort.

Lehua offered a thin smile to hide her discomfort. She couldn't get the image of the older man on the staircase in the service wing out of her mind. *Daisy hadn't seen anyone.* She considered telling Melia about the encounter. But when Lehua looked at her, she reared back, her eyes widening.

"Lehua," she murmured. "Are you all right? Your nose is bleeding—and you look like you've seen a ghost."

Ghost. The word was like striking flint. "It's not—" *that*, Lehua was about to protest, until a familiar peevish voice coming through the house's opened door interrupted her.

"Empty houses. Rows of them." *Leigh.*

This time, Lehua didn't have to ask if Melia heard anything. They ducked at the same time. Melia shut the house's door, then huddled with Lehua by the window, crouching out of sight.

"He doesn't understand the gold mine he's sitting on," Lehua heard Leigh say. She squinted, trying to see through the glass, but the painted window was like thick smog. "I told him he could have fifty guests at a time, and you know what he said? The same thing as last year: *Many are invited, but few are chosen.*" Leigh snorted as he paced. "He has a waitlist a mile long and he brings up scripture as if this isn't a business. Unfortunately, I don't think the others will be much help. They're all scared of this island."

Scared? Lehua grimaced. *Who is Leigh talking to?*

A low voice answered Leigh. Too soft and muted to decipher.

"They're comfortable." Leigh sneered the word. "No one wants to cross him after how easily he cut off Willa." Mockery poisoned Leigh's voice. *Who's Willa?*

Lehua saw the same question reflected in Melia's brown eyes. Was Willa another planter? There was something familiar about the name that tugged at Lehua.

A long silence stretched, and Lehua wished she could hear the other person. Who was it? Oliver? Sacha had said all the two men ever did was talk business. Lehua looked down, thinking. Red dust coated her feet.

Her pulse jumped. *Shit.* If Leigh saw their red shoe tracks covering the porches, there was a chance he'd check the houses. That was her and Melia's cue to leave.

Lehua pulled the girl's sleeve, lifting a finger to her mouth. She pointed toward the far end of the printing room. There had to be another exit. Melia's eyes narrowed; then she followed Lehua in a crouch toward the back of the house.

They rounded the long room's corner, dodging the massive wooden press. A mirror hung at the base of a small staircase. It reflected the stairs and a closed door on the upper floor under a sheen of dust. But behind the stairs was another door, leading outside.

They'd almost made it all the way to the door when Lehua heard Leigh arguing with whoever was outside, his words coming out twisted and garbled: "You want me to check?"

The two girls didn't hesitate. They bolted to the door. Lehua grabbed the doorknob, but met resistance. Was it locked? She pulled, tugging the door hard. And then she saw the nails, driven through a board over the door.

The two girls stared. Why was the back door nailed shut?

There was no time to talk. They threw their weight against the door. Nails scattered, plinking out of the wood as Lehua wrenched the door open.

Melia leaped out the door first, running toward the cane. She jumped over a shredded ti leaf plant, then looked back, waiting for Lehua.

When Lehua turned to pull the door shut, she glimpsed the stairwell's mirror in the shrinking gap of the doorway. She gasped.

A Hawaiian man was reflected in the mirror, looming at the top of the printing room's stairs. And his eyes . . .

Lehua recoiled, feeling the hair rise on her neck. But the man with his silver-dime eyes had vanished. Breathing hard, she chased after Melia.

As they ran through the cane and Kōpaʻa's green hills disappeared—devoured by the tall grass, black as ink even during the day—Lehua heard Leigh's words echo: *They're all scared of this island.*

THIRTEEN

The silence stretched as the two girls shouldered their way through the cane field. Red clay had settled into the creases behind Lehua's knees and clung to the roots of her hair.

She could tell from the way Melia kept looking at her that she was waiting for Lehua to bring up the unsettling question of why the back door had been nailed shut. The thick and rusted nails piercing the door had been smashed flat against the wood, leaving no doubt someone had intentionally hammered in each one to keep something *out.* The disconcerting thought sent goose bumps down her legs. But Lehua was too embarrassed to admit how unnerved she was.

Melia broke first. She stopped walking, resting one hand on her hip. "Are we really not going to talk about what happened?"

Lehua sighed. "What is there to talk about? Maybe it was a prank," she said, her eyes darting to her feet. A growing part of her wanted to just ignore what they'd seen, to pretend it hadn't happened at all.

The truth was, the discovery of the nailed-shut door was another addition to the list of strange occurrences Lehua had experienced on Kōpaʻa. The constant feeling of being watched, the town's weird noises, the missing bird carcass, and that unsettling photo of Horace all deepened the dread pooling in her.

Melia's stare was disbelieving. "Pretty elaborate prank, requiring no less than twenty nails, a wooden board, and a hammer," she said dryly. "C'mon. Why do you think that door was nailed shut?"

Lehua's mind flashed to last night, to those menacing eyes hunting her through the cane field, glowing in the dark.

The back door had been facing the sugarcane fields.

When she woke up this morning, her fear had felt exaggerated, her memory an unbelievable nightmare. The sinister gleam of the women's eyes muted by the morning's soft light. But now . . .

Lehua shook her head, driving the unsettling feeling away. Oliver hadn't seen anything strange. This island was getting under her skin. That was all.

"There's a lot of reasons that door could've been nailed shut," Lehua finally said.

"Really? Because you look like you're trying not to freak out."

Lehua forced a smile. "I'm not. The house could've been boarded up because of the abandoned printing press."

Melia gave her a look. "From the inside?"

Lehua's mouth clamped shut. Melia had a point. "Fine. What's your theory?"

"I don't have a theory," Melia admitted, moving through the sugarcane again. "It's this island—it's ʻeʻepa. A lot of people have died here, and that kind of history leaves its mark on the land."

You don't believe that, do you? she almost asked, but Melia's belief shone in her tawny eyes like amber in petrified wood, and Lehua remembered the man on the stairs and how his gaze had shone, piercing the dusty gloom of the house.

You don't know what you saw. Her eyes squeezed shut but the man and his uncanny eyes haunted the darkness under her eyelids, shaking her certainty. What if Melia was right? What if there was something unexplainable about Kōpaʻa?

Her grandparents flashed through her mind. *We never sleep with our feet to the door,* they had cautioned, shaking their heads at the way she and Ohia had arranged their beds. *You're inviting ghosts to spirit you away. And we won't know how to find you.*

Lehua pushed the memory away. *Don't be ridiculous.* The superstitions and myths her grandparents had believed in were relics now.

A hand touched her shoulder.

Lehua's eyes snapped open, snagging on Melia's worried face. "You all right?"

"I'm fine—I just need a moment to think," Lehua muttered, trying to hide the rush of humiliation and anger she felt. Ohia going missing was bad enough. She didn't need to be distracted by island superstitions. She needed to figure out what happened to her sister—and they didn't have any new leads. She'd been right: The town was abandoned and investigating it had been a waste of time.

The morning had been a bust.

Trying to clear her head, Lehua walked off into the sugarcane, almost stumbling across the cane field's uneven ground.

The fallen leaves and stalks shifted underfoot with each step. She stiffened as a sickening crack echoed. It didn't sound like sugarcane.

Lehua knelt, pushing aside the thick layer of cane mulch, then reared back at the dull and twisted shape buried in the soil.

"Lehua?" Melia called behind her. "Did you fall?"

"I found something," she said, trembling, still staring at the pale, broken rib cage. "Look."

Melia came closer and peered down, then tensed. "Iwi kūpuna."

Lehua licked her chapped lips. "What's that?"

"Ancestral remains," Melia answered, pulling out her phone. She turned on her flashlight and the beam vanished as it hit the cane wall enfolding them, unable to pierce the dense thicket's darkness. Her eyes flicked to Lehua's. "This area might have been an old Hawaiian burial ground before they built the plantation."

Lehua pushed herself to her feet shakily. She'd seen a lot of corpses but never outside of the mortuary. "You don't seem surprised that they built a plantation over a graveyard. Shouldn't we tell Chiyo what we found?"

Melia's lip curled. "She probably already knows."

"What do you mean?"

"It's not that unusual to find iwi kūpuna like this. Hawaiian remains turn up at construction sites on the other islands all the time. Beaches, too."

"Really?" Lehua couldn't hide her shock. "Why?"

"Our ancestors hid their families' remains to prevent desecration, so when developers break ground to build more hotels and high rises, they sometimes uncover bones in old caves and sand dunes."

Lehua frowned. "What happens when they find them?"

"For decades, they used to ship the remains off to museums or just lay concrete over them," Melia said, her voice laced with bitterness. "It wasn't until Honokahua Beach that things changed."

Shame curdled Lehua. She didn't recognize the name. "What happened then?"

"When they were constructing the Ritz-Carlton on Maui in the eighties, the construction crew found nine hundred skeletons there."

Nine hundred. Lehua's eyes widened. "They stopped digging, right?"

"Only after our people staged protests. It turns out more than two thousand Hawaiians were buried in the beach's sand dunes, so the developers built a cultural landmark next door to the Ritz and reburied the iwi kūpuna there—two years later." Melia rolled her eyes. "Now there are laws protecting iwi kūpuna, but they're still moved."

A wave of nausea churned Lehua's stomach. "Don't people know they're vacationing next to a graveyard?"

Melia made a face. "I mean, it was all over the news, but a lot of tourists probably don't care. It's not the only hotel they've built on top of our people's bones, or even the first plantation." Melia gave the rib cage hidden in the cane a pointed look. "Honokahua Beach used to be part of the pineapple fields."

Lehua swallowed. She knelt and scooped away the dead cane

leaves and stalks; then she softly pushed the rib cage back into the earth. She hadn't meant to break the fragile bones.

When Lehua rose to her feet again, Melia was facing the ground, saying something low in Hawaiian. The heat rose in Lehua's cheeks as she watched Melia speak—the Hawaiian words flowed so effortlessly from her lips, sounding like music. Lehua couldn't understand a word.

A deep silence hung over the sugarcane when Melia finished; then the two girls turned to leave, their feet crunching on the fallen leaves, gently breaking the quiet.

"What did you say?" Lehua asked, tucking her hands into her pockets. "It sounded beautiful."

Melia smiled. "That was a chant from a part of the Kumulipo, a creation chant about our people and our genealogy. The chant begins with the birth of Kumulipo, the source of darkness, and Poʻele, the source of night, and traces the beginning of the world to our people. According to the chant, the first burial was for Haloa-naka-lau-kapalili, the stillborn son of the gods Wākea and Hoʻohōkūlani, and from his buried bones grew the first taro plant, the staple food of our ancestors. All taro is said to originate from him. Afterward, the gods had another son who they named Hāloa in honor of his older brother." Melia's throat bobbed. "It is from Hāloa that our people, the Kānaka ʻŌiwi, or the people of bones, are said to have descended."

The people of bones.

Lehua was leaning toward Melia, drawn in by her warm voice. A part of her wanted to know more, but the shame of her ignorance kept her from asking Melia more questions. And old stories about Hawaiʻi wouldn't help her find her sister.

"If we're gonna search the barracks, we should hurry," Lehua said, pushing her way through the cane. Ohia was all she had left—she and Ohia had already been pruned, cut from that family and those Hawaiian roots.

When they reached the barracks, the sun was pummeling down, even with the breeze pushing her short curls apart. As she walked through the screen door, Lehua saw rows of empty bunk beds with mosquito nets pitched around them. The quarters were tidy and practically empty, but unlike the grandeur of the beautiful hotel up the hill, mold crept down the walls like ink and the lightbulbs hung from the ceiling on twine.

"C'mon, I'll give you the tour. There's *so* much to see," Melia said. "Daisy said I could take whichever bed I wanted."

"Ohia probably slept in one of these," Lehua said, scanning the bare bunk beds. Despite the rows of beds, she and Melia were the only people in the room. The one thing Lehua saw out of place was Melia's emptied duffel bag next to a chest full of clothes.

Lehua bent down to pick up a framed photograph nestled inside the chest. It was of a younger Melia. Missing two front teeth, Melia smiled in front of a blue house with a plumeria tree, sandwiched between two people who looked like they were her parents. Lehua's eyes swept from the photo to Melia. Now alone.

Lehua remembered the way Melia's face had shuttered on the boat when Lehua asked about her family. Maybe she wasn't the only one who'd been pruned from their roots. Melia's jaw tightened at her look. It was clear she didn't want to talk about the photo.

Melia came up to Lehua and took the photo from her. "Come on, let's keep looking to see if Ohia left anything behind. I'll take this side of the room, and you take the other." She started searching, opening the drawers and chests next to each bunk bed. "So who all is up there at the resort?"

Lehua blinked. "In the resort? A couple rich people." She began looking through the chest and drawers on the other side of Melia's bunk bed. Both empty. "Sacha Tasse."

"The influencer?" Melia made a face. "Huh. Maybe it's not so bad being out here all alone."

Alone? Lehua straightened. "But what about the other workers? I was gonna try talking to them about Ohia—to find someone who worked with her before she left."

"You mean the resort staff?"

"No, the other field-workers."

Melia's brow furrowed. "What other field-workers?"

"Melia," a voice scolded gently.

Chiyo.

FOURTEEN

Chiyo glided into the barracks in a crocheted white blouse, light denim jeans, and a pair of laced-up work boots. Her dark hair was tied into a loose knot that spilled down her back like poured oil, her pale cheeks rose-stained by the afternoon sun.

"I'm sorry to interrupt, but Daisy's been looking everywhere for Melia. Her orientation starts today." She glanced at Melia, her eyes soft. "Daisy is waiting for you by the main house. She's going to show you around the island today."

Melia rose to her feet. Her eyes flashed to Lehua's on her way out. *Sorry.*

Lehua swallowed, wondering how much Chiyo had heard. "It's my fault Melia's late."

Chiyo laughed, waving a dismissive hand. "All is forgiven, Lehua. I heard what you were discussing—and I understand completely."

Great, that answers that question. Lehua cringed. She and Melia hadn't exactly bothered with subterfuge. "You're not upset?"

A crease appeared between Chiyo's brows. "Why would I be? You're worried about your sister. We all are. If there is any way I can help you in your search, I want to. Even if you just need to talk to someone."

"I appreciate it," Lehua mumbled. Again, her sincerity seemed genuine. But her direct gaze had Lehua shifting uncomfortably on her feet. She wasn't used to people looking at her like that—like she had something important to say. When she dropped out, Uzzy hadn't even looked up from his clipboard. She had left her uniform on his desk and seen herself out.

"I was actually hoping I'd get the opportunity to check on you today." Chiyo gave her shoulder a reassuring squeeze. "How are you settling in?"

Lehua blinked, unsure if Chiyo was being serious.

At her expression, Chiyo smiled sympathetically. "I understand it's not ideal to be stranded here given your search. But you're our guest until Monday, Lehua. I want you to be comfortable." She pointed to the ivory resort in the distance. "Come, let's head back together. I can give you our signature historical tour along the way."

"A tour?" Lehua repeated. Her twin was missing, and Chiyo wanted to give her a history lesson? She had a lot more pressing things on her mind. She kept replaying last night, her rising anxiety, and what Melia had said, *What other field-workers?* "I'm fine—"

"Participating in our historical tour is a long-standing tradition for our guests," Chiyo interrupted, already offering her elbow. "I'd hate for you to miss out on such an essential experience. Consider this a welcome gift."

Lehua forced a tight smile to hide her irritation. "Fine," she said. When she returned to Maui, she'd need Chiyo's help with the police, and she didn't want to risk upsetting her. Kōpa'a wasn't a large island, so a tour shouldn't take long. It might even give her a better sense of where Ohia had spent her time, which would narrow down Lehua's search for Ohia's phone.

Chiyo steered Lehua onto the resort's red dirt path, leading her uphill. The plantation diminished with each step they took, the barracks blending into the cane behind them. As they reached the summit, Lehua's breath caught.

Kōpa'a unfolded before them, a green sliver against the vast expanse of dark blue ocean. It was easy to see why the planters spent so much money to come here. Fields of sugarcane bent toward the plantation town, the bluffs, and the chain-linked orchard as Chiyo gave Lehua a brief sketch of the island's first settlement. According to her, the island had been covered with wild grass and dense ʻōhiʻa forests, too hot and inconvenient for many families to inhabit before Horace and his father arrived. Under their stewardship, Kōpaʻa flourished as hundreds came to live on and work the land, leading to the town's construction.

"Horace ensured the church was built first and that his workers were given Bible translations," Chiyo said, guiding Lehua along the path. "As his father would've wanted."

Lehua bit the inside of her cheek. She doubted Chiyo's claim that Horace and his father had been good stewards, considering the illegal overthrow of the Hawaiian Kingdom.

Her grandpa had told her the story many times. A group of sugarcane farmers and businessmen, supported by the United

States military, had forced their queen to vacate her throne—or her people's blood would've dyed the islands red. "But there was no treaty of annexation," her grandpa used to say, his dark brown eyes shining with tears. "There's *still* no treaty."

Lehua had never known how to feel about that loss. How could she mourn something she'd never truly had? But looking at that abandoned town, and thinking of her grandparents buried in a mass grave hundreds of miles away, Lehua felt an ache behind her ribs, a longing for this place where her family had once belonged, now owned by someone else.

She knew an empty home when she saw one.

"What happened to all those people?" Lehua asked.

"People used to say sugar was king in Hawaiʻi. But as the sugar industry grew, profits slowed and Kōpaʻa needed to adapt, so Horace tried other crops. He planted pineapple, and Kōpaʻa became more successful than ever." Chiyo nodded toward the center of the island where thorny pineapple crowns unfurled. But north of that field was a giant plot of blackened ground, cracked like charred clay. "Until the cannery burned down."

Lehua stiffened. So that was what had happened to the cannery.

"After that, Kōpaʻa was never the same."

"What do you mean?" Lehua asked.

"The fire killed that year's crops and ruined Kōpaʻa's fields for years to come. After that fire, each sugarcane field turned, one after another, until all of them eventually spoiled. Some people think that the cannery's materials must've seeped into the soil. But others think this island is cursed."

Cursed. Lehua resisted recoiling. "Because of what happened?"

Chiyo shook her head. "Because the soil never recovered. It's like salted earth. Nothing grows there."

"Why didn't they burn the fields and start over?"

"The Jacobs family tried. No matter what they planted, nothing worked." Chiyo met Lehua's disbelieving look. "I'm sure Melia has told you the stories about Kōpaʻa."

Melia's flinty gaze flashed through her mind. *Kōpaʻa is ʻeʻepa.* Carefully, Lehua said, "I heard the plantation had a history."

"Yes, Kōpaʻa is rooted deeply in history," Chiyo said quietly, and Lehua wondered if she imagined the faint mockery tainting her voice. "I take it you don't believe in curses."

"No." Lehua crossed her arms, ignoring the uneasy flutter in her stomach. "Do you?"

"Living here, it's hard not to."

Lehua could still smell the dried blood inside her nose from earlier. Now its metallic taste was hard to ignore. "Have you seen something?"

Chiyo cleared her throat. Her hotelier smile returned, as if it'd never disappeared. "Sorry, Lehua. After giving this tour so many times, it's difficult not to get carried away sharing Kōpaʻa's rich history." She turned away from the destroyed cannery. "Let's return to your tour."

Chiyo climbed down the hill, but Lehua was slow to follow. When Chiyo had pointed to the sugarcane, a green cuff had dangled on her wrist. A woven ti leaf bracelet, just like Melia wore. Lehua stared at the ti leaf corralling them and thought about what Melia had said: *It brings good luck and wards off evil spirits.*

The resort manager's bracelet was a testament to her own belief in the superstitions.

"The island's troubles continued when the US entered the Second World War," Chiyo said, seamlessly picking up where she left off. "Martial law was established, and by the time the war ended, no workers remained on Kōpaʻa. The island might've stayed abandoned, if the Jacobs family hadn't switched crops again."

"Tourism," Lehua said, thinking about Honokahua Beach.

Chiyo nodded. "Yes, tourism. But Kōpaʻa has never forgotten its heritage." She pointed toward the faraway orchard, sealed behind its tarp-covered fence. Heavy persimmons hung on ebony branches. "While the persimmon orchard is a recent addition, it allows Kōpaʻa's legacy to live on. Do you know the Hawaiian word for land?"

Lehua shook her head.

"*ʻĀina*, but its literal translation is *that which feeds*." Chiyo drifted toward the field's verdant edge. "If you took care of the ʻāina, it was believed, it would take care of you in return." *Just like it provided for our ancestors*, Lehua heard her grandma whisper, and the memory of her soft smile and her papery, thin hands cradling Lehua resurfaced. "As Kōpaʻa's manager, I've tried to remember that principle while preserving the plantation's history and traditions. Now our fruit is famed throughout the world. We even ship our persimmon wood to the finest golf club makers."

"But you don't ship the fruit?"

"Mr. Jacobs prefers that his guests get the full experience and flavor by harvesting the fruit on the island. But I make sure nothing is wasted here. Including the buildings." Chiyo gestured toward the mill. It looked abandoned during the day, bleached and rusted under the hot sun. "Like the house, most of what you see is original. I preserve what I can, but some things can't be saved."

Chiyo swept a hand toward the barracks. "That building is the only cabin to survive. When the plantation was open, there were a dozen work camps, all segregated by race. That one used to house Kōpaʻa's Filipino workers."

Lehua could feel Chiyo's eyes on her face. "What happened to the others?"

Chiyo's smile sharpened. "I let them turn to rot."

As they walked, the sugarcane closed in, a wall of dagger-toothed leaves surrounding them.

In a quiet voice, Chiyo said, "Kōpaʻa's history runs deep, but that doesn't mean it can't be changed under the right hand."

FIFTEEN

The loch was reflecting the hundred trees flanking the resort like stained glass when Lehua and Chiyo returned. Coconut fronds blocked the midday sun while pandan leaves poked through the surrounding ti leaf, looking like an overgrown wonderland.

"Thanks for the tour," Lehua said, eager to return to the resort. Despite her efforts that morning, she was no closer to finding answers about her sister. But the heavy atmosphere and oppressive heat weighed on her, pushing her to retreat inside, where she could at least wait out the intense heat while she figured out what to do next.

"Of course. I'm hoping what you've seen today shows you how important it is to follow the marked path." Chiyo gave her a stern look. "Daisy told me you were wandering the cane last night. Now look at you."

The resort manager's gaze roved over Lehua's copper-stained skin to all the cuts the cane had left on her bare arms. *Shit.* Daisy had warned her she'd inform Chiyo. "I know, but I was in a hurry this morning," she said. "And last night—"

"It's against the rules, Lehua." Chiyo's clipped reprimand stunned her. "Kōpaʻa may seem small, but there's a reason we mark the resort's paths. The fields are dangerous. If you got lost or injured, it could take days to find you."

Lehua imagined herself trapped under the sugarcane's canopy with an unsettling wave of claustrophobia. Some of the stalks towered over twenty feet tall. "Wouldn't the workers—"

"I wouldn't rely on them," Chiyo interrupted, and her concerned expression cowed Lehua into silence. "That's why I need to warn you."

"About what?"

"I don't want to sound unkind, but you shouldn't get too close to Melia. She's a very troubled girl. We're very selective with the people we hire—we try to take in those who really need an opportunity like this and are unlikely to get a second chance anywhere else." Chiyo's voice dropped. "Unfortunately, our selection criteria have led to some *incidents* between our guests and field-workers. That's why we have our rule encouraging everyone to keep to themselves."

From the way Chiyo looked down when she said the word *incidents*, Lehua understood she meant violence. She thought of the strange field-workers she'd encountered last night, before realizing Oliver had been outside after curfew, too. What did Chiyo think about one of the *esteemed* guests ignoring her rules? Lehua doubted Chiyo had given the film producer the same lecture and mandatory tour when she found out.

"You're dealing with so much," Chiyo continued. "I wouldn't want you to get caught up with someone like Melia—"

"I get it," Lehua ground out. When they'd arrived on the island, hadn't she thought Melia looked like a girl running from something? Even so, she felt annoyed listening to Chiyo talk about her like that. Because Lehua knew firsthand what it was like to be "troubled." It didn't matter that she and Ohia were two coins cast from the same mold. Her star sister's currency had always run higher. "Can we move on now?"

Chiyo's shoulders tightened at Lehua's tone. She'd opened her mouth to reply when a gunshot pierced the air.

They jumped.

"What was that?" Lehua asked once she caught her breath.

Chiyo looked at the resort's terrace, her displeasure apparent. "Leigh."

The resort manager didn't seem surprised that one of her guests had a gun. She looked resigned, striding toward the terrace.

"Does he normally carry a gun?" With all of the resort's rules, firearms were allowed?

"He's ex-military," Chiyo said, her steps slowing as she caught herself. Talking about the guests wasn't allowed, either—and Chiyo seemed to realize a second later that she had said too much. But then she sighed. "He always brings a gun when he visits."

"Always?" Lehua repeated under her breath as another loud gunshot reverberated, raking her composure. Why would one of the guests need a gun on a wellness journey?

"Always. Now, why don't we head to the yard to join the other guests?" Chiyo strode away, expecting Lehua to follow, but Lehua paused at the entrance. Based on the conversation she and Melia had overheard in town and Leigh's sneer—*they're all scared of this island*—Lehua wondered if there was more to the manager's warning about the fields being dangerous.

Lehua looked up at the intricate glasswork of the cupola and thought of the resort's extensive security system. She couldn't see the hidden cameras, but the fact the resort had such intense surveillance suggested there was something to be afraid of on the island.

The women's shining eyes rose up and Lehua shook the memory away. *You don't even know if that was real.* But when Lehua glanced at the glass cupola again, a shiver raised her skin.

Last night, the glass had been threaded with thick shadow, impossible to see into.

Now a tall man lurked behind it. He looked like a younger—and less decayed—version of the pockmarked man who had appeared in the service wing last night.

This had to be Mr. Ira Jacobs, Horace's descendant. They had the same narrow and gaunt face, except his waxen features were devoid of wrinkles and too dark to discern in the cupola, leaving the impression of a hollowed-out skull.

When another gunshot broke the resort's heavy quiet and startled Lehua, the man vanished, leaving the white curtain fluttering.

"Lehua?" Chiyo called, and Lehua hurried to catch up.

Lehua followed Chiyo around the corner. Last night the yard had been empty. Now the guests sat in pretty lawn chairs artfully arranged atop the terrace's thick mat of buffelgrass. Except Leigh—and Oliver. The film producer was missing.

Lehua glanced at Chiyo. The resort manager had picked up a cold pitcher from the patio and was already pouring a tall glass of water. "Please take a seat. Daisy and I will be bringing out lunch shortly."

Lunch? "But I was hoping to use the computer to email my boss," Lehua reminded her in a low voice. "Did you ask Mr. Jacobs? What did he say?"

"Don't worry, he's aware of your request," Chiyo said calmly. "I will let you know his decision. In the meantime, please remember that using our computer would be a favor. In return, I only ask that you follow our rules. Now sit. We will talk after lunch."

Lehua resisted making a face as Chiyo handed her the water. Despite being hungry, she was reluctant to sit down for a picnic. But . . .

She thought of Oliver reaching for her last night and Daisy's warning to stay away from him. The film producer wasn't here. She could try prodding the guests for more information. Did they know what he was up to late at night, walking around the fields and breaking curfew?

So Lehua obeyed the resort manager and sat in one of the lawn chairs, sandwiched between Jennifer and Sacha. As Chiyo and Daisy delivered lunch, Lehua saw Leigh aiming a handgun at three cane-grass targets, lined up at the property's edge. They were bundled like straw puppets, looking uncomfortably human-shaped. He squeezed the trigger and the gun's deafening crack had Lehua instinctively shrinking back. The bullet pierced a target. Grass exploded from its chest.

Lehua shivered as Leigh turned around. She couldn't shake the memory of Leigh entering the printing house. If they'd been a second too slow and had surprised Leigh, was he the type of person to shoot first and ask questions later? What if he *had* seen them, and that was why he kept glancing back at her? The fear burrowed deep, refusing to let go, even after the chilling silence of the island replaced the sounds of the gunshots.

"Such a fragile ego," Sacha said, smirking, as she leaned over to Lehua. "Hi, stranger. Where have you been all morning? Please tell me you didn't do something fun without me."

"Chiyo gave me a tour." Lehua somehow managed to smooth on a smile. "We saw a lot of cane grass. Then Chiyo lectured me on breaking curfew."

Sacha laughed slyly. "Ah, so you know how dire the situation is here."

"I wasn't the only one, though," Lehua said, aiming for that same air of ease. Maybe she could get some information on Oliver. "Guess who I saw last night?"

Sacha's eyes brightened. "Who?"

"Oliver. He was walking around outside with his camera—"

Sacha sighed, disinterested. "Oh, that. He's obsessed with photography."

"But he was outside after dark. Isn't that against the rules?"

"Can you blame him? It's not like there's a whole lot to do here. I can't tell you how many times I've told Chiyo, *Do you know what Palm Island and the Maldives have that you don't?*" Sacha bent toward Lehua, her breath sliding warm over her cheek. "*An infinity pool!* And do you know what she said?"

"What?"

"*We offer a different experience, Sacha,*" the influencer said in a mocking voice, before switching back. "Can you believe that? It wouldn't kill Chiyo to add some cute beach bungalows, a glass-bottom kayak, or a tiki bar. I mean, we are in Hawaii! Where's the *experience*? We're supposed to be on vacation."

Lehua lifted her fork, hoping her face didn't betray her distaste. Sacha Tasse was a purebred heiress, whose biggest hardship was the lack of an infinity pool at her chosen resort. Not for the first time, Lehua wondered how Ohia had heard of the resort—and how she stomached the company. Lehua took a petulant bite out of her lunch—a platter of striped mullet and roasted vegetables—then asked, "Can't you heal a broken heart somewhere else?"

Sacha had her drink tipped toward her mouth, and her face tightened behind the glass as she sipped. But then she wiped her lips and her smile returned full force. "What do you mean?"

"You're on vacation to heal a broken heart, but you don't seem to even like it here. Why not escape to the Maldives or Palm Island?"

Chiyo said their guests came for the island's unique level of privacy, but that profile didn't seem to fit Sacha.

"Honestly, it's a family thing. Usually, my mom and I come here every year, but her age is starting to catch up to her. I took her spot."

A family thing? Sacha had said she'd come to heal a broken heart. Of course, she'd been so cavalier about it that Lehua hadn't quite believed her. Was that why Leigh had mentioned her mom in the lounge last night?

Lehua had assumed the guests were a random handful of people who happened to be vacationing at the same resort at the same time. But they didn't act like total strangers.

If Leigh knew Sacha's mom, the other planters could be connected outside the resort, too. It would be hard to ask if Oliver's unwanted advances had forced Ohia to quit, perhaps even driven her from the island, if all the planters were such close family friends. She'd have to be careful who she asked about Oliver—or run the risk of her questions getting back to him. She'd lose her only lead.

Lehua paused with her fork halfway to her mouth, catching a flicker of movement from Jennifer on her right. The widow sat with a sun hat obscuring half her sunburned face, but her pinched blue-eyed gaze was on them. Lehua hadn't gotten the chance to ask her about Ohia yet. But from the annoyed way Jennifer was glaring at her, she got the sense the widow's feelings hadn't changed.

Lehua almost rolled her eyes. Being a planter didn't seem much different from being in a private club. "Why are the resort members called *planters* again?"

"It's dumb. It's because of Horace, and the whole plantation fetish this place has." Sacha raised her glass toward the sugarcane field in the distance in mock-salute. "Kōpaʻa was his beloved Garden of Eden."

As Sacha continued to ramble on about the resort's exclusivity,

Lehua tuned her out, nodding along. She hadn't learned much about Oliver, just that the resort being a membership-locked private island was the main draw for Sacha. Lehua's skin itched as she remembered the bones she'd uncovered with Melia. *A lot of tourists probably don't care.*

Suddenly, Lehua noticed the feeling of unseen eyes on her back. She turned, expecting to see Daisy and Chiyo, only to find a gaunt man watching her.

It was the waxen man she had seen in the cupola, now standing shrouded under the terrace shade. Ira Jacobs.

His hollow cheeks and sharp brow highlighted his sculpted jaw and watery blue eyes. He may have even been striking once, but his face and body had been scraped out by whatever illness had taken root. From Leigh's conversation and Chiyo's description, Lehua had expected someone much older. He looked surprisingly young, somewhere in his early fifties, with his blond wavy hair slicked back. But there was a disturbing stillness about him, as if the sickness Chiyo had spoken of was tangible and thickened the air around him like a veil.

Lehua stared, wondering if she was imagining him, but then Chiyo looked over and stiffened. Then a quick smile appeared, hiding the subtle tightening of her jaw.

"Good afternoon, Mr. Jacobs. I didn't expect you to join us." Chiyo offered her arm to him on the veranda, but his gaze was still locked on Lehua, his lips peeled into a strange smile.

The weight of Ira's prolonged attention left Lehua feeling exposed, until Ira turned to Chiyo, speaking lowly. Chiyo had told her to not bother him during their tour of the resort. But this was the first time the elusive Mr. Jacobs had appeared. Even though he made her uneasy, she might not get another chance to ask him about Ohia or the resort's computer.

As Lehua rose to her feet, there was movement in her periphery. Suddenly, someone grabbed her elbow, sending a chill through her warm skin.

Daisy stood next to her with a warning look in her eyes that stopped Lehua cold. *Don't.* The sudden alarm on Daisy's pale face was in sharp contrast to her familiar wide smile.

Lehua was about to ask Daisy what was going on when something buzzed out of the girl's ear.

Lehua took a heavy step back, her breath hitching as another fly crawled out. She glanced at the other guests. But no one else turned to look. Beside her, Sacha continued to prattle on, even though Lehua could hear the buzzing growing louder.

"Is something wrong, Miss Sayers?"

Lehua whirled. She and Daisy locked eyes again. A shiver climbed Lehua's neck as Daisy's smile widened. There were no flies buzzing around the blond girl now.

Lehua tried to slow her uneven breathing. *Get your shit together.* This island was just giving her the creeps—and probably heat exhaustion, too.

"No, but I was hoping to speak to . . ." Lehua looked over at where Ira had been standing, but he was gone and Chiyo was now making her way toward them.

"Mr. Jacobs is looking forward to meeting you tonight during our dinner service. However, I should warn you he is rather eccentric," Chiyo said with a tight smile, leaving Lehua to guess what she meant.

Lehua cleared her throat. "What about the computer?"

Chiyo's eyes brightened. "Yes, Mr. Jacobs approved your request. I can take you to our staff computer right now if you're ready."

Lehua nodded quickly. "I'm ready."

As they headed toward the resort's entrance, Lehua glanced at Daisy uneasily again, remembering that strange buzzing she'd heard. But no insects circled the smiling girl.

Once again, there was nothing there.

SIXTEEN

A persimmon was waiting on Lehua's vanity when she returned to her room.

Chiyo had hovered while Lehua had emailed Avery, offering her and the resort's contact information—*In case your boss has any updates about Ohia*, she'd said. Lehua had hoped to dig around on the computer, but as soon as she completed the email, Chiyo had firmly closed the laptop and encouraged her to take a rest and prepare for dinner. It seemed enduring Chiyo's eager attentiveness was the price she'd now have to pay for breaking the resort's rules.

After Chiyo had dismissed her, Lehua found her room had been tidied up. Her bed remade with fresh towels folded on top. The fruit had been wrapped in a napkin on the vanity.

Lehua eyed the fruit suspiciously. It had to be from Daisy based on the girl's insistence that she try the resort's famous persimmons. She was unable to think about her without hearing the buzz of insect wings. She wondered again if it was heat exhaustion, but a cool shower did nothing to clear her mind.

By the time she finished showering, the afternoon sun bathed her room in shades of gold. She was planning on going downstairs to ask more about Oliver before dinner started. Even though she hadn't learned much from Sacha about the film producer, he was the only real thread Lehua had to pull on. She still suspected Ohia might have been a failed conquest—based on Daisy's warning and Oliver's crude attention last night. But when Lehua sat on the bed with her damp hair drying, she closed her eyes, and betrayed by her exhaustion, accidentally drifted off into a dream.

Her surroundings faded in and out of the dream before metamorphosing into a bedroom of resplendent trim and ornately carved furniture. Instead of white, the room was furnished with blue drapes, a chaise of steel blue, and curtains that topped the bed's headboard, dripping like rainwater. She saw a hairbrush threaded with long blond hair—and knew she was in another nightmare.

"Shh," a voice whispered. A girl flitted behind Lehua's eyelids as she tried to force herself awake. She could already *feel* the edges of the dream darkening, the beautiful curtains splitting like hair, turning into rags in her peripheral.

The fair-haired girl gripped Lehua's jaw, her long nails skimming her throat and neck.

"Open your mouth, Alana."

Lehua winced, hearing that name. Here was the nightmare—just as she'd expected, but she still couldn't wake up. Lehua ground her teeth shut as the girl's nails clawed into her skin. The girl's other hand shoved at her, pulling at Lehua's neck, pressing ice into her veins. The girl was colder than a corpse pulled from the mortuary's body fridge. Her fingers picked at Lehua's mouth and something *jellied* was pushed between her teeth. Lehua recognized the smell and felt sick.

Persimmon. The fruit burned her mouth, but the girl kept her in place until she swallowed it whole, the persimmon slicking down her throat.

"The taste isn't so bad," the girl whispered while her fingers dug into Lehua, freezing her from the inside out before she finally let go.

Lehua gasped awake.

Her eyes fluttered open to the wind groaning against the eaves. Footfalls landed outside her door. She sat up, still tasting the overripe persimmon mixing with her saliva. Lehua thought of flies bloated on rotten fruit—and gagged. With a shaky breath, she spat into her hand. But of course, her saliva was clear.

Lehua had never experienced such vivid nightmares before coming here. Even during that first year after her grandparents had died, when she and Ohia had slept in a dozen different beds, Lehua had slept deeply. It'd been Ohia who had cried herself awake, her hands clenched to her chest, and Lehua would wrap her arms around her twin, holding Ohia until her hammering heart slowed.

Of course, when Ohia had woken, she'd had no memory of those nightmares, of Lehua cradling her as she begged her to never leave. Lehua had stroked her sister's hair, enjoying her new nighttime role as protector, until one day Ohia stopped crying and Lehua's twin matured beyond the cocoon of her arms.

Lehua shoved aside the painful memory, her eyes sliding open. It was this island. *Did Kōpaʻa weigh on Ohia, too? Is this why she left?* Her skin prickled at just the thought of staying on Kōpaʻa past Monday. She'd only been here a day, and the people seemed unable to reap anything but dread from the island's burnt earth. None of the guests looked happy about being on vacation here. She thought about the way Leigh had outright said it—*they're all scared of this island*—and an angry wave washed over her.

You sound ridiculous, she thought, going into the bathroom to splash water onto her face. Lehua wondered if her worry at not finding Ohia had left a crack, a hole for their grandparents' stories to grow through. There was nothing unexplainable about Kōpaʻa—it was probably just being in Hawaiʻi and Ohia being missing that was causing her to dwell on their grandparents and their superstitions.

Lehua slogged out her bedroom door. Her loaned dress had wrinkled on the floor and now hung limply on her, clinging like a lace shroud. But she had nothing better to face the resort's guests in, and she needed every buy-in she could get if she was going to squeeze any information about Oliver or her sister from them. She was running out of time—Ohia being missing was what she should be worrying about, not island superstitions. She had two days to learn what she could about Ohia.

Lehua climbed down the stairs and found Chiyo waiting at the bottom landing. "Daisy is preparing the dining room, so I'll be your escort," Chiyo said. She clicked her tongue as she took in Lehua's wrinkled dress. "This won't do. Please, follow me."

Lehua trailed Chiyo out of the lobby. The manager opened one of the first-floor hallway's doors to reveal an immaculate, windowless room filled with ebony cabinets. A tiny chandelier left rainbows on a foliate carpet and a dark trunk in the corner. Some cloth was stuck between its closed teeth.

Chiyo waved Lehua inside. "Welcome to Kōpaʻa's lost and found. This is where we store the belongings that our guests and staff have left behind. Feel free to use whatever you'd like."

Lehua opened one of the dark cabinets. A cropped blazer embellished with gold buttons hung alongside a denim coat with a braided metallic trim and a patchwork jacket. On the cabinet, a handwritten label with curling script read *Outerwear.* "Won't someone eventually want their jacket back?"

Chiyo was flicking between another cabinet's wooden hangers. An embroidered shirt, a satin halter, and an oversized poplin shirt. "Not at all. You'd be surprised how disposable some things are to our guests. Most of the time, they do not even realize they've left something behind."

"Why don't you throw this stuff away, then?"

"Nothing goes to waste on Kōpaʻa," Chiyo said, reciting the words like they were her own personal tenet. "Besides, I like collecting them. It's fun to look at these clothes and to imagine the people who wore them—and what lives they lived." She pulled open another cabinet full of trailing dresses, some of them old-fashioned, in styles Lehua had never seen except in movies.

Chiyo held the luxurious clothes in her hands, almost reverently. Yet regret softened the curve of her lips. *To imagine the people who wore them—and what lives they lived.* Chiyo may have served the island's guests as the resort manager, but it was clear she didn't enjoy the same glamorous lifestyle.

"Do you get to leave the island often?" Lehua asked. She couldn't imagine staying in that place and never leaving.

"No, not really. When I first came here, I thought this would be the start of a new life for me, that everything that had come before could be changed. I didn't think I'd stay for so long. But I am no different from the sugarcane, the pineapple, or the persimmon trees. I am planted here now and you can't change a seed's soil once it has taken root." Chiyo smoothed her hand over a satin dress with pearl-buttoned cuffs wearing an unreadable look. Then she proffered the dress to Lehua, surprising her. "Would you throw this away?"

The satin sank through Lehua's fingers like water. "Never."

"*They* do. All the time." Chiyo closed Lehua's fingers over the dress. "Keep it, and feel free to take whatever you need."

"I couldn't—"

"You can and you will. Don't let anyone make you feel small, Lehua." Chiyo tipped Lehua's chin, making Lehua meet her sad crescent gaze. A tightness cinched her throat at Chiyo's unexpected tenderness. "You're as deserving of this place and these things as the people who cast them aside."

Lehua held the dress to her chest. How often had someone told her, and Ohia, otherwise? "Thank you."

Chiyo waved away Lehua's thanks. "Please. At least this way the clothes aren't left to decay, eaten by moths. I'll see you at dinner." She patted Lehua's shoulder, the same way her grandma would caress her back. The lump constricting Lehua's throat didn't disappear after Chiyo left.

Lehua circled the room on her own, grabbing a pair of pearl-studded flats and a bucket bag that she shoved her Nikes into. She changed quickly, wanting to get to the dining room early so she could ask the guests about both Oliver and her sister. Then she'd regroup with Melia tonight.

Her new dress glided like liquid mercury, its pearl cuffs winking with light. She looked around for a place to stash the dress she had changed out of. Her eyes landed on the storage trunk. She nudged the lid open, freeing the fabric caught in its teeth—then froze.

The clothes inside were less designer-worthy. Ripped jeans, denim shorts, and thin graphic tees were folded in a row, bracketed by holey sweaters and faded hoodies. But perched on top was a burgundy Adidas jacket with yellow racing stripes.

Lehua knew what the tag beneath the collar would say. Still, her hands shook as she lifted the jacket, and she read the Sharpied name on its tag.

O. Sayers.

Her sister's track and field jacket.

Lehua raced to her room with the black bucket bag and her sister's track jacket bundled against her. She tossed the bag on the bed, then ran into the bathroom and tried to breathe evenly, to keep herself from throwing up. She leaned on the bathroom's sink and looked down.

The jacket lay on the marble basin.

After they had signed with their university, the school had sent them two matching Adidas jackets in burgundy and yellow. Smiling defiantly, Ohia had signed her jacket's tag, then passed the Sharpie to her. "We made it, Le. Together."

They had been a matched pair wearing their jackets, up until Lehua quit the team. Now her own jacket, signed *L. Sayers*, was buried at the bottom of her apartment's closet. But Ohia had worn hers every day. She'd even had it on when she stormed out after their fight.

It wasn't unreasonable to find her sister's jacket in the lost and found—it was proof Ohia had been at the resort, as Chiyo had said. What Lehua didn't understand was *why* it had been in the resort's lost and found. And why the jacket was caked with mud and loose dirt.

And torn.

What happened, Ohia? Lehua reached out a hand, her fingers trembling against the familiar fabric. The once-rich burgundy was a stained mess of dirt and something red that Lehua was too afraid to look at. Ohia's jacket painted a terrifying story.

Lehua traced the familiar stitch lines of the jacket's racing stripes, now lined with dirt. The fabric still smelled like her sister. Jasmine, tuberose, and subtle coffee. Her sister's favorite perfume. The unmistakable scent wafted from the jacket's collar, as if her twin had just spritzed some on.

She held Ohia's jacket up to the light and her chest hitched. One of the sleeves was ripped through and smudged with . . .

Rust. Lehua exhaled low. *Not blood.*

The old plantation's shadow loomed outside the lanai's window. The decayed building was the same earthy shade as the stains marring Ohia's jacket. From the bathroom, Lehua could see the rusted mill through her balcony. *What were you doing in there, Ohia?*

Her gut feeling about her sister's disappearance had been a persistent, nagging doubt. She suspected something more had to be going on than she'd been told—that something bad had forced Ohia to leave in such a rush—and now Lehua had proof that someone was lying to her.

Could Chiyo be involved? The lost and found seemed to fall under the manager's purview, but Lehua couldn't imagine the immaculate and tidy manager tossing the jacket inside that trunk so carelessly. So how had it ended up there? Was it possible someone else in the resort had hidden it in the trunk, thinking no one would find it?

Lehua's throat tightened. The room hadn't been locked. Anyone could've hidden Ohia's jacket in there. Until she learned who was involved, she couldn't point fingers.

As Lehua stared at Ohia's ripped jacket, her heart pounded against her ribs, a frantic drumbeat of fear and uncertainty, not just from grief for her missing sister, but from the chilling fear of what the resort's powerful guests might do if she dared accuse them. Chiyo wouldn't be able to help her. They were rich enough that their influence extended far beyond the island. One wrong move and her life could be ruined. They had connections, lawyers, and money; she barely had enough to cover a plane ticket back to Arizona.

To find Ohia, she would have to tread carefully, without alerting those responsible—or risk her safety. She shuddered at the thought of Leigh's gun and Oliver's creepy leer. If the guests had made Ohia disappear, they could make her disappear, too.

Lehua didn't know what exactly had happened to Ohia yet, but she knew that it was worth lying about.

And the thought of what the truth might be was even more terrifying.

SEVENTEEN

The other guests were already seated and sipping from glasses full of amber when Lehua joined them, her palms slick with sweat.

The dining room was decorated in cream with light chinoiserie wallpaper. Pale candles glowed on a heavy wooden table, wax pearling onto silver platters. Through the wall of windows, the sky was a bruised plum, light spreading like a stain over the white room.

Lehua noticed Oliver first. The film producer was watching her, his half-hooded gaze slipping under her skin. She wished she could disappear into the wallpaper as the memory of his cold fingers grazing her face flashed through her mind.

Leigh sat next to him, eyeing the door impatiently. Lehua remembered the conversation she and Melia had overheard in the town. If he and Oliver had been talking about business before, they definitely weren't speaking now.

Sacha was glumly lounging. Her arm was draped over the

velvet chair, her skin shining like bone in the firelight. She turned away from Jennifer, who sat on her left, sniffing at her drink. There were two open seats at the table, one next to Sacha, and a plush velvet-backed chair at the head of the table. Ira hadn't arrived yet, and Chiyo was nowhere to be seen.

"There you are," Sacha said when she saw her, and Lehua forced a smile onto her face as she sat down next to her, trying to look relaxed, despite her churning stomach. When she left her room, she'd done her best to compose her face and slow her frantic breathing. But the sight of Oliver less than five feet away washed cold dread over her and threatened to undo her.

"Why didn't you find me after lunch?" Sacha asked, lathering some sort of cream on her hands that carried notes of persimmon and something musky. "I didn't think I was being that subtle."

"Sorry." Lehua didn't know how to respond as the influencer placed her hand on Lehua's. She'd played into the influencer's attention before, but now her smile felt strained as she looked at Sacha, her eyes darting from her to Oliver. "I dozed off. I didn't sleep at all last night."

Sacha's face softened. "It's this place. Here." She opened her clutch and pulled out a travel pill case, pushing aside two Kōpaʻa-branded tubes and her slim phone. She palmed two pills and handed them to Lehua. "They're sleeping pills. I take them before the noises start because *it's a working farm, Sacha . . .*" Sacha stopped her Chiyo impression. "What?"

Lehua realized she was staring. "I thought guests weren't allowed to have phones."

Sacha laughed a little too loudly. "Oh. *That.* Yeah, they said

I should leave my phone behind, but why would I? I'm in a total dead zone anyway. And I'm so bored, Le."

Lehua's jaw tensed at the nickname, but she hid her reaction with a sip of her drink, the same sour elderberry tonic Chiyo had poured her yesterday. She wished it were actual alcohol.

"I get it," Lehua managed, even though Daisy had been adamant about the resort's no-phone rule. Then again, someone like Daisy didn't get to tell someone like Sacha *no*.

Sacha talked about Kōpaʻa needing a *bigger* spa, and Lehua used the influencer's chatter as a cover to survey the other guests. Who else had a phone? She thought about how disinterested Sacha had been in Oliver breaking the rules. Did everyone else get to ignore the rules?

She wished Ira would show up already or that the other guests would start eating. Maybe she should've skipped the dinner entirely and shown Melia her sister's jacket. The rust stain seemed to be a clue; they could've explored the mill together.

"Lehua?" Sacha was looking at her, tight-lipped and annoyed. "Did you space out?"

"Sorry, yeah. What did you say?"

"I asked if you'd go swimming with me tomorrow. Kōpaʻa is *not* Wailea Beach, but I'm getting too pale. TMZ knows I'm *somewhere* in Hawaii, recovering from"—she put up air quotes—"*heartbreak*. I can't go back to New York looking like I spent every day crying in my room. That's not attractive or aspirational. Besides, I cannot spend another hour stuffing persimmons into jars or making intention candles with that creepy blond." It took Lehua a second to realize Sacha meant Daisy. "Don't get me wrong. She can mix a great lotion, but she does not know the meaning of the word *relax.* Look at her. I feel like I need another three hours in the spa so I can unwind *for* her," Sacha said, sighing.

Lehua cringed, avoiding Daisy's eyes. Sacha hadn't exactly tempered her tone. Lehua had no doubt Daisy had heard every word.

Sacha cupped her cheek, shaking a friendship bracelet with enamel charms spelling *home* that was stacked between two diamond-studded cuffs on her wrist. "Where's your head at, anyway? You seem so distracted."

Lehua noticed Jennifer's eyes on her. She was seated only a couple feet away and watching Lehua again, like she had during lunch. Lehua couldn't shake the feeling the widow was listening in on their conversation. "I was thinking about my sister . . ."

Sacha's lips curled with sympathy. "Still no word?"

What do you *think? I'm stuck here.* Lehua tried to curb her expression. "No one has a clue where she's gone."

"Didn't Chiyo say she quit and returned to Maui?"

Then why is her jacket here?

Lehua was spared from answering. Heavy footfalls echoed down the hall, loud enough to catch everyone's attention. Only Lehua turned to look.

Ira hovered in the doorway dressed in a black suit, the top of his head brushing the frame. The way he was lit by the dining room's candlelight, it was now clear he was all sinew and bone, his skin translucent. Clusters of veins were visible, branching out like boughs—completely at odds with the harsh angles of his face, which looked *wolfish.*

Chiyo was at his side, steadying him as he maneuvered to the table. His knees curved outward as he walked, his tendons pulling taut under the fabric of his black suit. When he sat, he took a heavy gulp from the stem brought to him, and his cologne filled the room. Lemon and smoky rum barely concealed the rot wafting off him, a decaying odor like fruit wasting on the branch.

Ira Jacobs wasn't sick. He was *dying.*

He acknowledged the resort's guests with a smile, revealing a full set of unnaturally white teeth. But when he turned to Lehua, he gave her a cool assessment.

"Lehua Sayers," he said, leaning back in his chair. His voice eased through the room like a rasping wind, husky and dry. "Quite the surname for a Kanaka. Chiyo said this is your first time visiting Hawaiʻi. How are you finding the islands?"

For a Kanaka. Lehua bit her tongue. "I wish I was visiting under better circumstances."

"Yes, I heard about your sister. There are a lot of Kānaka twins, aren't there? Kameʻeiamoku and Kamanawa, the royal twins adorning the Hawaiian coat of arms, and of course, Laʻieikawai and her twin sister Laʻielohelohe, the two princesses who were separated and hidden away." He savored another sip of his drink. "And now you and . . ."

"Ohia," Lehua answered. She didn't recognize the names and felt another pang of embarrassment. *You sure you're Hawaiian?* "Did you meet her? My sister."

"Unfortunately, I am too unwell to leave my home and visit every worker that comes to my island. Chiyo handles that business now." He patted Chiyo's hand as she walked past him, balancing a silver tray with platters of food. "She was once a worker like your sister. A child, really. But she came to my island and found her calling, and now look at her. How are you enjoying my island?"

Lehua bristled. *My island.* It chafed her to hear Ira call it that. She searched for something civil she could say. "It's warm."

"The perfect climate to grow our crops. Do you know what *mālama ka ʻāina* means? It means *to take care of the land*. The early Kānaka believed that land was life—that it was a relative to be cared for and respected; so you see my island is the natural habitat for the Kānaka. Your people's temperament and constitution are uniquely fit for what we do here. In fact, I'm sure your new *friend* Melia will thrive here." Lehua's eyes widened as Ira went on. "It's good you found another Kanaka to spend your time with. You know what they say about birds of a feather."

Lehua's fists curled under the table as the image of the black bird, the ʻalae ʻula, splayed dead flashed into her mind. *How does he know about Melia?* Had Chiyo mentioned her? She remembered the resort's surveillance system, the security cameras planted all over the island, and a sudden thought sparked: Could he have been watching her and Melia?

But Ira didn't give her an opening to ask. "Do you work?"

"I'm a mortician's assistant. I handle the dead." It was the blunter answer Lehua used, one that had people desperate to change the subject, and she relished the look of discomfort the other guests wore as they predictably leaned away. *Good.* She wanted to ask about her sister.

Ira's attention was unwavering now. His pronounced blue eyes charted her features like she was a new species, a new kind of human altogether. A lump of unease grew in her throat.

"Mmm, interesting," he mused, flashing his unnaturally white and glossy teeth again, and Lehua realized they were porcelain veneers. Daisy and Chiyo set down plates around the table, serving bleeding cuts of red meat, soft potatoes, and grilled vegetables. "Do you prepare bodies the traditional way or," he paused, and looked toward his guests, his eyes darkening with strange mirth, "do you follow the Kānaka method?"

"Excuse me?"

Ira's gaze was adhered to her face and that unsettling feeling persisted. His attention reminded her uncomfortably of the women in the cane. "My apologies, I forget you don't know your people's history. I'm referring to the final voyage of Captain James Cook. It's a morbid fascination of mine. Are you familiar with the story?"

"No." She could feel the other guests' gazes vaulting back and forth between her and Ira, clearly more interested in the conversation than their food as none of them touched their plates.

It was plain everyone else feared the man, even in his thin and weakened state. Back in town, Leigh had mentioned something about a girl named Willa when she and Melia had been hiding. *No one wants to cross him after how easily he cut off Willa*, he had said. Lehua wondered if whatever had happened to Willa could explain the planters' silence now.

The other guests had quieted, turning into glass so brittle that it seemed the smallest move from him would tilt them over the edge, shattering their careful smiles. Was it his money? Was he richer than them?

She thought of Sacha beside her, with her mother's luxury empire and her own beauty brand, and tried to imagine a fortune large enough to intimidate her and every other person at the table.

"Captain James Cook was an exemplary explorer of the South Pacific and the first European to set foot in Hawaiʻi. Unfortunately, his encounter with the Kānaka went off course. They were ruled by chieftains, bloodying their land and their own people with savage warfare, and they honored Cook and his men at first. But when Cook left the islands, a storm damaged his ship, forcing him to return. This time, the Kānaka were less hospitable. They stole a cutter, leading to a skirmish between them and Cook's marines, and Cook and his men were overwhelmed by the Hawaiians' brutality. He was murdered by the Kānaka mob." Ira steepled his fingers. "When his second-in-command assumed control of the ship, he attempted to trade for Cook's body so they could give him a proper burial, but the Kānaka had already *cooked* him."

Ira's smile widened, his veneers peeking through. Lehua couldn't speak. She didn't know what to say. The implication was clear enough in Ira's contemptuous blue eyes and smirk.

"The Kānaka . . . ate him. When his crew asked for his remains, the scalp, the long bones, thighs, legs, arms, the skull, and even the hands, feet, and jawbone were missing. They found out all had been scraped clean, except for the hands, which the Kānaka had preserved with salt."

Lehua looked at her plate, at the red meat bleeding toward

the silver edge, and unease slithered behind her ribs. She couldn't reconcile Ira's history lesson with the stories her grandparents had shared—or the bones she and Melia had reburied that morning. "Why? Why would they do that?"

Behind Ira, Chiyo looked uncomfortable for the first time. Her back was ramrod straight. Was this what she'd meant when she called Ira *eccentric*? It was a hell of a euphemism.

"The Kānaka believe there is power—what they called *mana*—in a man's bones. They believed Captain Cook's spirit resided within his bones, and to them he was a chief they'd felled in battle, so they distributed his bones among the villages to be shared, with only some of poor Cook's remains being returned to his crew after their uneasy truce." Ira grinned at her again. "You see, when I asked about your job, I'd made a clever little joke that I thought you'd enjoy, considering your people's history with bones."

Lehua bristled with disgust at Ira, the guests, and the spread of rare meat. Flies had started to descend, breezing from one dish to the next, covering the glistening red meat with their buzzing. The thick smell of decay clung to the air. But no one batted the flies away.

Anger hummed under her skin. She wanted to spit at Ira and lock herself in her room. The resort rules be damned.

She wanted to find Ohia. She wanted her twin back. She knew what the *joke* was supposed to be—and at whose expense the other guests were quietly chuckling. She didn't find it clever at all.

Ira's grin deepened.

"Sorry," Lehua said, pushing away from the buzzing table. The flies scattered. On her left, Sacha didn't budge. Despite the influencer's big speech decrying racism last night, she was remarkably quiet now, not daring a look in Lehua's direction. "I'm actually not hungry."

Ira's husky voice turned into a robust laugh. "Apologies, everyone," he said, blotting his wet mouth with his napkin. "The grim details of Kānaka culture compel my curiosity, but I should know what is and is not proper dinner conversation at my age." He looked from Lehua to Chiyo. "Perhaps we can serve dessert early to lighten the mood. Do we still have that persimmon ice cream?"

"Yes, and molasses. But I've prepared something else."

Lehua could hear the steely note in Chiyo's voice. Maybe she was angry on her behalf. But Ira didn't seem to recognize the bitterness lacing his manager's tone. He shook his head. "Lehua's a guest. She should enjoy Kōpaʻa's most famous crop." He turned to Lehua. "Did Chiyo give you a tour? She's the one who suggested we plant persimmons. The tree belongs to the genus Diospyros. It's a Greek word, meaning *fruit of the gods* or *divine fruits*. But the curious thing about persimmons is that when they're ripe, they don't look ripe. They have to be soft to the touch and almost rotten before their flesh turns sweet enough to eat."

Lehua knew plenty of men like Ira, who liked to talk and talk and talk, sharing their knowledge, like it was food and everyone else was starving to partake. She thought of the smell permeating the resort, the rotten trace of Ira's cologne, the odor haunting the hallway outside her door—and she hated everyone in the room for indulging in her discomfort.

"Honestly, I'm exhausted," Lehua said, not bothering to sound tired at all.

“If you insist,” Ira said, leaning back in his plush chair, where he held himself so perfectly still Lehua couldn’t help but wonder if he’d died, choking silently on his half-empty drink, his sickly lips beaded with amber.

But Lehua had never been that lucky in her life.

In the downstairs hallway, she counted to three and took a deep breath that did nothing to cool her anger. Even here, the persimmons soaking Ira’s drink burned her nose with their astringency. Unfortunately, she hadn’t left the dining room alone.

The lobby door clicked softly. Lehua glanced toward the threshold to see who’d followed her, and bit her tongue. It was Jennifer.

Her eyes were downcast as she walked toward Lehua, her open-back cotton gauze dress whispering with every step.

“Could we speak somewhere privately?” Jennifer asked.

Lehua hesitated at the insistence in Jennifer’s eyes. It was off-putting—but maybe Jennifer had information that would help her. She remembered the way Jennifer had been ostracized by the other guests. If the feeling was mutual, the widow might feel less loyal to the other planters. Maybe she could tell Lehua something useful.

“All right.”

Jennifer opened one of the hallway’s ebony doors and held it wide, leading Lehua into her room. The door thudded shut behind them.

Jennifer's room was full of ivory, walnut, and gold thread, and it was massive. A second adjoining room had a king-sized bed piled high with plush blankets, warm quilts, and a dozen pillows. Her suite had a direct floor-to-ceiling view of the faraway town.

A blackwood desk was pushed against one wall, an antique desk lamp and jars of skincare and Kōpaʻa-branded persimmon lotion spilled across the wood. An unzipped suitcase sat next to the desk with a framed photograph laid on top of designer clothes haphazardly thrown in.

In the photo, a younger Jennifer smiled next to a wizened old man who Lehua assumed was her late husband. It was obvious he and Ira were related in some way—Lehua noted the man's similar features, the pale blue eyes, the skin beneath them trenched purple. Except this man's lips and jaw were hollower than Ira's, erased by an obvious illness, a spreading decay. *Cancer.* Lehua had seen the disease's victims in the mortuary.

Miss Jennifer, Sacha's nickname for the widow seemed much crueler now.

Jennifer picked up the silver frame. "I apologize for the mess. And I'm also sorry about the way I behaved yesterday. When I saw you, I thought you were your sister. She'd been working inside the resort. She left days after we arrived."

"She was inside the resort?" Lehua asked, and Jennifer nodded.

Lehua bit her lip. None of the other guests had mentioned Ohia working *inside* the resort before. All she could think about was Ohia, orbiting the guests like a star lost in their solar system, being called a ghoul here. "Did she seem . . . happy?"

The widow looked uncomfortable. "This is going to sound awful. But to be honest, I don't remember. You know the rules about interacting with the workers." She lifted a shoulder. "But I am sorry about tonight. You shouldn't have been treated that way."

Lehua didn't acknowledge her apology. Jennifer had sat silently while Ira went on with his "history lesson," so the sentiment was more than a little late and pointless. She nodded to the woman's open suitcase. "I thought your group's wellness journey was ending Monday."

"It does. The others will likely stay until then," Jennifer said, checking her golden watch, its face inlaid with small pearls and diamonds. "But I've arranged to leave tomorrow afternoon." Lehua felt a flare of bitterness that Jennifer could arrange her own private yacht rescue while she was forced to wait until Monday.

"I don't see you hanging around the other guests much," Lehua said, trying to sound casual. "Why?"

Jennifer's grip tightened on the picture frame. "To be honest, I'm sort of an outsider here. The other planters have their cliques—as silly as that sounds at our old age—and some of them care more about legacy, and how you got your membership, than anything else. Old money versus new." She laughed bitterly, rolling her eyes. Her derision for Sacha, the heiress influencer, was heavy in the air. "This was more my husband's scene, I guess you could say. Sylvan was the real planter," she said the last word with twisted lips, staring at the photo. "He loved Kōpaʻa and this house. He used to visit every year before his health declined and, well, there are some things even a yearly wellness retreat can't cure."

She returned the photograph to her suitcase face down. "But he was the one everyone knew. This was actually my first time coming back to the island without him."

"I'm sorry for your loss."

Jennifer waved a hand. "It was his time. He lived a long life. In the end, nothing could be done about the cancer. We were only delaying the inevitable."

Lehua ran her teeth over her lips. "Sacha mentioned you had married into . . . all of this."

"Sacha's always so quick to air out everyone else's business." Jennifer scowled, and Lehua sensed there was more she wanted to say. "Did she tell you her mom used to come here?"

"Yeah, she said it was a family thing."

"Oh. *A family thing.* How sweet." Jennifer rolled her eyes. "It was, right up until she put Marguerite in a psych ward." She looked at Lehua's shocked face. "Didn't mention that part, hmm? She did that to her own mother to take her spot here."

"She said she used to come here all the time with her mom." Sacha was shallow and entitled, but was she capable of locking her own mother up? All she did was complain about Kōpaʻa. "Why would she need to take her spot?" Lehua asked, searching Jennifer's expression for the slightest tremor or hesitation that she was lying—and a cold certainty filled her.

Jennifer was telling the truth.

"Her mother was going to cut her off. She wanted her daughter to grow up, act her age, experience the real world—and that was reason enough for Sacha to put her away."

"And the other planters didn't have an issue with that?"

Jennifer waved a hand, gesturing toward the fine furnishings around them. "Do you think moral or ethical scruples matter to them? Ever since I married my husband, I've been swimming with these sharks and, you know, you stay here long enough and—" Jennifer shook her head, exhaling a long sigh. "Let's say I learned to stay in the shallows. What Sacha did to Marguerite? That's the sort of ruthlessness they enjoy. Of course they let Sacha take her mommy's spot. They didn't care. Marguerite was the only one stopping Sacha's membership, anyway. Sacha has the type of pedigree you can't say no to, especially not on this island. What Sacha wants, she gets."

Trepidation sluiced down Lehua's spine as she thought of the influencer's intense focus on her, her flirtations. The more she learned about Sacha, the more inconsistencies she found. But why would Sacha lie to her? Did she know something about her sister's disappearance?

Jennifer pulled closer. "You can't imagine what else she's capable of. You shouldn't trust her. You shouldn't trust anyone here."

"Why are you telling me all of this?"

"I debated not saying anything, but . . ." Jennifer sighed. "You need to stop asking so many questions, Lehua. You don't know this place like I do."

Swimming with these sharks. What exactly had Jennifer witnessed over the years? Lehua licked her lips, dried from anxiety. She thought of her sister's jacket, stained with rust and mud. "Did Sacha hurt my sister?" Jennifer evaded her searching gaze. "You know something. Please tell me."

Lehua held her breath and waited, but Jennifer shook her head, unwilling to look at Lehua's desperately pleading face. "No. You're not listening, just like your sister and Willa. You have to stop digging. This place isn't safe. It swallows people like us up. Don't you understand I'm trying to help you?"

Like your sister and Willa. Lehua's eyes widened. When she and Melia had been eavesdropping on Leigh that morning, he had mentioned that name—*No one wants to cross him after how easily he cut off Willa.* Who was Willa—and how did she and Ohia know each other?

"Ohia talked to you about the resort?" Jennifer froze and Lehua's breath hitched. "Please. Who is Willa? Did something happen to her, too? You have to tell me. Whatever happened, maybe it's not too late; we can go to the police together."

But at this insistence, Jennifer started forcing Lehua toward her suite door, surprisingly strong. "When the boat comes back Monday, make sure you get on it and leave this island. I'd offer to take you with me, but I can't risk you slowing me down."

"What has you so scared?" Lehua demanded, struggling to stay in the room as the widow pushed her toward the door.

Jennifer smiled. There was no warmth in it. "If you'd seen what I have—you would be afraid of this island, too." She shook her head at Lehua's foot blocking the door. "I'm trying to warn you. But if you continue to make a scene, I will scream—and you'll have to explain to everyone in that dining room why you're harassing me."

"Just tell me what happened to my sister," Lehua pleaded, leaning toward Jennifer, desperate. "Is she safe?"

"Haven't you been listening at all?" Jennifer's voice dropped into a grating whisper. "None of us are safe."

The widow shut the door, abandoning Lehua in the hallway alone.

None of us are safe.

The widow's words chased Lehua to her room. She wanted to turn back and demand Jennifer answer her questions. But she knew Jennifer wasn't bluffing about her threat. The fear in her eyes had been unmistakable.

Whatever Jennifer was afraid of, it was obvious she was more frightened of it than of Lehua.

Lehua climbed the stairs angrily. She had to share what she learned with Melia. Then they could search the mill for clues about what might have caused the rust stain on her sister's jacket. But as Lehua considered what she should do next, Jennifer's fearful warning filled her mind. *You're not listening, just like your sister and Willa.*

The truth was the widow's fear, combined with her sister's torn up jacket, scared her. She desperately wanted to believe that Ohia was somewhere safe, but that was becoming harder to believe the longer she stayed on this island—and the more she learned about Ohia's disappearance.

The hallway's sconces flickered as Lehua passed the resort's faded photos. Outside her door, she sucked in a breath. Green light illuminated the seam beneath her room's door, puddling near her feet. She knew she had turned the light off when she left.

Lehua pushed the door open, her hand curled into a ready fist. But there was no one inside.

Her room was empty—and ransacked. The bed's quilt was tossed aside, the vanity's drawers hung out, and her backpack was upturned.

Steam hissed through the bathroom door. Was someone in there? The resort's thick silence was punctuated by the sounds of running water and her pounding heart.

Lehua unplugged the green-shaded lamp and pulled it off the table. She gripped the heavy base and rushed the bathroom door.

Dense steam obfuscated the bathroom and wet the walls. Steaming water rained from the showerhead. But no one was inside the bath—and her sister's jacket was gone. *What?*

Lehua heard herself panting. She had set the lamp down and turned the tub's faucet off when she saw it. A message on the fogged white mirror.

Written in the drippy steam was a single word: LEAVE.

EIGHTEEN

Within seconds, the message started to fade, dissipating with the bathroom's steam like it was never there. But Lehua could feel where the steam had dried on her arms, and she felt a cold piercing into her, sliding deeper into her bloodstream as the droplets glided down the mirror.

She backed away from the mirror, her breath ragged, until the porcelain tub struck the back of her trembling legs. A laugh, full of unease, bubbled up in her throat as she desperately clung to the hope this was someone playing a "joke," but terror gripped her. *How would they know?*

She thought of the messages Ohia would daub in steam in their high school locker rooms—*Gone to class, had a meeting, see you at home*—all of them signed with a swirled *O*. Except this message wasn't signed. Because Ohia wasn't there. *She left.*

What if she didn't? A sinister voice rose in her mind, spurred on by Jennifer's warning to stop investigating. *What if Ohia never left?*

Suddenly, Lehua was twelve years old again, huddling against her grandmother's side as she lay in her hospital bed. A spot her grandmother had never left alive. "Come here, my Lehua."

Lehua had hesitated, scared to flatten the IV bleeding morphine into her grandma's veins. But her grandma had brushed away the tears staining her skin. "This isn't the end. I'll visit you and your sister." Her grandma had smiled. "Promise you'll watch for me."

Lehua rose to her feet and white-knuckled the sink basin at the memory of her grandma's hands on her cheek. If her grandparents' stories had been real, they would have been there for her and Ohia when they were shuffled through foster homes. She had watched for her grandparents every day for years—and she had never found a night moth looking after her or Ohia. She had never felt their presence. Not even in the mortuary.

No. She refused to believe her sister was dead and that her spirit wrote this message.

LEAVE looked like a threat, streaking the glass, dripping rivulets down the reflection of her face like cuts. But who would have written this? As far as the other guests knew, she was stranded, waiting for the boat to arrive.

Lehua swept a look toward her room, her heartbeat ticking in her ears, growing louder. Every guest had been seated at the dinner table. She and Ira had been the last two to arrive, and frail as he was, she couldn't imagine him ransacking her room in that short amount of time. Chiyo and Daisy had been the only ones revolving out of the room, carrying platters of food. After she and Jennifer spoke, Lehua hadn't seen anyone on the stairs on her way up.

Lehua stopped cold. The balcony door was ajar. She could

hear the night exhaling through the opening, alongside a rumble of laughter from the lounge. She walked outside. Her trembling hands gripped the balcony as she leaned over. Her breath caught.

The ti leaf outside her room had been trampled, parts of it torn and shredded.

Whoever wrote that message and stole her sister's jacket had jumped down as Lehua climbed the stairs.

Lehua scanned the fields. A bloom of light flickered beyond the old plantation's silos, silhouetting the darkened mill—and she remembered the rust staining Ohia's torn jacket.

She didn't know who ransacked her room, but the rusted mill, the place her sister's jacket had been ripped, held answers about what had happened to Ohia.

Melia was bundled up in a hoodie in the barracks with her back curled against her bed frame. She had been lying down but sat up when Lehua raced inside.

Lehua felt a rush of relief at seeing the girl's face. She wanted to tell Melia everything and hear her say her name, so it would shoot through her like an electric current, easing the fear that had shaken loose after she'd talked to Jennifer and had seen the message scrawled on her mirror. But when Lehua stepped toward Melia, the first thing she saw was the ashen pallor of her bronze skin, her upper lip beaded with sweat.

"What happened to you?"

"Nice to see you too," Melia laughed, short and reedy. Her

fingers were shakily holding a plate with dehydrated persimmon slices splayed like dried flower petals. "That bad, huh? I feel like I have the flu."

Lehua sat down on her bed, her legs bumping into Melia's. Even through her jeans, her body was cold. "You look . . ."

"Awful?"

"You said it, not me," Lehua said, trying for levity, despite her worry. She'd investigated the town with Melia only hours ago. What happened after they'd split up? "Did something happen during your orientation?"

Melia sighed. "No, Daisy just served me lunch while I asked her a couple questions about the job. She mostly gave me a lot of nonanswers, then told me to wait until my first day. But that was it. According to her, I won't even start working in the fields until Monday."

Lehua frowned. Maybe it was something Melia had eaten then. Except she'd looked pale earlier, too. It'd been hot when they'd run through the cane fields, and Melia had been wearing long sleeves and a pair of jeans—the same clothes she wore now under her hoodie—and the night was still balmy. Sweat pooled down Lehua's back and neck.

"Maybe it's heat exhaustion? Do you have a headache?" Lehua knew she sounded overly concerned—overprotective, but something about Melia's sudden decline didn't sit right with her. Not after everything that had happened.

Melia brushed her away. "I'll be fine. Now tell me why you're here." She looked at Lehua and her tawny eyes were incisive. As usual, Melia had missed nothing. Her voice softened. "What happened?"

Lehua took a shaky breath. "Someone was in my room. Before the dinner, I found Ohia's track and field jacket. Except it was torn up and had rust on it. I hid it in my room. But when I got back, it was missing, and someone had ransacked the place. They left a message on the bathroom mirror, telling me to leave."

"Holy shit. Are you okay?"

Lehua's shoulders drew in tight at the tenderness in Melia's voice. "No," she admitted. "Nothing makes sense." She told Melia about everything that had happened after they split, recounting it all for the other Hawaiian girl, who listened intently. When Lehua finished, her gaze swept the bunker.

"Do you think it could have been one of the field-workers?" Lehua asked. She never got to ask them about her sister. Perhaps one of them knew something. But even as she looked around, she could tell the camp house was as neat and tidy as they'd left it that morning. There were no signs any of the workers had even entered.

"No one's been in here. I don't know where the others are," Melia said, looking worried. "Lehua, I think it's this island."

Lehua's teeth ground together at the idea that Melia was about to suggest something supernatural might be responsible for her room being ransacked. Half a year at the mortuary said otherwise. Six months at the dead's side—and she'd seen the dead in every stage of decomposition. But she'd never seen a damn ghost.

"My sister isn't a ghost story for you to tell, Melia," Lehua snapped. Her sister was missing and someone on this island knew something about it and they were *lying* to her. Yet Melia wanted to talk about ghost stories? She thought of how Chiyo had described Melia: *troubled*. "Maybe I should've listened to Chiyo."

"What's your problem?" Melia sat up straighter at the growl in Lehua's voice. "I'm trying to help. You'd trust Chiyo over me? What did she say about me?"

"Chiyo told me to stay away from you." Lehua was angry—about the dinner, Jennifer, her sister's stolen jacket, Sacha's phone, and that damn message—and she knew she was taking it out on Melia, but she couldn't stop herself. It wasn't Melia's fault, but her anger had nowhere else to go.

Melia stiffened and pulled away. "What *exactly* did she say?"

"She said I shouldn't get caught up with a girl like you, said you were troubled."

Melia's eyes latched on to hers, flickering with betrayal. "And you believed her?"

No. Lehua didn't believe Chiyo. Melia didn't deserve any of her anger—she knew that. At the sight of Melia's hurt expression, Lehua's fear and sorrow filled her, overtaking her anger.

"I honestly don't know what to think or who to trust, Melia. All I know is that my sister is gone and I . . . I can't think she's dead." Lehua whispered.

I'd know, she thought, but Lehua didn't say that.

You didn't even know she was missing until Uzzy told you, a low voice whispered. Lehua felt frantic and exposed, waiting for Melia to shove her away, order her outside the barracks, to lock her out, leaving her on her own.

I'd deserve it, Lehua thought. Another wave of shame crept up her neck as she thought of the way she'd lashed out at Melia. But Melia didn't yell or shove at Lehua. She stayed silent.

When Lehua dared to look at Melia again, she was deflated. Without her anger, all that was left was a girl, young and grieving.

"Troubled, huh? I guess that's one way of putting it," Melia said, averting her eyes. "Sure, I applied to work here. Because no one would hire me on Maui after I was blacklisted. That's why I was at the unemployment center. I'd been sleeping in a tent for a month."

"What happened?" Lehua asked. "Why were you blacklisted?"

"I used to work at a resort as their 'cultural advisor,' meaning I slipped leis on tourists and was another part of the scenery. Well, until they asked me to perform a stupid ceremony." She huffed out a pained laugh. "Some bullshit 'land blessing,' so they could build another ugly-ass hotel and say *we* wanted it. So yeah, I said no, and they blacklisted me. I couldn't get hired anywhere else on the island, and when I couldn't keep up with the payments . . . I lost my parents' house. The only thing I had left of them."

Tears settled in Melia's eyes. Lehua remembered the framed photograph she'd seen in Melia's trunk. A young Melia, missing teeth, standing with her parents in front of their blue house. She wanted to reach for Melia and hold her, but Lehua knew what it felt like to lose your home. There was no balm, no comfort for that loss.

Melia rubbed the tears away and stared out the window at the glowing resort. "I didn't want to become another Hawaiian priced out of paradise, driven out of my homeland. Instead, I lived on the streets so I could stay *home.* I thought that would be it. But then Chiyo emailed me saying a spot had opened up and that I could do a month-long trial period. It felt like my luck had changed. Except nothing's changed, has it? I'm working for another resort, a resort that isn't much different from the last one—only they treat their employees like charity cases and have a higher-class clientele. I guess to someone like Chiyo, I *am* troubled. But it's because of people like her and resorts like this that I don't have a home. Why I can't get a job doing anything else." Melia smiled, but it was empty, her grief palpable. "To them, I'm troubled because I tried to stop them from taking *more.*"

"I'm sorry, Melia. You don't know how sorry I am. I didn't mean what I said."

She couldn't bear to look at Melia's face and see her broken trust. There would be no coming back from this—whatever tether she'd felt between them, whatever growing attraction they'd had would be gone, carried out on the tide.

"I know you didn't." Melia wiped her face, smearing the tracks her tears had left. "I guess if you'd believed Chiyo, you would've stayed away."

Then Melia stood up suddenly, surprising her. She strode toward the door, wiping her hands on her jeans. "If you want to look inside the mill for clues about why your sister was there, we should probably head out now."

Lehua blinked. "You still want to help me?"

"I said I would, didn't I? C'mon. We should get going."

Lehua followed Melia outside. The night had darkened, and the cane seemed to loom taller, grasping skyward. As Melia stepped into the sugarcane fields, the leaves engulfed her. "There's not a clear walkway to the older buildings, so we'll have to cut through here."

Lehua stumbled into the dark after her, guided only by moonlight.

"Watch where you step," Melia warned, without turning. "There's an irrigation ditch and you'll want to avoid any holes you see. Yellow jackets sometimes make nests there. Well, usually."

"Usually?"

"I haven't seen or heard any since we got here."

Now that Melia had mentioned it, it was *odd* that Lehua hadn't seen any wildlife since arriving—except for flies and that dead, half-eaten bird they'd found in the abandoned town. In Lāhainā, katydids had chittered outside her window all night long, echoed by a handful of gecko trills. But not on Kōpa'a. The darkness enveloped them with its silence.

Kōpa'a is 'e'epa. Unexplainable. "You said you'd read some stuff about the resort—before you came," Lehua began carefully. Their earlier camaraderie was gone and their partnership felt tentative. Brittle. "What else did you find out?"

"A lot of the usual bullshit. Kōpa'a was bought by some sugarcane planter right after the overthrow, whose dad was one of the original missionaries who'd settled in Hawai'i, bringing their mission of 'merry and uplift.' " Melia scoffed, surprising Lehua.

"You don't believe in that stuff?" Lehua asked, surprised. She wondered where Melia's belief began and ended. Where did the other girl draw the line between something like religion and island superstition? How did she delineate the two? Lehua's grandparents had never been religious. The first time Lehua and Ohia had entered a church, they'd been dutifully following one of their foster families into a pew.

Judgment flickered in Melia's eyes. "No, but my family converted."

There was more there, but Lehua didn't push. She climbed a low hill after Melia, exiting a pineapple field. Their crowns stabbed the girls' legs as they overlooked the island and the great house in the distance.

"There's a saying. About the missionary families," Melia said, staring at the whole of the island: the abandoned mill, the empty camp house behind them, and the fields spreading out like a ripple from where they stood on the hill. "They came to do good, and did very *well* instead.

"When Horace built his plantation, he tried to hire the same families he'd pushed out, but they weren't interested in the low wages, so they had no choice but to leave—the provisional government, which was run by white planters, wasn't going to intervene on their behalf. So, like most plantations, Kōpaʻa hired overseas workers and kept them practically indentured. Until they all went on strike, shutting the plantation down."

"I heard there'd been a fire . . ."

Melia's eyes flashed to hers. "Oh, there was a fire. The workers lit up one of the pineapple fields in protest, so Horace locked the cannery. The workers that were stuck inside burned up with the building and fields." Melia was looking at the scorched acre, at the ruined plot of earth Chiyo had pointed out to Lehua earlier that day. *Nothing grows there.*

The tour had conveniently skipped that part about why.

The photograph she'd seen earlier that day ran fleetingly through her mind, the number of people Horace must've locked inside the cannery to burn. An oily feeling sank down Lehua's legs. She felt like she was going to be sick.

"Of course, when he was asked about it, Horace claimed it was untrue. That the fire was an accident. But there've been a lot of 'accidents' since. Workers would warn their friends away from the island, saying *Don't work at Kōpaʻa, you'll only become fertilizer for the cane.*" Melia shook her head. "Before I saw you in Lāhainā, I thought about leaving and taking my chances. But I knew if I left, I'd have to leave Hawaiʻi—and I couldn't do it. I couldn't give them the satisfaction of chasing me away. At least here, I'm still *home.*"

Melia took a breath, then guided Lehua back into the cane. Before long, the mill came into view. "We're here."

NINETEEN

The two girls descended the hill, two shades against the night, their footsteps stirring up red grit, the mill growing on the horizon.

Lehua tipped her head back, taking the building in. The old plantation blocked out the sky. "Wow."

The mill was a mess of rust and yellowed sheet metal slanted to the side, its foundation sinking into the ground. Next to the creepy building, large piles of hulled sugarcane were stacked like loose pyres.

Lehua sniffed. The sugarcane was soaked in something with a sour, almost fermented odor. She lifted her phone's flashlight onto the cane heap. Something red covered the severed sugarcane, smeared like blood. She did a double take; then she realized the harvested cane was full of rot. Lehua covered her nose. The freshly reaped sugarcane wept sap smelling like alcohol and mildew where their stalks had been cut.

"This looks—" *spoiled*, Lehua was going to say, until a metallic shriek lacerated her ears, making her whirl around.

Melia had shoved the mill's door aside. Overgrown weeds wreathed the derelict doorway, climbing the mill's peeling paint. Melia whistled low.

"Yikes. It almost looks like a mouth, doesn't it? I'm getting chicken skin already," she said, showing Lehua the goose bumps scaling her bare arm.

Melia was right. The mill's jagged doorway gaped like a dark toothy maw. A disconcerting feeling knotted Lehua's gut, warning her to turn around.

Something was genuinely wrong.

Why would Ohia have come here? Lehua's gaze split between the dilapidated mill and the spoiled harvest lying outside. The cane still oozed. Someone had hulled all of this sugarcane very recently, even though Chiyo had said the plantation's cane had spoiled decades ago.

Lehua had seen a stream of workers enter the mill yesterday. But the door was so worn and rusted that it didn't look like *anyone* had been inside the mill for years. Its darkened windows were empty and vacant like the eyes of the dead. How had Ohia and the field-workers gotten inside?

Melia flashed her a weak grin. "C'mon. We definitely won't find anything if we stay out here."

Lehua hesitated, taking in Melia's sickly pallor. Sweat dampened her lips. "Are you sure? Maybe you should sit down."

"I'll be fine." She rolled her eyes, then slipped through the rusted entrance.

Despite the warning in her stomach telling her to retreat, Lehua followed Melia inside, the doorway's corroded edges grazing her like teeth.

The mill was like a giant warehouse inside, bent and broken. A cavernous graveyard of rusted scaffolding hung above their heads like an unnatural skeleton. The copper walls had oxidized into a ghoulish green and scars stained the metal where decades of mill smoke had once flowed.

Strangely, Lehua could still smell that smoke haunting the air—stale and sharp, like cigarette smoke left to linger, like something burned in the back of her throat.

This building was the aftermath. A leftover terror from the plantation's history.

She and Melia drifted through the mill, untethering the spiderwebs dusting their paths. The silence encircled them, and Lehua let it pool around her while her mind tried to reconcile the place with what she'd seen last night. The overhead lights had been on, illuminating the workers hacking their blades through the grass outside. Those same massive lights were shattered tonight, their glass shards crunching underfoot.

"I could've sworn I saw all these lights on last night," Lehua admitted quietly.

"I'm almost positive we're the only two people to step foot in this place since the nineties," Melia said, running her hand down one of the copper walls, over a long line of tallies scratched into the metal. A wooden plaque was mounted above the tallies, reading *No man, having put his hand to the plow, and looking back, is fit for the kingdom of God.*

When Melia turned around, she looked disappointed. "I thought there would for sure be more in here."

"Like what?"

"I don't know—something. Your sister came in here for a reason—and the whole island's a relic." Melia let out a shaky laugh as sweat beaded her skin. "Why else would they bother keeping all of this around?"

"Chiyo said Horace instructed that his island be kept in perpetuity. To preserve history."

"Uh-huh. This doesn't look *preserved* to me."

"I'm surprised Ohia came in here at all. She doesn't do ick."

"Is this ick?"

"It's full of spiderwebs and mold, Melia."

Melia shrugged. "You work in a mortuary, handling who knows how many dead bodies. I didn't think this was a huge leap for you."

Lehua's lips flattened. "Yeah, but . . ." *Ohia's not like me,* she'd been about to say. But maybe she'd been wrong about Ohia. Her jacket had been smudged with rust. Her sister must have entered this place. But at the reminder of Ohia's jacket, Lehua remembered one of its sleeves had been torn, too.

Melia pointed toward a thin metal stairway. It twisted toward a catwalk that overlooked the mill floor and the abandoned carts of hulled sugarcane left to rot. "We can get a better look from up there."

"Here, let me go," Lehua said. Melia looked far too pale for Lehua's liking. "I'm the one holding the light," she added, though she doubted Melia bought that reason.

She looked like she might argue with Lehua until she sighed. "Fine. Be careful. Those stairs look rusted through."

Lehua stepped onto the staircase. The metal whined loudly, protesting her weight. She had a feeling if she showed any hesitation, Melia would push past her, despite how awful the girl must've felt, so Lehua drew in a sharp breath and forced her feet up the stairs.

Each step clanged, shuddering through the swaying metal as she climbed higher. She exhaled low when she reached the top, then muffled a cry.

A man stood on the dark catwalk, less than an arm's distance away. A sheath of moonlight crept along his body and slumped shoulders. His head was tilted, his face bowed. Until her flashlight reflected his shining eyes.

The man smiled a flat rictus grin. "You shouldn't be here, kaikamahine."

Lehua stumbled back with a scream. She tripped, her foot catching on the grating as the worker lurched toward her, grinning wildly. It was the same painful smile that the women in the field had worn, stretched so wide it peeled the skin. She scrambled to run as his fingers closed around her biceps, icing her blood.

She tasted grit, pineapple, something coppery. Blood. She was convulsing on the walkway, twisting beneath the man's grasp, when the staircase rattled behind her. *Melia.*

"You shouldn't be here, kaikamahine," the man repeated in a low hiss, his spit running down Lehua's cheek. His other hand closed around her throat. "You can't let the foreman see you."

With a grunt, Lehua kicked free but before she could scramble away, he grabbed her and wrenched her back.

"Run, Melia!" Lehua cried. "There's someone up here."

As Lehua struggled to break his grip, her chest clenched tight with cold, the freeze after an icy bath. When she finally pulled free, she whirled to face the man—only to find the metal walkway dark and empty. There was no one there.

TWENTY

Lehua and Melia slid to their knees in the grass, panting after their dash through the field.

The air was warm, yet Lehua's teeth were chattering and her heart thumped low in her chest, like it was trying to pump the ice out of her blood. She drank in heavy gulps of the night, the smell of dirt, cut grass, and cane leaves churning her stomach.

"What happened?" Melia demanded, and Lehua winced.

What happened meant she hadn't seen a damn thing.

"I thought I saw someone," Lehua said, wrapping her arms around herself, her fingers grazing the cold patch the man's touch had left on her biceps. A shudder rocked through her.

She half hoped Melia would brush her off, protesting what she'd seen with her own eyes: the catwalk empty except for Lehua curled on the ground. But Melia was staring at her now. "Who'd you see, Lehua?"

Lehua averted her eyes. "A worker."

"That's it?"

Lehua hesitated, remembering with dread the percussive slam of her body hitting the walkway's grating. She didn't want to talk about how the man had seized her and how she'd felt the calluses marking his fingers pinch her skin, soaking cold and terror through her. She could still see his horrible frozen grin. *You shouldn't be here, kaikamahine.*

"He . . . grabbed me," she confessed, exhaling hard. "He told me I shouldn't be here."

She was afraid to look at Melia. Even though the other girl said she believed in the unexplainable, a part of her worried she wouldn't believe *this*. What if she thought Lehua was losing her mind? But when she met Melia's gaze, exhaustion smudged the underside of her eyes and damp sweat soaked her face.

A wave of guilt rolled through Lehua. "Jesus. Are you okay?"

Melia shook her head. "Yeah, I'm fine—just thinking."

Lehua didn't buy it. "About what?"

Melia laughed. They were far enough away that the mere sight of the mill no longer made Lehua feel uneasy. "Ghosts."

Lehua hated the sideways look Melia gave her. "Melia, I didn't see some dude in a white sheet."

"I didn't say you did. But I know you saw something. Something ʻeʻepa. Unexplainable."

Lehua held Melia's gaze this time. Not a ghost, but something not quite right. Fine, she could accept that. "What's that mean exactly?"

"This island is a storied place. There are a lot of stories and legends that can't be explained, Lehua. Have you heard about the Night Marchers?"

"No. Another ghost story?" She heard the defensive edge in her voice and regretted it.

Melia smiled. "Sort of, but not really. Not like the ghost stories you know. The huakaʻī pō are the ghosts of ancient Hawaiian warriors. They rise from the ocean and their old burial grounds to march toward ancient battle sites until sunrise. You can see where they've passed by the footprints the warriors leave behind."

Lehua remembered the footprints she'd seen tracking through the graveyard that morning and resisted a shudder. "How do the warriors leave footprints if they are ghosts?"

"I told you our ghost stories are different. Our ghosts aren't just apparitions. They're corporeal. The legend says you'll know they're coming if you hear a conch blown in the night, and see a line of torches getting brighter and brighter."

"What are you supposed to do then?"

"Bow," Melia said, completely serious. "Or hide."

"Or what? What happens?"

"You'll die violently, unless you have an ancestor who is marching with them. Someone who can claim you as their family."

Lehua's shame rose. If the Night Marchers were real, would she even have an ancestor to claim her? Her grandparents were buried in Phoenix and her mother had abandoned her. Lehua couldn't imagine being claimed by her. In life or in death.

The only person she could see emerging from a ghostly vanguard to call her theirs was Ohia, but now she was gone, too. Lehua had no real past to cling to, no other family.

"This is the first time I've heard that story. My grandparents used to tell us stories about our homeland, but—" *I buried them.* She sighed. "I feel like I don't know anything about Hawai'i."

"That's not your fault," Melia said. "Our culture and language were banned until the seventies, Lehua. They wanted it to die out—for *us* to die out—but we're still here."

"Are there other stories?" Lehua asked quickly, hoping Melia didn't hear the gravel in her voice.

"Like the huaka'ī pō? I mean, there are 'aumakua, and 'unihipili, but they're not specific legends. More like . . . spirits."

Spirits? Lehua's skin crawled at the word. The man in the mill had felt like flesh and blood, not a ghost. But . . .

Our ghosts aren't just apparitions, Melia had said—and Lehua licked her chapped lips. "What kind of spirits?"

"In old Hawaiian legends, we believe the spirit could rest happily in eternity, but a part of them would always linger in their bones, and that sometimes a departed spirit might make their presence known through nature, like a rush of wind or in the pattern of a bird's flight. But 'aumakua are different. They're the spirit of an ancestor passed on who protects their descendants and loved ones after death by offering advice and sending them messages through their dreams. Sometimes, they visit as animals."

Lehua thought of her grandparents and her strange nightmares—of Ohia running away, and the changing wallpaper in her room. She bit her lip. "And you believe all of this?"

Lehua saw a flash of amber in Melia's eyes. "Of course."

"Do you have an . . . 'aumakua?"

"Our family's 'aumakua is the 'alae."

Cold slipped down Lehua's shoulders. "That was the dead bird we saw, right?" She thought of the bird they'd found in the abandoned town and its shredded black plumage—and how still Melia had stood over it. No wonder the girl had been frightened when it disappeared. Lehua had seen the same bird taxidermied, entombed in a glass case in the lounge.

"Yes," she said, staring at the ground. "My tūtū said her parents used to see dozens in Lāhainā, before the planters cleared the wetlands and diverted the water for their cane. She used to find handfuls of their feathers."

Lehua yearned for the pride in Melia's voice, the deep connection she had with these stories and their homeland. Did she and Ohia have an 'aumakua? Had her grandparents known their 'aumakua? Or was that something you lost when you left Hawai'i?

She was still thinking about it when they arrived back at the barracks. Melia surprised her by not going in right away. Instead, she sprawled out on the grass, throwing her arms behind her head.

"C'mon," Melia encouraged. "It's still early. I have one more story to tell you."

Lehua hesitated. "It's after midnight." *You should be resting*, she almost said. But the truth was she didn't want to return to the resort or her room. Not yet.

"Early enough." Melia smiled, and Lehua felt that pulling tide rising. It was hard not to stare at Melia, to keep reminding herself that she was only here for Ohia. What would happen if she stopped resisting that feeling?

"What story did you have in mind?"

"The story of Lehua and Ohia," Melia said. "Do you know it?"

"Our grandma told us that story all the time. She was the one who named us, so we'd never be apart." Lehua's throat closed on that word. Because it hadn't worked.

"Hey. It's a good inoa for you." Melia rolled onto her elbows so she hovered over Lehua on the grass. The stars shone like silver pins, holding up the sky behind her. "A good name. That's how I know you'll find your sister, Lehua."

Her name on Melia's lips thrilled her. It was like an electric current, sparking that tide drawing them together. She'd worried she'd severed that connection earlier.

"Thanks," Lehua murmured, realizing how close Melia's face was to hers. "Does your name have a story?"

Melia looked at Lehua's lips and curled toward her like a crescent moon. "It means *plumeria*. My mom's favorite flower. She was reading a book under the tree outside our house when she felt me kick for the first time. *Oh, so that's your name*, she used to say. My dad wanted to name me Sam—can you imagine?" She laughed. Then her warmed eyes dimmed. "I still can't believe they're gone. I thought it'd get easier, but every day is just as hard."

"I'm sorry," Lehua said. "I know it doesn't help to hear that, but I am sorry they're gone. I wish you weren't alone." She knew what it was like to be pruned from your family.

"Yeah." Melia tucked her knees to her chest, then rested her cheek against them. "It's part of why I couldn't leave, why I chose to live on the streets instead of finding a job on the continent where life might've been easier. That's not where I belong. Hawai'i is the land where my parents, their parents, and their grandparents lived and died. It's where their bones are buried.

As long as I stayed on the ʻāina, I figured I could never be alone. Because they're here."

Lehua thought of her mom. She went home, to the place she could never be alone, to the place her people's bones rested. Looking at Melia and the soft sadness in her eyes, Lehua thought she understood her mom's decision for the first time.

That's life in Hawaiʻi. You don't have a lot of options unless you're here on vacation.

"What are you thinking about?" Melia asked, tucking a loose strand of hair behind her ear. Lehua watched it slip free again almost instantly and resisted the urge to fix it. Melia was leaning toward her again with a soft smile.

"My mom," Lehua said, and Melia doubled over, laughing.

"Your mom?"

God, why had she said it like that? "I mean, my mom—She . . ." Lehua trailed off, her own embarrassed laughter leaking away. "She left us when we were born to come back to Hawaiʻi." Lehua swallowed as each word became harder than the last to pry out. "And she never returned."

Melia's mirth disappeared. "Do you know what happened?"

"No. The police tried looking for her when our grandparents passed away, but—" Lehua shook her head. "They never found her. I don't know if she's alive or dead—or happy, even. I was angry as a kid. I felt like all those social workers were telling us our mom didn't want us. I started to believe it and I hated her. To be honest, I am still angry. But I think I get it now—why she came back to Hawaiʻi.

"She'd been nineteen when she had us and she wasn't ready to be a mom. She hadn't had great options, but our grandparents had loved us," Lehua said. "Perhaps leaving us with them had seemed like the best option."

Her grandma had understood. *She left, going to the one place she knew*, she'd once told her and Ohia. *Home.* But Lehua had been too young to fully comprehend the depth of her mom's grief for her lost homeland. Lehua had been hurting too much to accept it. As she got older, her hurt had spread into a rot that had decayed the memories of her grandparents, too.

"You said you and Ohia were the only ones left. What happened to your grandparents?"

"They died when we were twelve. We grew up in the foster system after that."

Melia grimaced. "I'm sorry."

Lehua's eyes prickled with tears. "Do you know what the worst part is? I didn't get to bury them. I didn't get to take care of them like they took care of us. The state put their ashes in an unmarked plot after they died—I found out last year when I was just starting college."

The injustice burned to life in her, surprising her. She hadn't known a smoldering fire could come back so quickly, razing everything she'd thought she had hidden all these years.

Melia reached for her hand. "Is that why you went into mortuary work?"

Lehua blinked. "What do you mean?"

"You found out what happened to them when you and Ohia were in college, a year ago. And you started at the mortuary after, right?" Melia pulled Lehua's hand into her lap, spreading her fingers wide with her own. "You painted night moths onto your arm when you took the job," she pointed out, running a finger down the moths hidden in her garden of tattoos. "You have three of them."

Lehua tried to swallow the feeling in her chest. It extinguished the flames. "I didn't realize," Lehua said, staring at the three dusty-winged moths on her arm. Her grandma's smile flashed through her mind. *This isn't the end. I'll visit you and your sister. Promise you'll watch for me.*

Maybe, Lehua conceded, she hadn't been watching close enough. Memories of her grandparents welled up as Melia lay back down next to Lehua, her hair grazing Lehua's cheek. She could feel Melia breathing next to her.

"I wish you and Ohia had come home last year. You could have come to Pāʻia, and met my parents. My dad would've taught you how to hand-pound poi and my mom would've shared her haupia recipe. Then you two could taste home wherever you and Ohia went."

"And what about you?"

Melia's cheek caressed hers as she turned, her eyes shining with delight. "I would've taken you to the old sugar mill in Pāʻia, and we would've explored the plantation as I told you stories about Hawaiʻi."

Lehua laughed. "Well, after tonight, I think we can check *that* off the list."

"No, I wasn't finished," Melia said, and a shiver crept down Lehua's neck. "That isn't all we'd do."

This time, when Melia's gaze sank to her lips, Lehua leaned

in. Melia's fingers skimmed her throat, reaching for her. She was now close enough that Lehua could feel Melia's breath exhaling against her open mouth. But there was a question in her hesitation, her sudden shyness. *Can I?*

Lehua thought of the stubborn tilt of Melia's chin and pressed her fingers against the hollow column of her throat, lifting her mouth toward her. She brushed her lips against Melia's softly, barely exerting pressure. If Melia wanted to, she could pull away, breaking the loose cage Lehua had made, Melia's pulse fluttering like a trapped bird's wings against her fingertips.

Instead, Melia pulled Lehua on top of her. Lehua's body shielded Melia's face from the sky. Their hands curled into each other's hair. Lehua cupped her cheek, feeling that desperate undertow tying them together. She kissed Melia without hesitation, their bodies melting together until all the space between them disappeared.

Lehua didn't want to spoil the moment, but she couldn't let herself fully sink into the soft way Melia was nestled against her, how her head fit next to hers. Not when Ohia was out there.

When Lehua drew back, it was like the tide receding, leaving her skin cold.

"Lehua?" Melia said as she moved away. "Is something wrong?"

"Sorry, I'm just worried about Ohia," Lehua whispered, thinking of the torn jacket. What if that man who had attacked her in the mill had attacked Ohia, too? If she hadn't been so shaken, they could've followed him. "Do you think she's okay?"

Melia offered her hand and Lehua took it, leaning gratefully against her soothing presence. Her eyes flashed to Lehua's, sending a wave of warmth into her. A balm against the chilling fear. "What does your naʻau say? Your gut," Melia asked gently.

"My gut?" Lehua repeated. "What do you mean?"

Melia rested her hand on her abdomen. "Our naʻau is our physical and spiritual center, representing our emotions and innermost thoughts." Melia laid her other hand on Lehua's stomach. "Our ancestors would use their naʻau as their guide for making decisions. So what does yours say when you think about Ohia?"

Lehua closed her eyes. She thought about the terror she'd felt in the mill and the dread that had overwhelmed her when she saw her room had been ransacked. Her sister's phone and jacket pointed to her being in trouble. But . . .

"I don't think she's dead," Lehua said, looking at Melia.

Melia leaned back. "Trust your naʻau, Lehua. It will steer you toward your sister." In her other hand, Lehua saw Melia had her ti leaf bracelet curled in her fist, and she was holding it out to her. "And take this for good luck, too."

"What about you?" Lehua searched Melia's warm gaze.

Melia smiled softly. "I'll just make another lei."

Lehua nodded despite the bitter fear coating her throat. She wanted to know everything about Melia, about her life, about Hawaiʻi. For all the time they'd spent together the last two days, Lehua wanted more. But their time was frustratingly finite. They had less than two days. She wanted weeks, months, a year to unravel her, and the homeland she'd never known before now.

In two days, she had learned more about Hawaiʻi and her ancestors than she had in her entire life, and she wondered if that was what Ohia had come to find. If her sister, like her, had wanted to feel that faint connection again, like they had before their grandparents had died.

But something Melia had said earlier soured the thought. *Bones.*

"At the dinner tonight, Ira Jacobs said something about Hawaiians."

Melia's gaze darkened. "Oh yeah?"

Lehua watched the darkened resort where only two lights glowed in the windows, looking like eyes, as she repeated the story about Captain Cook. "He said we—that the Kānaka ate him."

Melia's beautiful face was fierce in the moonlight. "We didn't eat anyone, and the attack wasn't unprovoked—it was retaliation. Captain Cook and his men had spread syphilis and gonorrhea to the women and stolen sacred wood from a burial site to repair their ship. The tension between Cook and our people rose, so he kidnapped the island's ruling chief for *leverage*. Our people tried to stop the abduction and Cook's men shot at them, starting the attack. After he died, Cook was given the same funeral rites that any Hawaiian elder would have received. His body was baked, and his bones cleaned. It was more than he deserved, but to this day, haoles"—Melia paused, her eyes flickering to Lehua's—"*foreigners* insist we ate him."

Lehua looked toward the resort again, remembering the shame she'd felt at the table, and how Ira had insisted it'd only been a well-meaning *joke*.

Melia nudged her shoulder. "Remember, Lehua. They want to be the only ones telling our story, because in their version they're fucking heroes. But we can't let them say our history is done and written. Not by their hand. That's how they get to keep what they stole." She extended her hand, and Lehua took it.

"Mai poina, Lehua. Don't forget."

Lehua climbed her balcony, clutching the ti leaf woven around her wrist. Despite the leaves, a knot of fear tightened her chest as she stepped through the lanai door. Her bags were still upturned on the floor inside, the vanity's drawers leaning out of their homes. Anxiety clung to her as she locked the balcony door.

She had mentioned the possibility of Melia spending the night in her room to recover. The suites were a good twenty degrees colder than the rest of the island, but Melia had insisted on staying in the barracks, only promising to consider it after Lehua had badgered her. But when Lehua had suggested she abandon the ʻeʻepa island with her on Monday, Melia's face had shuttered.

"I can't, Lehua," she'd said. "I know something bad happened on this island. But Hawaiʻi is my home. It's the only home I've known, and . . . ʻai pohaku." Her smile had twisted into something angry, her gaze petrifying into amber. "I'd rather eat the stones of our land than leave."

Lehua had nodded, knowing her hope that Melia would join her had been selfish, considering how much their homeland meant to her. Still, the rejection stung.

Looking out the slatted window, she thought of her grandpa, sitting in his car and staring at a colorless sky, knowing exactly where Hawaiʻi was when she and Ohia had asked him. She hadn't felt that tug, that tether to the land, when she stepped into the sea in Santa Monica. But walking away from Melia, she'd felt it pulling tight between them. She felt it now.

Hawai'i's that way.

A sad smile curled her mouth as she braced for their coming separation on Monday, when she'd get back on the boat to Maui—hopefully with Ohia if her sister was somehow here. Lehua liked Melia and could feel herself drifting closer to her every day on that current joining them together through their na'au like a fetter. But this would be the second time someone chose Hawai'i over her.

Melia's decision was not Lehua's to make; Lehua knew that. Yet she couldn't imagine leaving Melia to fend for herself. Not after what Lehua had experienced in the mill.

She touched her phone's jagged screen, and the broken glass pricked her fingertips. It must have cracked when the man wrestled her to the ground. She remembered how his eyes shone an uncanny silver, and the way he vanished.

Something 'e'epa. Something unexplainable.

Something dangerous.

Because after everything she'd experienced and learned, she had to accept there *was* something unnatural about the island, something unexplainable, as much as it terrified Lehua to admit it.

Workers prowled the island every night, cutting and hauling cane grass, yet Melia was the only worker sleeping in the barracks and had never seen another field-worker inside. Lehua's ransacked room and her sister's disappearing jacket with the ominous message on the mirror. That strange notification she'd gotten when she first arrived. And now the mill's broken lights . . . The mill floor was full of dusty, fragmented glass, but those shattered lights had been intact the night before.

Melia was right: There was something ʻeʻepa about Kōpaʻa, and Lehua had no doubt it was dangerous. She'd felt the danger in the man's grip, in the barely leashed violence that had tightened around her neck like a noose. There was something ʻeʻepa on Kōpaʻa—and she and Melia were trapped on the island with it.

Lehua washed the dried blood and red clay off the night moths inked onto her sugarcane-cut arm. The island and her combined, dissolving down the drain together. When she got into bed, she stared at Ohia's photo on her phone's lock screen. *What happened, Ohia?*

If Ohia had encountered something unexplainable, Lehua wanted to believe her sister wouldn't have thought twice about fleeing the island. *She doesn't do ick.* Ohia would have deserted the resort and her favorite jacket and her phone as quickly as possible.

She would have run.

Lehua closed her eyes, feeling the man's icy touch on her biceps, his voice echoing in her mind. *You shouldn't be here, kaikamahine.*

Even though Melia had told her to trust her naʻau, it was hard to listen to that instinct. Because Ohia had gone into that mill. Her torn jacket proved it. Her sister might not be dead . . .

But that didn't mean Ohia was safe.

TWENTY-ONE

SUNDAY

Lehua chased Melia through the cane. Her dark hair bled behind her, trailing through the stalks, never snagging. Melia turned a corner, then another, until Lehua lost her in the grass. She spun in a circle, her nails digging into her palms. "Where are you going?"

She was barefoot and the stalks beneath her feet were wet from rain. Even her hands were slippery. The air smelled rank and wrong. Lehua pushed her way through the sugarcane, but the cane pushed back. The sharp leaves sliced at her skin, ripping it open. From somewhere in the slatted darkness, a cry echoed. A wet gasp.

"Melia?" Lehua ground her teeth and pressed forward. "Melia?"

Only her own footfalls answered her. Her hands started to sweat. The wind rustled the leaves, echoing the fast inhale of her breath, pulsing in and out of her chest.

"Lehua?"

A chill crawled down her back at the thin voice. That wasn't Melia.

Lehua took a step back and the ground gave way. Blood, not rainwater, seeped up between her toes, welling like a wound in the island.

Lehua choked back a scream. She hauled herself out of the sinking ground, grasping at the sharp cane. Leaves snapped as she tried to outrun the rising tide of blood. But when she saw a young Hawaiian woman with a mauve bandana cowering on the ground, Lehua froze. A puddle of blood soaked her knees.

"Melia?"

Melia looked up and flickered, transforming into Ohia. Juice ran down her chin, ruby red.

Her twin grinned at her, her eyes glowing silver. Pale pink viscera shone between her teeth. Severed muscle and swollen flesh were in a torn pile at her feet. Behind her sister, the gleam of silver-dime eyes watched from the cane, glittering above a dozen rictal grins.

"You shouldn't be here," a mass of voices whispered. The gore around Ohia seeped like crude oil, lathering the ground with a red foam. It swelled toward Lehua's ankles. But her feet had fused to the cane floor and blood wetted the plants.

From the cane stalks, their eyes winked like stars. Lehua's terror rose as the blood swirled into a susurrant river with the voices speaking in unison: *"Leave."*

Lehua woke with a start, gripping the bed's quilt in a clammy fist. Morning light sliced the darkness, thin and blue. A soft humming droned, the echo of the workers and their knives cleaving the nearby fields.

Lehua exhaled hard. Sweat soaked her back and bed. A copper taste glazed her mouth. Blood. She'd bitten her tongue in the night. She checked her phone, lying beside her head. A little after seven.

Shit. She pushed up, untangled her legs from her damp sheets, and padded toward the bathroom. In front of the mirror, she rolled her tongue, feeling a sting against her gums. She washed her mouth and teeth, letting the cold water and crisp morning air clear her head.

There was no chance she'd fall back asleep. When she met her eyes in the mirror, it was hard not to conjure the Ohia she'd seen, her wet mouth, the chewing squelch of viscera—and her sister's shining gaze, something ʻeʻepa glowing within.

Lehua remembered Melia's flash of fear as she'd shared how ʻaumakua could send messages through dreams. A wave of dizziness overtook her when she thought of the gore coating her sister, and her molten silver eyes, matching the eyes of the man in the mill. If the dream was a message, was it an omen—or a warning showing her where Ohia was?

Lehua looked queasily at the bracelet encircling her wrist. She wasn't sure she trusted a bunch of ti leaf to keep her safe from whatever lurked in the fields. She recalled Ira's remarks at dinner last night and his interest in the grim details of "Kānaka culture." How deep did that curiosity go? Was it just a casual interest, or was it possible that living here had encouraged his morbid fascination?

Ira's family had lived on the island for over a hundred years. Given everything she'd witnessed in two days, she couldn't fathom how anyone could live here and remain ignorant. She wondered if she could check the small library in the lounge for clues about the island. Daisy said the lounge used to be Horace's library. Considering how obsessed the resort was with memorializing the island's history, she might be able to find some sort of record there, perhaps even an account of the ʻeʻepa events that Chiyo had mentioned during their tour. If Jennifer had warned Ohia to stop asking questions, maybe Ohia had been trying to uncover something ʻeʻepa about the island. That could explain why her sister had been inside the mill.

Lehua resisted a shudder and stripped out of her sleeping clothes, taking one look at the long scratches on her arms and legs, red gouges like claw marks from the sugarcane, before pulling on jeans and a sweatshirt that she'd packed for the plane.

She quietly treaded into the plush hallway, downstairs, and into the dark lounge. The sun hadn't quite risen yet. A cold sweat rolled down her neck. It was easy to imagine something unknown watching her from the room's silent corners. She flicked on a light and took in the brimming bookcases, full of cloth- and leather-bound books with browned and cracked spines.

Lehua flipped through a handful of books. Detailed anatomical sketches and paragraphs full of indecipherable medical jargon swished past her fingers. She traded the medical journals for another stack, using the table in front of the fireplace to sort the books by subject matter. Nothing she read talked in-depth about the island itself.

She reached for the least damaged of the books, one bound in indigo cloth. A handwritten note gripped its front. *Vol. IV, The Journal of Horace Ira Jacobs.* She pulled the cover open slowly, and a flimsy creased paper fell from its pages. It was a letter from Jacobs & Pacific dated 1903, confirming a list of needed supplies: *bolts, bone meal (200 tons), Chinese (order 20 men, 10 women), dried blood, two horses, 20 ft. iron bar, Japanese (order 30 men), lumber, two mules, olive oil, tobacco.*

Lehua felt her stomach churn. It read like a grocery list. She eased the letter back into the front of the book, then flipped through the other pages, but all she found was a script too faded to read, and another loose page at the end of the journal, reading *Thou hast multiplied the nation, thou hast increased their joy: they joy before thee according to the joy in harvest, as men rejoice when they divide the spoil.*

Underneath the Bible verse, the curling script continued, *Caucasians are constitutionally and temperamentally unfitted for the harvest, but the Kānaka is peculiarly adapted. They do not have the character for shrewdness and knowledge of mankind, but are tethered to their land. The Chinese, Japanese, and Filipino workers make do, but the spoil is not as sweet, and the fruit does not last—*

Lehua shut the book, jamming it angrily into its shelf. Dust fell from the bookcase. She remembered Ira's glee and ill-disguised derision for her, for Kānaka. Apparently, his racism had been inherited. Horace Jacobs wrote about workers like they were commodities to be traded and bought.

Chiyo and the other guests would be up soon, and Lehua was considering abandoning the library and her search when she saw it. The outline of the service wing's hidden door, barely perceptible atop the wallpaper and the lounge's wood paneling. *Daisy didn't lock it.*

A nagging tug in Lehua's gut, in her nāʼau, pushed her toward the secret alcove. It connected the lounge, the dining room, and Horace's bedroom, according to Daisy. Maybe Ira had kept some of his ancestor's collection in his personal room after the library's transformation into a resort lounge. She was reaching for the thin wallpaper seam outlining the door when she paused, remembering the old man she'd glimpsed on the stairs that first night. *Horace.*

You look like you've seen a ghost, Melia had said in a wavering voice, thick with worry after they'd found the photographs of Horace and his children. What if Lehua had? What if that man had been ʻeʻepa like the workers and could answer her questions about the supernatural?

The question kindled a reckless flame inside of Lehua. She opened the hidden alcove, emboldened, then slipped inside.

TWENTY-TWO

A deep gloom veiled the walls and spiral staircase of the service wing. It seemed darker than before, despite the light welling into the alcove from underneath its hidden doors. The last time Lehua had been here, only moonlight had silvered the edges of the room. But she hadn't been alone.

And she hadn't been hoping to see a ghost.

Lehua placed a single foot on the staircase and felt a low creak clamor through her, echoed by the fear humming beneath her skin. *I'll be in and out*, she told herself, feeling like a child afraid of the dark, bargaining with herself as she hesitantly took each step.

Once she had made her way up, she eyed the door leading to Ira's room with wariness. *What if Ira is in there right now?* Maybe she'd be lucky and he'd be sleeping. Chiyo said he was sick, and Lehua could smell the disease coating him like rot.

Lehua held her breath and nudged the secret door open, then crept inside, bracing for the sound of Ira's voice. As her eyes adjusted, Lehua saw another hallway with a second corkscrew staircase leading to a higher floor. *The resort's cupola.* At the end of the hallway, candlelight flickered. Lehua's blood drummed at the sight, but she kept moving. *You've already come this far.*

Lehua skulked forward, pressing herself against the wall when she turned the corner. Light slid in through the gaps of the hallway's hidden doors. A hum drifted through the porous wall at the end. Ira.

He was not asleep or outside his room like she'd hoped. The rasp in his voice was gone while he hummed softly to himself. *He's distracted.*

Good. Lehua felt that wild recklessness flare in her chest again, encouraging her to move toward the hidden wall panel. As she grew closer to the sound of Ira's low humming, she thought it sounded familiar, like a hymn she'd heard in the mortuary, at one of their funerals. Then she smelled the overpowering persimmon rot.

Lehua's stomach jumped, almost heaving. She didn't dare press herself directly against the door's seam, but she had to at least look. Breathing slowly through her mouth, Lehua shielded her eyes and peeked through the gap.

A human skull grinned at her.

Lehua reared back. Her teeth clanged painfully, biting down on the scream threatening to break through. She clamped her hands over her mouth until her heartbeat slowed.

She didn't know what to make of the skull in Ira's room, but Lehua couldn't shuffle her way downstairs with more questions than answers. This time, when she stared through the gap, she was prepared for the nauseating sight of the toothy grin and cleaned-out eye sockets glaring back.

What she wasn't prepared for was the dozen other skulls on display all over Ira's large bedroom. By the wavering candlelight, Lehua could see a desk strewn with papers and journals and skulls, the corner of an ornate library peeking at her with more skulls stacked next to open jars of heady fermenting persimmons. Upon a massive bed lay the island's owner, humming quietly to himself. But Lehua's gaze kept sliding back to the skulls next to the jars of persimmons.

They shouldn't be that close together, some faraway part of her brain insisted. Lehua would've laughed at herself if she wasn't so afraid of being caught. As if Ira's biggest problem was with handwashing and basic hygiene.

He keeps bones in his room, she thought, and she remembered the gleam in his blue eyes when he'd talked about Captain Cook and how his remains had been treated. Hypocrite.

As she peered at the persimmon jars, thick syrup surrounding those orange carpels, Lehua caught a whiff of something pungent and distinct that stung her eyes and nose like vinegar. *I know that smell.*

Ira had risen from his bed and was admiring a jar on his bookshelf. As he lifted the vessel, Lehua saw something drift in the glass . . .

A pale hand had been sundered at the wrist, its delicate nails magnified by the syrup it floated in. *A human hand.* Lehua retreated from the door, biting into her knuckle so she wouldn't heave.

She couldn't believe her eyes, but there was no mistaking that smell. Formalin. Liquid formaldehyde and methanol. It soaked the hand, preserving it in that viscous treacle mixture that was competing with the stink of overripe persimmons. She'd come to find a record of the resort's supernatural events and the unexplainable to protect her and Melia from whatever lurked in the cane. But the bigger threat might be here at the heart of Kōpaʻa.

Lehua's vision swam. Whose hand was Ira holding? She had to get out of here, but a part of her wanted to charge into Ira's room and demand answers. As she hesitated, an icy hand enveloped her face, covering her mouth so she couldn't scream.

Cold filled Lehua, dropping like a wave over her head. She could still hear Ira humming on the other side of the hidden panel, unaware. Lehua spun, frantically trying to fend off whoever had grabbed her in the dark. Until she glimpsed Daisy's fair face and striking pale eyes.

Daisy let go of Lehua and held a finger in front of her mouth, a silent warning. She peered around Lehua into Ira's room.

Then Daisy bolted, hurrying down the spiral steps Lehua had climbed on her own, and Lehua knew that was her cue to follow. Each creak of the stairs sent her heart thudding and she wished she could be as quiet as the lithe blond girl. Daisy hadn't made a single sound when she descended the corkscrew stairs.

When they finally reached the ground floor, they caught their breath.

"You scared me," Lehua whispered.

Daisy stared at her with disbelief. "What are you doing here? I warned you to follow the rules, Miss Sayers."

Great, we're back to Miss Sayers, Lehua thought. "I mean, the rules seem kind of ridiculous when he's keeping *human remains* in his room, right? Shouldn't there be a rule against that?" Why wasn't

Daisy more freaked out about the bones or the human hand Ira had? Then Lehua realized. "Wait, you and Chiyo know about this?"

Daisy's expression was unmistakable. *Yes, she knew.* "It's what he studies."

Right, and budding serial killers torture small animals because they're interested in veterinarian work. Lehua gave Daisy an incredulous look. She'd seen the medical journals in the library, but she didn't think Ira was a doctor. Even if he was, she didn't know a single doctor who kept remains at home. "I bury the dead. You don't see me keeping them on my bookshelf."

"It's because he's dying. He's fascinated by death but fears his own."

We're all dying. Lehua wanted to shake her. "Doesn't it matter whose hand that is? What if he had something to do with my sister's disappearance?"

Finally, Daisy's usual mild expression broke, turning into anger. "You don't get it. Do you?" Her voice sent Lehua stumbling back a step. "Whose hand did that look like?"

And the words cut through Lehua, silencing her. Because it'd been a pale white hand. It clearly wasn't Ohia's.

Maybe Ira had shipped a hand in formalin to his island—he was rich, so Lehua didn't think finding a supplier of human remains would be that hard.

Daisy's nails needled her palms. "I'm sorry I broke the rules again, Daisy," Lehua said, and the girl flinched, making her feel worse.

Why are you here? Lehua almost asked. Chiyo had told her they prioritized the workers who *needed* the opportunity. Whatever Daisy had left must've been really terrible if she was staying here, after everything Lehua had seen over the last two days.

She reached for Daisy, wanting to offer her a hug or something, but the girl took a step back, keeping her eyes on the floor.

"I am sorry I lost my temper," she said. "It wasn't appropriate. It'd be best if you pretended to have never seen those things."

"How am I supposed to do that?"

"The same way I'll forget I saw you here," Daisy said forlornly, pointing toward the lounge's hidden door. "I won't say a word to anyone—and neither should you. But only if you go right now."

Lehua didn't appreciate the ultimatum, but when she tried to meet Daisy's eyes, the blond girl turned away, resolutely facing the service wing's walls. Lehua sighed, slipping through the alcove door. It had barely shut when she heard the click of a lock on the other side. Of course, Daisy would make sure Lehua never wandered in there again. Still, Lehua was relieved Daisy had agreed to not tell anyone that she'd seen her.

Until Lehua heard someone clear their throat.

Sacha leaned against the lounge's double doors. She wore a shawl, a tight-fitting top, and high-waisted silk pants that gathered in puddles of fabric on the herringbone floor.

"Morning." She waved her fingers, giving Lehua an expectant look.

"Hey." Lehua forced a smile as nonchalantly as she could. Had Sacha seen her coming out of the hidden door? Lehua didn't know. She'd been so focused on Daisy locking the other side, she hadn't bothered looking around the lounge.

"You ready for our swim? Although . . . Huh." Sacha paused, cocking her head. "That doesn't look like any swimsuit I've seen."

"Sorry, it slipped my mind." *Dammit.* Lehua had completely forgotten Sacha had asked her to swim yesterday. Had she said yes? She couldn't remember.

"Please, it's fine. I mean, you probably didn't pack one. But you can come to my room and try on one of mine," she said, flinging herself into one of the wingback chairs, the picture of ease. *Thank god.* Sacha hadn't seen a thing.

"My question is, What are *you* doing in the library?" She sniffed. "You're in Hawaii. Why would you spend that time stuck indoors reading?"

Up close, Sacha's lotion was impossible to ignore. Persimmon and musk—and something pungent like cigar smoke.

"Boredom," Lehua said with a shrug. She wanted to track Melia down and tell her what she'd found, but she needed to get rid of Sacha first. "This place is kind of creepy, isn't it?"

"Oh, I hadn't noticed, but I don't hide in dusty lounge libraries," Sacha said. "I know of a private white-sand cove on the east end of the island if you want to go with me . . ."

The invitation was clear enough but Lehua couldn't forget the way Sacha had sat silently as Ira insulted Lehua in front of everyone. Sacha's attention hadn't seemed to matter much then.

"Really?" Lehua crossed her arms. "I didn't think you were interested anymore."

"Why would you think that?"

"You were pretty quiet last night," Lehua said, unable to hide the venom lacing her voice.

"Wait. Are you talking about that whole thing between you and Ira?" Sacha asked with a laugh. "He's an old man, rotting on an island. It's a waste of time to say anything, believe me. He won't change. He can't see the privilege he has or how he affects people."

Lehua thought that was rich coming from her.

"You shouldn't punish me because he doesn't have any table manners," Sacha said, pouting. "C'mon, Le."

He won't change. The same could be said about the influencer. Sacha wouldn't—couldn't—understand, and Lehua didn't want to waste her time arguing with her, either.

"No, you're right," she said, faking a tight smile.

The influencer's contrition melted away. "Now that that's over, let's go before it gets too hot to do anything but swim." She raised her eyebrows meaningfully.

Lehua feigned a yawn. "I might go later. I didn't really sleep."

Sacha's eyes narrowed, making Lehua's pulse jump. Why was Sacha watching her like that? "You said that yesterday. If you're that tired, you should try one of my pills."

"I still have the last one you gave me," Lehua lied. After everything that happened last night, she had no idea where she put the influencer's sleeping pills.

"Ohh-kay," she said, stretching the word out with a full-lipped smile. "Maybe you'd get more rest if you stopped sneaking out every night."

Lehua froze. "What did you say?"

Sacha pretended to check her manicure. "Last night, I went upstairs to look for you and your room was empty. I saw you and that girl outside. I didn't know I had competition." She fanned her nails out, her dark look melting into a smirk. "Looks like I'll have to raise the bar."

Without warning, Sacha reached for Lehua, pulling her into an unwanted kiss, plunging her mouth toward hers. Citrus coated her lips like perfume. Sacha's mouth was urgent, prying the kiss from Lehua's lips like it was a tithe, a toll she had always expected to collect. Perhaps kissing her, a Hawaiian, was just a part of the *Hawaiʻi experience* for Sacha.

"I couldn't wait any longer," Sacha whispered against Lehua's mouth, skimming her teeth over Lehua's bottom lip. Then she bit down.

Lehua flinched as the coppery taste of blood hit her tongue. She tried to pull free, but when she placed her hands against Sacha's shoulder, she stilled. Sacha's skin felt *wrong*, like dried fruit, the coarse flesh scouring her palms.

Repulsed, Lehua jerked away, attempting to shove the influencer off her. But Sacha clung to Lehua, refusing to let go. Sacha's strength surprised her. She struggled against her firm grip until Sacha finally released her, her swollen mouth grinning at Lehua in a way she assumed was meant to ease her. It did the opposite.

"Sorry, I had to know how you tasted," Sacha said, laughing softly. "I was too subtle last time, and I wasn't about to make the same mistake." She ran her manicured nails down Lehua's cheek, then her other hand pulled Melia's ti leaf bracelet off her wrist. The influencer held it up, smirking. "Don't forget whose room you're supposed to visit tonight. I'll be waiting."

Lehua backed away, her bottom lip throbbing and skin still

crawling from the sensation of Sacha's flesh. She raced out of the lounge and the resort's west wing as fast as she could. Sacha's hands had sunk into her possessively, like she'd been laying a claim on her. *We are in Hawaii! Where's the experience?* Lehua didn't want to be used—consumed—by the influencer.

When she got to the resort's entrance, she'd meant to run outside and find Melia. But as she opened the door, a flash of movement had her shrinking away. Leigh stood outside, peering into the sugarcane fields alongside the resort.

Lehua held her breath as she watched Leigh through the front door's narrow opening. He hadn't seen her yet as he circled the resort exterior, staring into the fields. He looked like he was searching for something. Given the red field dust coating his black suit, it didn't look like he was trying to hide what he was doing, either. It was obvious he'd been looking inside the sugarcane fields. Out of all the guests, Leigh had seemed the strictest regarding the rules. Why was he breaking them?

As Lehua hung back, a chill exhaled down her neck. She remembered seeing Sacha's phone in her purse last night and the disinterested way she had reacted to learning Oliver broke curfew. *I saw you and that girl outside,* Sacha's words rose in Lehua's mind and her anxiety clung to her. Did none of the resort's rules matter to the guests? Or . . .

Lehua thought about the way Sacha hadn't agreed with her about the island being creepy, Jennifer's fear of the island, and her late-night encounter with Oliver outside the cane fields—and what he'd said when Lehua told him the workers had been acting strange. *You mean working?* Could the guests know about the island's workers? But if they knew the island was 'e'epa and some of them were afraid like Jennifer was, then why would the guests return to the island?

She scanned the resort's ivory façade for the camera hidden there. She recalled the security room, the heavy surveillance, and shivered. Perhaps those cameras weren't for watching the guests, they were for watching the unexplainable hiding around the resort.

Daisy had told her to forget what she saw in the service wing. That wasn't possible. The hand in Ira's room hadn't been her sister's but it had been someone's. Lehua didn't know how it tied to her sister's disappearance, but she had a queasy feeling in her nā'au that it was all connected. That the reason why the guests would still come here, even knowing the dangers of the island, was connected to whatever had happened to Ohia, too.

You need to stop asking so many questions, Jennifer had told her. If Ohia had been asking questions about the island, maybe her sister had uncovered something she shouldn't have. Something dangerous. She eyed the thick cane where Leigh had been searching, and a wave of trepidation moved over Lehua.

She turned toward the barracks. Melia knew the island and its stories. Maybe together they could figure out what Ohia had found.

TWENTY-THREE

The cane grazed her cheeks as Lehua made her way to the barracks, and her chest tightened. It felt like the island was closing in on her with its stray leaves and eerie chorus. Only the sky's pallid blue, spreading like dye overhead, soothed her rising claustrophobia, reminding her of Phoenix and Ohia.

They used to hike outside the city together, talking among the saguaro cacti, red rock, and blue sky. Far from their guardian of the week, month, or year, Lehua would invoke the past while Ohia's umbra eyes would go distant, then lost. The last time they hiked together, trudging up one of their favorite peaks, was before high school graduation. They had reclined on a slash of sandstone like two lizards in the sun, and Ohia had sighed. "We made it, Le."

Lehua had immediately understood the double meaning of her twin's words. She hadn't just been talking about their hike; they had finally secured their future as university track stars. But that was before Lehua quit.

Lehua's gaze swept over the island. She wondered if Ohia had been happy here, before she learned how the past could rear its ugly head into the present. She imagined her sister's hair highlighted by the sun and her charred eyes bright. But the Ohia in her mind was the opposite of the sister she argued with three months ago, that stranger who had tried to coax her back to school. If Lehua had returned, would that have stopped Ohia from running away? She doubted her refusal had caused her sister's grades to drop or made her leave the team. But if Lehua had stayed, maybe Ohia would've invited her to Hawaiʻi. *Would I have said yes?*

The awful truth was Lehua didn't know the answer. She loved Ohia. But she had *wanted* to grow apart, to see who she would become outside of her star sister's orbit.

"Now you know."

Lehua's breath caught in her throat. She stopped walking and slowly turned toward the cane. *Who said that?*

The field was empty. Only the wind whispered through the tall grass.

She wiped her wet eyes and brow, slick with perspiration. The sudden silence enclosed her like a fist—and the world tilted.

A disorienting fever gripped Lehua. The dirt road ahead blurred and shimmered, draining like an artery over the hill's vivid edge. An ache pressed down on her distorted vision. She felt like she was peering through a broken kaleidoscope.

Why can't I move? Her heart rattled as her feet refused to obey, her chest shaking violently as if caught within an electric current, like her body was failing to resuscitate. Until . . .

The wind whipped the grass, choking off the ringing silence

in her ears. A cold wave washed over her, finally unmooring her from her trance.

Released, Lehua gasped. Her hoodie was soaked in sweat, and she used it to mop up the streaks running down her face. Just how long had she been standing there? She checked her phone—3:23 p.m.

Lehua did a double take. *Four hours?* Could it really have been that long since she left the resort? She aired her shirt, noticing something shredded on the path ahead of her. Ti leaf.

The protection plants hedging the field had been hacked into bare stalks, their vibrant leaves stamped into the road. But when she left Melia last night, there hadn't been any torn leaves or plants here. It was unlikely someone from the resort had destroyed the ti leaf after she left, which meant . . .

A rustle disturbed the field. Unease crawled over Lehua as the oppressive feeling of more than a dozen eyes suddenly bore down on her. Dread raced down her back, an unrelenting warning.

Something had destroyed the plants, and it was still here, hiding.

The wall of sugarcane was well over twenty feet tall, and their leafy crowns blanketed the field with a darkness as thick as night. But now a glow shone through the stalks.

As the cane sashayed, Lehua remembered Melia's story about the huakaʻī pō. Torchlight heralded their arrival. *But it's daytime,* she thought defiantly, even as the sizzle of the lanterns hissed louder, growing closer. Lehua's fear spiked, an angry stab of adrenaline that left her dizzy. *I should run.*

She had nothing to protect herself—her wrist was bare. Because Sacha had taken Melia's ti leaf bracelet. She had whirled toward the jagged cane to hide in its dips and gulches when three workers emerged.

Lehua backed away, stumbling. All three had loose hair, black as burnt sugar; tanned leathery faces callused by the sun; and taut mouths, contorted into matching rictal smiles.

Worst of all, they were not alone.

Lantern light seeped like ichor out of the dark field, revealing a growing crowd of field-workers. They reaped the sugarcane, dragging their blades back and forth. But their gazes were on Lehua, glowing with eyeshine.

"You shouldn't be here," one of the three workers hissed through her cracked teeth. Despite her smile, her eyes were low, and her hands shook. She was hunched on the road, wearing a floral aloha button-up like Chiyo's, long jeans, and what looked like a straw wide-brimmed hat. But her uniform had a tear running through it, stained red, and her shaking fingers bundled empty air.

"Why didn't you run, kaikamahine?" one of the men asked, his lips smacking as he chewed something between his smiling teeth. Dusty wings and antennae painted his mouth in a mass of dead insects. *Night moths.* He was *eating* them.

A thorax fell from his mouth as he drew closer, his head lolling to the side, his arms swinging a long blade, sawing at nothing.

Kaikamahine. Lehua shrank at the Hawaiian word. It was the same one the man in the mill used before lunging for her.

Behind her, a smudge of shadow eased into the cane, and

Lehua realized there were workers there, too. Sharp panic and terror coiled in Lehua, circling like a riptide. They were herding Lehua and she was blocked in, cornered by the ʻeʻepa workers and their sawing blades. But . . .

They weren't moving closer—and these workers didn't tackle her to the ground like the man in the mill had. Despite their grins, their eyes were wide, *afraid*. But of what? No one else was around.

Lehua pictured Ohia, her lips drawn into a smile, and it was like she was on the island with her. *You're looking for answers about the supernatural, right, Le?*

"Why are you here? Why are you following me? Do you know where my sister went?" The words bubbled out in a desperate stream along with her worst fear: "Did you hurt her?"

Lehua's eyes darted from their faces to the weapons they carried. A cane knife, a machete, and a sickle swayed close. Yet their sharp edges stayed low, pointed toward the ground.

The workers stood stiff, their eyes showing too much white. The same unnatural silence and encompassing stillness shrouded the dead. But then the other field hands slowly turned and disappeared into the sugarcane, as if devoured by the plants. They departed without a sound, like smoke dissolving in the air, raising the hair along the back of Lehua's neck. *I told you our ghost stories are different,* she heard Melia saying in her mind.

Only the man who had just called her kaikamahine remained, staring at Lehua, his eyes shining.

Lehua panted, her chest frantically rising and falling. "Well?" she demanded.

"We told you to run, kaikamahine." The man's gleaming eyes

were sad, at odds with his wide smile. His next words sent a shudder down her spine. "They know you lied, *Alana*."

Alana. The name sank into Lehua like teeth.

The man turned, starting his retreat toward the field. *No.* Lehua couldn't let him leave. She had more to ask.

"Wait!" she cried, desperately bolting after him into the dark mouth of the sugarcane. She didn't care that it could be dangerous. The worker's words drummed in her ears, stoking that reckless fire in her chest. *He said Alana. He knows what happened to Ohia.*

Lehua ran after him, shoving apart the stalks and leaves blocking her way. She didn't care if the man attacked her. He knew more about Ohia. He'd even *warned* her sister.

"Come back!"

Sugarcane snapped against her skin, reminding Lehua of her nightmare—and the blood she'd run through. But she kept going, charging deeper into the thicket. Until the retreating worker vanished into the green with his lantern, leaving no trace—and no light.

Lehua screamed after him, a guttural howl that pierced the silent field. Her head spun in the sugarcane's oppressive darkness, her hands splitting with pain as she ran, desperately hoping she'd somehow find the man again.

Lehua tripped on what she thought was a rock. But when she stumbled onto her knees, she saw it was a human bone.

The bone was half buried in the cane field.

Lehua stared, unable to make sense of what she was seeing.

Like in Ira's room, she thought dully about how the bone didn't belong there. It was long, its head curved where it'd once connected to someone's hip, and it had been bleached by the sun.

Had she somehow found more iwi kūpuna? Lehua pushed herself to standing, her foot aching where it'd struck the femur. She fumbled for her phone and aimed her flashlight at the ground. The ruined femur was half submerged in the carmine clay next to a cracked skull and another buried rib cage.

All at once, Lehua was back at the mortuary, raking the remains of a young teen out of the cremation chamber into the steel bin at the bottom of the retort. In the bin, the hip bone of the boy cracked against his shin bones, falling with a clatter.

That day she'd learned not all the bones burned when a body was cremated, especially when the deceased died young. She and Avery would rake the ashes of the dead, removing the nails and screws from the coffin they had burned in, and gather their bones to be crushed in the cremulator and ground into fine ash.

"Young bones are stronger," Avery had told her after. "They're made to live long."

Now bile rose in her throat. Unlike the rib cage she and Melia had uncovered, there was a trail of bones leading deeper into the field. If these bones were iwi kūpuna, they hadn't been buried deep.

They were scattered above ground, atop the sugarcane's decayed mulch and spoiled roots.

The island's wind pushed through the sugarcane, sending a shiver down her skin. Fear twisted Lehua's gut—her nā'au—then she felt sick. She bent over, dry heaving. She needed to find Melia.

"Lehua?"

Lehua spun, frantically directing her flashlight's beam at the cane behind her. The light reflected off a pair of familiar eyes.

"What are you doing out here?" Chiyo asked.

"I was taking a walk." The lie drifted through the air, low as a whisper, unconvincing to her own ears.

She knew enough to recognize the bones behind her didn't belong to her sister. They were cracked and old, whitened by years in the sun. But that skull had belonged to someone, just like the hand in Ira's room—and instinct had Lehua retreating, shielding the skeletal remains from Chiyo's gaze. *They know you lied, Alana.*

She didn't know what questions Ohia had been asking. But human bones were hard to ignore.

Chiyo took in the sight of her—the stains on her jeans and sweatshirt, the rips in her cheek and hands—and pressed her fingers to her shocked mouth.

"Lehua," she scolded gently. "I told you not to leave the resort's marked path. Look at you. You're a mess."

Lehua felt the wounds stinging her hands. Undoubtedly grit and dirt had mixed with her blood, painting her palms black. But Lehua couldn't take her eyes off the resort manager. Had the worker been talking about Chiyo? Did Chiyo know Lehua lied?

Who else? a part of her mind reasoned, wanting to flee into the sugarcane to join the 'e'epa workers. Except Chiyo's tender look and the way she reached for her hands diluted Lehua's certainty. When she had asked Chiyo where her sister was, Chiyo's eyes had met hers unflinchingly as she told Lehua she didn't know.

"You fell?" Chiyo asked, looking over Lehua's hands.

"I tripped," Lehua said, making a decision. "Over this." She cast her flashlight on the bones, all while studying Chiyo. But if Chiyo was surprised to see human bones in the field, she didn't show it.

She met Lehua's gaze without hesitation. "Oh no, not another one."

"Another one?" Lehua repeated, not sure she was hearing Chiyo right. Could the bones be iwi kūpuna after all? "You have human remains in your field, and that's all you have to say? Aren't you wondering how they got here?"

"Sadly, I know exactly how they got here, Lehua," Chiyo said. "Look."

Chiyo pushed the cane behind Lehua aside, revealing an open stretch of scorched land. The red dirt surrounding the cane turned into gray, dry, and cracked hard mud.

They were standing near the burned down cannery.

Chiyo stepped through the gap, her black hair falling loosely over her neck, dark strands gleaming beneath Lehua's flashlight in the dusky afternoon. The resort manager had traded her tiered dinner dress from yesterday for her usual aloha shirt uniform.

"When the fire happened, the cannery wasn't empty."

The words slid into Lehua like a knife, staying in the gap of her ribs. She remembered Melia's story and said, "Because Horace locked the doors, trapping the workers during the strikes."

Chiyo's head snapped up. "Where'd you hear—"

"Doesn't matter. Is it true?"

Chiyo's silence was answer enough.

"No wonder nothing grows there," Lehua spat, and that feeling of betrayal returned. Disgusted, she looked away from the resort manager, whose expression was full of contrition.

"I'm sorry I didn't tell you." Chiyo knelt and pushed apart the soil, unearthing another bone, small like the shattered piece of a hand. Lehua shuddered. "It's not a happy history, and I thought it'd be kinder to omit that part."

"Kinder to Horace, maybe. But not to those workers. People should know the truth." Was that why the island was full of ʻeʻepa workers? Lehua had no idea how hauntings were supposed to work, but maybe the truth was all the workers wanted.

"They do." Chiyo rose from her crouch, her gaze sweeping over Lehua, landing on the persimmon orchard, its chain-link fence, and the sea behind Lehua. Chiyo's eyes were distant, her fingers fidgeting with the ti leaf bracelet around her wrist. "But it's Horace's island."

"It *was* Horace's island."

"Well, Mr. Jacobs wouldn't allow me to say it during the tours—because it's his resort."

"But you run the resort," Lehua protested. Chiyo had been the one to tell her, *Kōpaʻa's history runs deep, but that doesn't mean it can't be changed under the right hand.* How did hiding the resort's past line up with that?

"Only as much as he lets me," Chiyo said, and Lehua winced. She thought of the way Ira had patted Chiyo's hand during dinner. *She was once a worker like your sister.* "I know it might surprise you. But

I don't make the rules here. Only enforce them." She gave Lehua a wry smile.

Chiyo began walking and Lehua knew she expected her to follow. They strode through the scorched field in silence, until they came to a hedge of untouched ti leaf and ducked under its splayed leaves, trading the packed earth for red dust again.

The path was a vein cutting through the fields around them, worn with old boot marks. Atop the dirt trail was a bucket filled with golden persimmons, the smell fetid and astringent. A dirty dish lay on the ground next to it. Lehua recognized it when she saw the dried persimmon slice sticking to its rim. Melia had been eating off that plate last night.

"It's for Mr. Jacobs," Chiyo said suddenly, confusing Lehua, until she realized she had meant the bucket of persimmons. "The sicker he gets, the worse his cravings become."

Something about the way Chiyo said *cravings* made the hair on her arms stand up. Lehua remembered the way the man had reached for her during their dinner. It'd been overly familiar. "Is Ira normally so . . . touchy?"

Chiyo's lips flattened with understanding. "No, Mr. Jacobs is not like that. I suppose you could call him a collector." She sighed as she picked up the pail. "He likes beautiful things."

Was that why her sister, Daisy, and Melia had been hired? Like Chiyo, all of them were pretty. They'd draw trailing looks wherever they went, especially from a lecherous man. Then again, all of Ira's guests were refined and beautiful, even Leigh. When she'd sat across from the guests at the dinner table and orbited them in the lounge, it was hard not to notice how coolly sculpted their milky white faces were, a sea of fair features, jeweled with blue eyes. Lehua's grimace deepened. Maybe that was the secret to getting invited to Kōpaʻa: You had to have a certain look.

"Is he dying?"

"He's been dying for a long time."

The path circled up to the resort. Lehua glanced back, toward the scorched earth, but the cane stole her view. She could only see the cut leaves sprawling out of the nearest field like seaweed run ashore by the tide. Lehua remembered Chiyo's story from the tour, and dread soured her stomach.

"Lehua, why were you wandering the cane fields?"

"I . . ." Chiyo wasn't going to let her get away with a full-on lie. But Lehua wasn't about to admit she'd been heading over to the barracks, either.

Chiyo would ask why, and Lehua didn't want to get Melia in trouble. Even if she wanted Melia to leave with her, she couldn't jeopardize Melia's employment—she couldn't do that to her. It had to be Melia's choice. But Lehua couldn't ignore her unease, so she decided on some version of the truth.

"I saw the workers in the field, just now," Lehua said carefully, assessing Chiyo's face as the words sunk in. *Prove I can trust you, Chiyo.* "I was hoping to talk to them, ask them about my sister, but . . ."

Chiyo shook her head. "At this hour, Lehua? You'll make yourself sick. It's too hot to be wandering the fields. And you already know talking to the workers is against our rules."

But they talked to me.

Their pleading eyes were wide in her mind. No matter how unexplainable the workers were, they were real—and they were afraid of something on this island, enough so that they'd tried to warn her sister. Yet Chiyo's face was unreadable, a still pond revealing nothing.

"Lehua, I said you could ask me any questions you'd like about your sister. Instead, you've continued to blatantly break our resort's rules."

Lehua hadn't missed the way Chiyo had sidestepped what she'd asked. That worker had been trying to warn her. He had led Lehua to that scorched field—that terrible graveyard—and Lehua recognized a message when she saw one. That field was like the message scrawled on her mirror. A warning to leave.

"But would you have told me the truth?"

Color flooded Chiyo's cheeks. "Of course, Lehua, and the truth is I've told you all I know. I honestly don't know where your sister is."

Once again, Chiyo's eyes were unwavering, meeting hers. *She's telling the truth.* Chiyo didn't know where her sister was. Lehua knew she was supposed to apologize, to act repentant. But the worker's warning was an unforgiving mantra. *They know you lied, Alana.* A wave of fear washed over Lehua. "Ohia left on that boat with the same captain? You saw her go?"

And there was the faintest pause before Chiyo laughed, a strange lilt. "This is an island. How else would she have left?"

Lehua feigned a smile as Chiyo held the resort's double doors for her. "You tell me."

Once inside, Chiyo turned the key in the lock behind them, sealing the resort's front door shut. *Locking me in.* The sound of the heavy lock struck the air off-key. Had Lehua pushed the manager too far?

Chiyo gave her a clipped smile. "Sorry, Lehua. Seeing your current state, I can no longer leave this door unlocked. I know you're worried about your sister, but you should be thinking about yourself and what you'll do after you return to Maui. I'm sure there's a good reason Ohia left. Maybe she realized what she was throwing away. Her track career, college, and you—"

Chiyo's mouth shut, and Lehua wondered if the resort manager realized she'd said too much about Ohia's track career—something Lehua had never mentioned to Chiyo—until her gaze swung, following Chiyo's attention.

Ira stood on the grand staircase, waiting with an elegant smile.

He was dressed in a black suit, reminding Lehua of the photo she'd found. He looked like a younger, harder, and more handsome version of Horace, despite his illness. Unlike his ancestor, his cheekbones were steep, descending toward an overly sharp jawline, not yet sunken by age. He was no longer bent over, his legs bowing with each step as he walked like they had during the dinner.

While he looked better than he had last night, his milky skin still looked translucent. *He's been dying for a long time,* Chiyo had said, and Lehua resisted a shudder, remembering the bones stored in his room. *He's fascinated by death but fears his own*, Daisy had told her.

"Hello, Chiyo, Lehua." His blue eyes brightened at the sight of the persimmons Chiyo carried. He reached for the bucket and Lehua spied a Bible tucked under his arm with raised golden lettering on the spine. *Jacobs* was embossed on the cover, barely visible under Ira's sleeve.

Chiyo's shoulders straightened, and Lehua watched her careful mask fasten back into place. "Good afternoon, Mr. Jacobs. I apologize for the delay. I ran into Lehua on my way back, and was escorting her—"

He waved a hand, silencing her. "Come now, Chiyo. I'm not going to bite. It's the Lord's Day, after all."

Lehua said nothing. She felt his eyes rove across her stained clothes, going up her neck, and finally ending on her torn cheek. *I'm not going to bite*, he'd said, and Lehua couldn't help feeling that Ira *would* bite if it were any other day, and her heart sped again. *I need to get out of here.*

"I was about to tell Lehua about tonight's dinner, and the boat . . ."

"When you're done, you can meet Daisy and me in the basement," Ira said, taking his Bible out from under his arm, revealing his ancestor's name. He caressed Horace's name, embossed with gold foil, and walked past Chiyo and Lehua. "We can plan the next harvest." His voice melted into a laugh as he turned the corner, greeting someone else.

Lehua was glad to see him gone—and she wasn't the only one. Next to her, Chiyo's lips quivered slightly. *They're all scared of this island*, Leigh had said, but Lehua didn't think that was true of Chiyo. She was afraid of *Ira*.

"Ira believes Sunday should be a day of rest and reflection for our guests. He thinks it's appropriate that the Sabbath falls on the last full day of their retreat, encouraging them to reflect," she said, her voice slightly shaky. "Bearing that in mind, dinner will be served in the rooms tonight. The other guests will enjoy their after-dinner reflections in the lounge, but . . ." Chiyo sighed. "Considering how you've flouted our rules, I'm sure you'll understand why I will not be inviting you to join us, Lehua."

Good. Lehua didn't want to be corralled with the other guests, locked inside the resort where Chiyo could watch her. Once Chiyo delivered her dinner, she'd jump her balcony's ledge, find Melia, and share what she had learned. But Lehua tried to look contrite. "I understand. You mentioned something about the boat, too?"

As they climbed the stairs, Chiyo's eyes were cast down like she was watching Ira through the floor. "Oh, yes. The captain confirmed he'll be back tomorrow night, and your return trip has been already paid for," she said as they approached Lehua's room. "I bet you're excited to return home."

Lehua forced a smile when Chiyo looked at her, acting out the role the resort manager expected: the stranded sister returning home at last. But Lehua was replaying their conversation outside. There'd been cracks in the resort manager's well-worn mask before they'd encountered Ira. When Lehua had asked about whether Ohia had gotten on the boat, Chiyo's laugh had been brittle, high, and thin, and a dark light had bloomed in her eyes. She'd had the same look after Ira had left. A knowing look of fear.

Lehua believed Chiyo didn't know where Ohia was, but the resort manager had been afraid when Lehua had pressed her. *This is an island. How else would she have left?*

Chiyo said goodbye, promising her dinner would be delivered soon, while Lehua slid into her room. Then she shut the door, turning the lock tight before dropping to her knees. Her eyes cut to the cane fields. The workers had mistaken her for her sister like Jennifer had—because they'd been trying to warn Ohia. *We told you to run.*

Had Chiyo known exactly who Alana was when Lehua had shown up? Had she already worked out that Ohia had lied about her identity before Lehua had told her Friday night? Her sister wasn't famous like Sacha. But it was possible someone could've recognized the all-star track runner Ohia Sayers the moment she'd arrived—and told the resort about her deception.

Maybe a guest had reported Ohia's lie to Ira, not Chiyo.

Because the resort manager had been wrong about the bones Lehua had found.

Lehua wrapped her arms around herself as she looked out at the moonlit cane field, swaying outside her balcony. Whoever those bones belonged to, they hadn't died in a fire. Bones charred when they were cooked in the body's fat, which meant whoever was in that field had been killed another way. Had Chiyo simply repeated what she'd been told? Or was she complicit and covering for Ira?

We told you to run. Lehua saw the bones laying in the field and the skulls decorating Ira's bedroom and the delicate hand preserved on his shelf. The human remains were scattered in different locations, but they shared one chilling connection.

Ira Jacobs and his fascination with death.

TWENTY-FOUR

Dinner arrived exactly thirty minutes after Chiyo left.

Lehua had spent the last half hour waiting in her room, the vanity chair pushed up against her door as a makeshift barricade, when she heard the knock.

She changed out of her dirty clothes, yanking on the shirt and cutoff sweats she usually slept in. She wanted to appear like she was heading to bed in case Chiyo or Daisy came to bid her goodnight. But when she opened the door, the hallway was empty except for a tall decanter of water and a silver plate piled high with thick spaghetti and diced red mullet. Lehua looked down the hallway, then claimed the food. She blocked her door with the vanity chair again, careful to brace it beneath the knob, then sat with her legs folded on the bed.

She was counting down the minutes until she knew the guests would be distracted at dinner. Then she would jump from her balcony undetected and find Melia, the only person she fully trusted. Once she told Melia everything she'd discovered about the island's owner, Melia would understand the danger living inside the resort—and they'd hide from Ira tonight. Then they'd figure out a plan to find Ohia before the boat arrived tomorrow. *They know you lied, Alana.*

Lehua nibbled at the food and drained the water in one long gulp. She put the silver platter back in the hallway, then paced her room, listening for the sound of someone taking her plate away. She didn't want anyone to discover she was gone until tomorrow afternoon at least.

She was unsure how much Chiyo knew about the bones in the cane field. But Chiyo had lied when she'd pressed her about Ohia's departure. *How else would she have left?*

If the workers had warned Ohia to run and her twin hadn't escaped on the island's boat—and Chiyo didn't know where Ohia was—maybe her sister was still on the island somewhere. Either way, Lehua wanted a bigger head start than her sister had gotten.

Why can't you keep up? Uzzy taunted in her mind when a wave of nausea struck her. Lehua shakily checked her phone for the time and squinted as the screen seemed to blur in and out of focus.

Lehua rubbed her eyes. Why did she feel so lightheaded? She waited for the wave of dizziness to pass and lifted her phone again. On her lock screen, Ohia's face was bright, her eyes dark like an eclipse. She looked softer, less intimidating somehow, than Lehua was used to.

She'd always thought no one could catch Ohia when she was running. But maybe Lehua had been wrong.

I'm sorry, she thought, meeting Ohia's eyes in the image, and the wound from their fight was there in her chest again. Except it was worse now. Lehua had the feeling if she prodded it, the pain would overwhelm her like pressing down on a contusion—or a broken bone. Despite what her naʻau said, Lehua still had no evidence her sister was safe. What if she was dead? What if Ohia's spirit had left that message on her mirror, telling her to leave?

The story of Lehua and Ohia. Do you know it? Lehua could hear Melia's voice again, the way her warm alto had resonated in her ears when they'd lain in the grass. *Remember the story of our names, Le.*

Lehua didn't remember the first time she'd heard the story—but she couldn't forget the last. Their grandma had been in the hospital, and she and Ohia had been lying next to her, one on each side. Their grandfather had been staring out the window while their grandma told them the ʻŌhiʻa Lehua legend in a whisper-thin voice one more time.

"Long ago, there'd lived a girl named Lehua on the island of Hawaiʻi, who was as beautiful as she was kind. She was beloved by a warrior named ʻŌhiʻa, whose heart was as full of kindness as bravery. But the volcano goddess Pele was also in love with the mortal warrior, until ʻŌhiʻa refused the goddess, saying his heart belonged to Lehua. In a fit of anger, Pele transformed the warrior into a gnarled tree. Heartbroken, Lehua asked the other gods for help, but they could not undo what Pele had done. Seeing her grief, the other gods pitied her, and turned Lehua into a flower, joining the two once again."

"Never to be torn apart," their grandfather had added, smiling at them from the window. Ohia and Lehua each held one of their grandma's hands, her skin cold and thin like paper. "In Hawaiʻi, they say that if you pick a lehua flower, separating ʻŌhiʻa and Lehua again, Lehua grieves, bringing the rain. When your mother left the two of you in our care, we wanted your inoa to remind you daily of the family you have in each other, and your homeland."

While Lehua fought the beginnings of a headache behind her eyes, she thought of her sister's tear-streaked face. The dizziness returned and soon Lehua's vision began to dim. She felt her knees buckling and slumped forward, collapsing onto the bed.

Then there was darkness.

She was lying in her bed. Her ears rang. When she looked around, her eyes couldn't focus—everything blurred, whirling with her frantic movement. She shakily gathered herself to her feet, taking a step toward the lanai door when she collapsed again, falling onto the bed. *What's happening to me?*

Lehua looked at her door. The vanity chair still blocked it. But her rising panic drowned out any relief she felt as exhaustion seeped in like a black vignette. She felt like she was wrapped in thick layers of wool, unable to grasp her terror. Why couldn't she lift her head?

A stale metallic taste coated Lehua's mouth, turning her lips tacky and dry.

Drugged. Lehua's head throbbed as she fought to keep her eyes open. Next to her, the bedside lamp cast a thin halo of green light, barely enough to pierce the night, as a siren pealed outside the lanai door. The mill siren.

It's this place, Sacha had said at the dinner yesterday, offering her two sleeping pills. *I take them before the noises start.* Lehua thought about the dark look the influencer had given her at their last meeting, that awful kiss, and her heart sped. *Don't forget whose room you're supposed to visit tonight.*

Had Sacha . . . drugged her? Her food had been left outside. Anyone could've messed with it. The influencer could've easily broken the pills and dissolved them into her water, and Lehua had gulped it down greedily. But why would Sacha drug her? *What's going to happen to me?*

Lehua's thoughts raced as her body became increasingly heavy. She tried to push herself up from the bed, but her body was unyielding. *Get up. Run.* Lehua heard Uzzy screaming at her—*I don't care if your legs are broken*—but her former coach seemed far away.

A thick fog covered her vision as Lehua faded in and out, watching the lanai door where the curtain waltzed from side to side in the breeze. The night grew darker every time she blinked. Then she heard it. The locked lanai door sighing open.

"Who's there?" Lehua croaked, her stomach capsizing with the effort.

There was the soft creak of the door, the click of it closing, then the sound of something being *dragged* across the room's wooden floorboards. She heard footsteps, until they were dulled by the carpet. Lehua couldn't move. It took all her strength to keep her eyes open, holding her breath as a shadow came into view.

Relief swept through Lehua.

Melia was there, her face gaunt in the lamp's green light.

"I'm so glad it's you. Can you help me up? I can't move . . ." Lehua mumbled, her words slurring. But she trailed off when Melia stood silent. Completely still. The hair rose on the back of Lehua's neck. She managed a panicked whisper. "Melia, are you okay?"

At last, Melia's shoulders lifted, then dropped in a shrug. With her skin stained green by the nimbus of light, Melia looked even more sickly than when Lehua had left her. Her mauve bandana was stained and her socks were dark with black dirt, her shoes gone.

Lehua's throat bobbed. "What happened to you?"

In answer, Melia moved closer. She climbed onto Lehua's bed, the mattress denting beneath her body.

Melia wrapped her arms around Lehua, drawing her close, then began to sob.

"Melia, what happened?" Her touch was cold, leaching Lehua of heat. An iciness poured into her veins. Chicken skin rose where Melia touched her. "Jesus. You're freezing."

Unease crept down Lehua's back, metamorphosing into guilt. *I was supposed to be there. Whatever happened is my fault.* Melia was drained of the warmth and weight Lehua had leaned into last night. When her mouth had been soft against hers, their lips stealing each other's breath with delight.

Now fear closed around Lehua's throat as Melia's grip tightened, her fingers clutching at Lehua's back. "Tell me what's wrong, Melia, so I can fix it—"

It was all Lehua could do to keep her teeth from chattering. She tried to pull away, but Melia's hands were digging into her,

her palms slick with sweat, and blood—blood from where her nails had scraped Lehua's skin. Melia's sweat seeped through her hair and clothes, carrying the stink of rotted persimmons.

Then their eyes met.

Her familiar tawny eyes were huge and devoid of their usual color. Tonight, her irises were gleaming and wholly black.

Melia smiled, her lips stretching open to reveal bleeding gums.

Lehua let out a strangled scream and tried to jolt back, but her body lay like a stone slab in the bed as Melia climbed on top of her, peering down. There was such raw anger in her wild smile that Lehua couldn't look away.

"Melia . . ."

But the girl showed no recognition at her name. She leaned in, her face pressing against Lehua's warm cheek like cold glass. Her hand dragged across Lehua's body and latched on to her throat, her frigid fingers encircling her like a noose, sliding where the sweat and blood dripped off the two girls.

All Lehua could do was gasp, her lungs heaving for air. Melia's throat quivered as her lips parted, her jaw unhinging. Her mouth opened, impossibly wide, and pain exploded in Lehua's head as Melia exhaled against her face. But there was no sound, no air, and no heat.

There was only an all-consuming cold, and the taste of plumerias and persimmons, astringent and floral, slicking down Lehua's throat.

Lehua coughed, sputtering, desperately trying to buck the other girl from her chest, but she was still weak from the drugs, frozen in place. A leaden wave washed over her, a black swell swimming across her vision. Her legs kicked twice, then stopped—as Melia's voice, hoarse and gravelly, whispered: *"Leave."*

When Lehua woke, she could taste the crematorium in her mouth and felt the sensation of something heavy weighing on her like a body. She couldn't remember passing out, only Melia's hollow voice and her hands around her neck—and the pounding nausea in her head and stomach, humming like a storm of insects.

Lehua reached for her neck instinctively, and her touch stung. Her throat was tender, raised with chicken skin. Nothing more. But . . .

The bed's quilt had been knocked to the ground. The light coming through the lanai was strong, brighter than daylight and hotter than the sun—and two umbra eyes stared at her through the shutters like a shadow waiting to be let in.

"Melia?" Lehua asked with a wave of déjà vu, her thoughts scattered. But at her voice, the shadow vanished, dying in the sunlight. Except—

Lehua stopped dead.

The light coming through the window wasn't from the sun. It was fire.

She stumbled forward and yanked the lanai door back. The early morning was flushed red by the flames. The cane fields were smoldering, thick with smoke, black as a river where the fire had already passed.

And on the balcony was a burgundy sports bag with an iPhone

tucked into its pocket, glinting in the light of the flames. Lehua recognized the small pearl charm hanging from a braided cord.

It was the same phone she'd been trying to find with Melia over the last couple of days, the same phone she'd been trying to reach from the moment she first heard her sister had been suspended.

Ohia's.

TWENTY-FIVE

MONDAY

Lehua hid her sister's duffel under the bed, then tucked Ohia's phone into her pocket before jumping off the balcony. She knew she was being reckless, running headfirst into a smoke-ringed field, a fire blazing in its center, but the thought of Melia, ill and weak, trapped within the workers' barracks as the fire spread, left no time for hesitation.

The nightmare replayed in her mind as she rolled to the ground—the gravel in Melia's voice, the white light filling her eyes. It didn't feel like a dream. It felt like a warning to find Melia.

Melia, who didn't know she'd been drugged last night, who didn't know about the bones in Ira's room, and who was sick and alone while a fire raged toward her.

Lehua ran across the island, past the cane fields, ducking where the plumes of smoke were thickest. Everything was wreathed with a sooty haze, and ash feathered Lehua's shoulders.

The cane glowed, lit by the blaze within. Something chittered in the dark. Lehua told herself it was animals scuttling to safety.

She raced down the smoke-filled path to the barracks. The fire had consumed the grass, cane, and hedges nearest to the resort. Above the inferno, the rusted mill loomed, seemingly unscathed even while its siren blared.

"Melia!" Lehua called as she reached the door of the barracks.

No answer.

Lehua threw open the door. The windows were drawn and the lights were off. Only firelight silhouetted Lehua. She turned toward Melia's bed, and her breath caught.

The room was empty.

Had Melia seen the fire and run? She held her hand over her nose and raced toward Melia's bunk bed. Her duffel was missing—but her bed was stripped clean. Lehua's heart hammered with fear as she checked the table nearest to the bed. Empty.

She searched the closet. The trunk. The drawers. Empty. Empty. *Empty.* Her fear swelled, cresting on a new wave with each place she searched. There was no trace of the other girl. *Where are you, Melia?* Even the photo of her family was missing.

"Melia?" Lehua panted, hoarse.

But Melia had disappeared, just like Ohia.

Lehua trudged back into the resort, her feet heavy with trepidation and fear. By the time she returned to the estate, the fire had burned out and smoke hovered over the island in dark clouds.

Inside the resort, the lobby was full of excited voices. Sacha was gossiping with Leigh and Oliver. Lehua could hear snatches of their conversation. But when the resort's doors thudded shut behind her, their circle broke apart. Their gazes swept down her smoke-stained cheeks and sooty clothes, drenched through with sweat.

Sacha's mouth dropped open. Disbelief flickered through her widened eyes, gone in an instant. "Oh my god, are you okay? Were you out in the fire?"

"I'm fine," Lehua whispered, her voice choked by the smoke. Sacha looked surprised to see her—more than the other guests—and the memory of Lehua's drugged stupor came back in a rush.

"I was trying to find out what happened out there," she said, her throat scratching against each word. Even with the prepared lie, her voice shook slightly. She pressed a hand against her tender neck. She hoped the other guests assumed it was the smoke that made her tremble—and not them.

Considering Sacha's access to sleeping pills, Lehua couldn't shake her suspicion that Sacha had drugged her last night after she hadn't gone to her room. *You can't imagine what she's capable of*, Jennifer had warned her. What if Sacha had done something to Melia, too? *I didn't know I had competition.*

Melia had to be responsible for the return of her sister's bag and phone. She must have found them without her—after Lehua didn't show yesterday. But she had no idea where the other girl had gone now. First Ohia, and now Melia. The thought unspooled pain from her chest, threatening to tear Lehua in two. Could the influencer be responsible for Ohia's disappearance, too?

Ever since she and Sacha had met, there'd been inconsistencies in the influencer's story. Sacha hadn't been up-front with what Chiyo had told the other guests in the lounge, she'd followed her and Melia and had spied on them, and Sacha hadn't been forthcoming with her reasons for visiting the island.

"No one knows what happened," Sacha told her now, buzzing with excitement. "But Chiyo's off investigating it."

"Was anyone hurt?" Lehua asked.

"No. Everyone was inside the resort," Sacha said. "Well, everyone except Miss Jennifer. She left early and missed it all."

With everything going on, she had forgotten that Jennifer was leaving early.

"What about the workers?" Lehua remembered the black clouds devouring the cane fields. A deep fear pinched her heart, thinking of Melia out there alone. *I should've been there.* "There was someone staying out in the barracks."

"The workers are the resort's responsibility," Leigh cut in. "Not ours."

"But this is an emergency," Lehua said as a stab of anger shot through her. She was acting reckless, but guilt shredded any sense of self-preservation. *Whatever happened to Melia is my fault.* She had involved Melia and let her help even after they suspected something bad had happened to Ohia. "We need to make sure she's not hurt."

"But why should *we* check?" Leigh scoffed. "For all we know, this worker could have started this whole mess."

"I'm sure Chiyo is checking on your friend," Sacha huffed.

Sacha's retort had been quick, too quick—and she had a sinking feeling. She had to find Melia, and fast. She wasn't sure she could trust Chiyo, but maybe there was another worker she could ask about Melia.

"Where's Daisy?" Lehua asked, and a long silence hung. The guests stared blankly at Lehua and a new wave of frustration swept through her. It was obvious they didn't know who she was talking about. If she'd called Daisy the creepy blond, she was sure Sacha would've recognized her then. "She served us at the dinner with Chiyo."

"Oh. *Her*," Sacha said, her tone flat. "I'm sure she's lurking around here somewhere, sweeping up ash or something." She laughed softly and there was a cruel undercurrent that pierced Lehua through. "I for one can't believe how *well* I'm feeling. I got the best sleep of my life during a fire—isn't that just like me?"

Lehua turned before Sacha could see her look of disgust. She was wasting her time talking to the planters. She'd return to her room and look through Ohia's duffel. Maybe Melia had left her a message inside. She was twisting around the grand staircase's tight corner when she nearly ran into Chiyo on her way down.

The resort manager startled when she saw her. "I was just about to check—" Chiyo's mouth shut as she took in Lehua's sooty appearance. "Really, Lehua? You were outside again. Why?"

Lehua stared at her feet. The smoke smudging her face and clothes made it clear that she hadn't stayed inside the resort during the blaze, so there was no point denying it. "I was just trying to figure out what caused it. But when I passed the barracks,

Melia wasn't inside. Have you heard from her? Is she all right?" she asked, tilting her head to watch Chiyo's reaction.

"That was kind of you to check, Lehua, but extremely unsafe." Chiyo shook her head. "I'm relieved you weren't hurt, but please rest assured I'm looking for Melia."

Lehua's gaze narrowed. She already knew how the manager's missing person cases went. To her credit, Chiyo was doing a great job feigning concern, but she couldn't be looking that hard for Melia—not in *those* plush shoes.

"Do you have any idea where she could've gone?"

"Unfortunately, as we have no clue what caused the fire, there is the possibility Melia may have started it and fled." Chiyo slid her a sad look. "I hope you now understand why I warned you away from her."

"Right." Lehua couldn't stomach Chiyo's pleasant façade right now. "You think Melia started a fire and fled—on an island."

Chiyo's face stiffened. "Like I said, Lehua, we are trying to figure out the cause," she said, her voice harsher than Lehua had ever heard it. "I know this is an unfortunate way to end your stay with us but I'll send Daisy up with a late lunch. Just think: only a couple of hours until you're back on Maui."

"Can't wait," Lehua said, knowing she'd toss the food as soon as it arrived. As she slinked up to her room, she tried to form a plan. She desperately hoped Melia had left her a message inside Ohia's duffel, telling her where to find her.

When her bedroom door was shut, she connected her sister's phone to her charger with trembling hands, then she went toward her bed. The ivory quilt and sheets were in a heap on the ground where she'd left them. She bent to grab them as she waited for her sister's phone to turn on. But when she flipped the sheets over to make space to sit—Lehua stopped cold.

Two footprints were stamped in dirt on the white quilt, on either side of a crumpled mauve bandana. *Melia's.* The same one she had been wearing in the barracks, and in her dream last night when she'd climbed atop Lehua's bed and strangled her.

Lehua picked up the bandana. An iron taste filled her mouth, sending her head spinning.

Melia hadn't been in her room since their first night on the island. It was only in Lehua's dream that Melia had drifted inside and climbed into the bed, covered in sweat and blood, smelling of rotten persimmon.

Lehua ran the bandana through her fingers, rubbing her thumb against the dried red stains. *It could be field dust.* But Lehua knew the difference. She could smell the metallic tang.

Lehua's stomach turned. She folded the bandana in her hand, hiding the bloodstains. Melia's breath had been perfumed by rot and her glassy eyes had flashed like pearls. Had that not been a dream?

The terrifying reality of finding Melia's bloodied bandana in her bed, laced with the scent of decay, suggested otherwise. A chilling dread gripped her. *Melia isn't coming back.*

Yet a small hope flickered that she would find Melia and Ohia safe. Somehow. When they saw each other, Melia's tawny eyes would lift and a divot would crease her lips, drawing Lehua's mouth to hers. *I was worried about you*, Melia would whisper. *I came to your room but you weren't there.*

Lehua held on to the image and her tiny seed of hope that her sister and Melia were safe. But when she heard the chime of Ohia's phone turning back on, Jennifer's warning resurfaced in her mind: *This place isn't safe.*

TWENTY-SIX

Lehua sat in front of Ohia's upturned duffel, clutching her sister's phone. Dirty clothes seeped out of the bag, wrinkled and smelling rank. Most of the clothes were cast-offs—old shirts, jeans, and running shorts Ohia had owned since leaving their last guardian's place.

Amid her sister's clothes, Lehua found a slim wallet with Ohia's fake ID and a couple of dollar bills. Ohia stared back at her, her eyes dulled by the ID's finish. *Alana Marie Holt. DOB: 06/11/2007.* Their shared birthday.

Lehua shoved the ID and wallet into her own backpack, then considered the spilled mess of clothing in front of her. She hadn't found a message from Melia inside her sister's duffel. But Ohia had packed enough clothes to last at least two weeks. It looked like her sister had intended to stay at Kōpaʻa longer than a week.

Until something happened, derailing those plans.

She'd hoped to find some sort of clue inside her sister's bag. But all she found were discarded protein bar wrappers and she felt a pang, remembering how Ohia would empty entire boxes of snacks into her bag for their track meets, always throwing in more than they needed.

That left Ohia's phone.

Lehua turned over her sister's phone, and her dark reflection stared back. Then Ohia's lock screen disappeared, unlocked using Face ID.

Quickly, Lehua scrolled through her sister's texts. The last message Ohia had received had been from Uzzy more than two weeks ago, demanding she talk to him before she did anything *rash*. Lehua saw her own name further down. Her last text to Ohia was her apartment's address, sent three months ago.

Lehua swallowed. The night they'd had their fight. But that was it.

None of her frantic texts or calls had made it through, because Ohia's phone had been in a cellular dead zone before its battery completely drained. Then how had her phone connected with Lehua's?

Lehua opened her sister's email. A couple messages were downloaded in the inbox. Beneath a reminder to appeal her college suspension was an email from Kōpaʻa Management. *Kōpaʻa Island Resort, Farm, and Orchard—Thank you for your message* read the subject line. A handful of messages were nested in the email.

Hi, I saw your ad looking for a farm worker. Could I get some more info about the job?

Best, Alana

Her sister had sent that email two months ago and gotten an

automated response: *We're so glad you want to join history by becoming a part of Kōpaʻa. Our management team thoroughly reviews every application and will reach out to you if your experience matches our resort's opportunities.*

Two days later, Ohia had received an email from Chiyo, asking for more information about her and what her goals were. *We only consider serious applicants*, Chiyo had written, including a PDF Ohia had saved in her downloads.

Become a Part of Kōpaʻa the pamphlet began, the white words printed on a photo of the resort at night. The terrace's grand windows splashed light on the sugarcane. The next pages of the pamphlet were full of vibrant island scenery, golden heads of persimmon, and pristine beaches.

Then Lehua saw the workers. A restored photo of the mill's interior showcased a line of field hands loading cane into the machines. She stopped scrolling when she spotted the man who had attacked her in the mill. *You shouldn't be here, kaikamahine.* He stood among the other workers, clad in all denim. The exact same clothes he had worn in the mill, only his eyes weren't silver.

Underneath the caption, *Kōpaʻa's committed to preserving its history and heritage*, was an impossible date. *1910.*

With a shiver, Lehua remembered how the island's workers had vanished into the cane's lengthy shadows. *I told you our ghost stories are different,* she heard Melia saying. Because if the photo's date was right, the mill worker was over a hundred years old—and it proved he had been a ghost.

Lehua hastily scrolled down, replacing the man's face with cane fields. *Let us empower you to grow, guiding you toward a greater purpose.* Under all the photos, a photographer was credited. *O. Orin Jacobs.* One of Ira's ancestors. She'd seen this name somewhere before. Had she seen this Jacobs on the portrait wall?

Lehua hesitated. During that tour, Chiyo had said Kōpa'a was still a family enterprise. *I'm jumping to conclusions,* Lehua thought, staring at the name. But . . .

The bones in the cane field had been old, far older than Ira. Whoever was responsible for scattering the bones had done it decades ago. It couldn't be Ira. But maybe it'd been another Jacobs. *But why?*

Lehua closed the pamphlet's PDF, feeling shaken. The bright photos paired with the smiling workers made Kōpa'a seem idyllic and ethereal. *Too good to be true*, she thought, remembering the field-workers and their too-wide smiles. A cold terror filled her.

Her sister had always been an optimist and a staunch pep talk believer. She used to study the motivational printouts their social worker handed out after every meeting. *Breathe,* one poster had said, *you'll get through this.* The same social worker had gifted Lehua *How to Win Friends and Influence People* as a birthday gift.

Lehua could imagine Ohia, giddy and hopeful, coming to the resort. *Why not, Le?* her sister would've said, fighting a smile. *It could be good for us.* Before they had both signed up for track, Ohia had said the exact same thing.

Lehua opened her sister's photo albums next. There was a screenshot of the contract Ohia had signed, and she'd highlighted: *You are forbidden from posting your experience on social media.* Then there were screenshots of three people's social media accounts.

Lehua didn't recognize any of the people as her sister's friends and flipped to the next image. Another screenshot. It was a social media post from more than three months ago, showing a Polynesian girl with a white streak in her hair and her back turned to the camera as she held a handful of sand. *You don't get many second chances in life, and I'm not letting go of this one #imua #kopaa*, read the caption.

Seeing that hashtag, Lehua understood. Ohia had found Kōpaʻa's previous hires before she'd arrived. Lehua scrolled back to the screenshot Ohia had taken of the girl's photo grid. It looked like she used to post every day but . . .

That photo was the girl's last post.

Lehua stared. A terrible feeling gutted her. Last night she'd realized that all of the resort's field-workers were ʻeʻepa, except for Melia—and Melia was missing now, just like Ohia.

An unpleasant shudder shook Lehua. If she scanned the faces of the resort's field-workers, would she discover a Polynesian girl with a dyed white streak among them? When Ohia arrived, had she realized this girl was missing from the barracks immediately and started asking about the island's previous workers? *You're asking too many questions,* Jennifer's words echoed.

Ohia was smart. She would have pieced together the missing workers, their abandoned social media accounts, and the unexplainable nighttime harvest. *We don't cut plants after dark.* Their grandmother had taught Ohia the same superstitions. *It attracts spirits.*

Her sister would've realized the island was haunted and that someone had killed all of the workers after luring them here. Lehua thought of the warning Jennifer had given her—to take the boat on Monday and escape when she could—and she wondered how much the guests knew. She saw the picture of Jennifer's husband in her mind. He'd looked related to Ira. *He was the real planter.*

When Lehua had returned to the resort, she'd thought Sacha had been responsible for drugging her last night. But if all of the resort's members knew about the workers being 'e'epa, maybe they knew who was responsible for killing them, too—and that was why they were afraid of Ira.

There were hundreds of photographs taken after the screenshots. A view of Maui from an airplane. The banyan tree in Lāhainā. The ocean from the boardwalk. Ohia had documented her entire journey from Arizona to the island.

Lehua stopped on a selfie. Ohia had her arm around a white girl with a sly smile and a sunburn blooming on the bridge of her nose, highlighting her platinum-dyed hair and pale eyes. Daisy.

Except Daisy looked soft and bright, happier than Lehua had ever seen her in the resort. She had her blond hair up in two matching buns, and wore a cover-up over her swimsuit with a familiar friendship bracelet around her wrist, its enamel letters spelling *home.*

Lehua stared. She'd seen that bracelet before. Except it'd been sandwiched between two diamond-studded cuffs—on Sacha's wrist. *That creepy blond*, she remembered Sacha calling Daisy, loud enough that the other girl had undoubtedly heard.

There were pictures of Daisy and Ohia on the resort's beach. Ohia had her feet nestled in the sand while Daisy was taking the selfie. *So Daisy knew her. Why didn't she say something? And what had* happened *to Daisy?*

When Lehua swiped forward, she heard her sister's voice.

The video, time-stamped, six days ago, started playing immediately. A blurry cane field susurrated in the wind as Ohia's feet pounded red dirt. Her breath blasted through her phone's speakers. She was running.

"Willa's been missing for a couple days now," Ohia said between gulps of air, and Lehua straightened at the name. *No one wants to cross him after how easily he cut off Willa*, Leigh had said. "They said she returned to school." Ohia's hands shook as she took a deep, shuddering breath, and Lehua noted the similarities between Willa's departure and the story she'd been told about Ohia. They were hard to miss. "But she never told me she was leaving. She said, 'If you don't see me tomorrow, you should run.' And I *didn't* see her."

Ohia turned the camera. Her hair had slipped free of its ponytail and fell in tangles. Her tears cut through the dust coating her cheeks. She looked taut, wary—*afraid*.

"I think they're lying to me about what happened," she said, her eyes darting from the camera to the cane behind it. "There's something going on that they don't want me to see." Lehua's blood roared in her ears as her sister headed into the leaves, the cane rustling eerily. Then Ohia's eyes widened, filling with alarm. "Someone is coming," she said, and the video cut off.

Lehua replayed the video's end and zoomed in desperately on the cane field, dragging her finger uselessly over the video and her sister's frightened face. She hoped to find some clue, some sign that revealed whether Ohia was alive or not. But the end was the same: the video cutting to black.

Lehua stared at the dark screen, the reflection of her scared face replacing Ohia's. That recording was the last thing in Ohia's album. She tried to imagine what happened next and the possibilities terrified her, coalescing into an overwhelming fear.

That feeling in her na'au had been wrong because Ohia was truly gone.

Lehua bolted to her feet as her breath hitched, turning frantic. *I need to get the hell out of here.* But would she even be allowed to leave?

Chiyo had claimed the boat captain had been forced to leave her stranded because of an incoming storm, but Lehua doubted that was even true now. *Maybe Chiyo wanted him to leave me here.* If the boat captain was in on it, there was no guarantee that the boat was coming at all. But if the resort was responsible for her sister's disappearance, why would they trap Lehua on the island?

To cover their tracks.

The thought loosened a panicked bubble of laughter. Lehua bit into her fist as tears slipped down her cheeks, mirroring the ones Ohia had worn in her video. What had Ohia been doing? It was clear her twin had been terrified and more than ready to flee the island. Why hadn't she run once she figured out something was wrong? Why had she stuck around to find Willa?

Who is Willa? she'd asked Jennifer after she'd let the name slip, and the widow had frozen. *Just like your sister and Willa*, she'd said, because Ohia had been caught in the same situation Lehua was. Her sister had been searching for Willa, another missing girl, and had been asking the same questions.

Lehua thumbed through her sister's photos again, and she

stopped on the ones with Daisy. Dressed in her swimsuit, the blond girl certainly didn't look like a worker in these photos.

She looked like someone on vacation. Daisy looked like . . .

A guest.

Lehua fled her room, and a chill followed her all the way to the resort's portrait gallery. There Lehua's steps stalled. Her eyes scraped across the wall, sinking down every glamorous photo, seeing all the resort's guests over the years. The photo wall depicted the resort's history alongside the Jacobs family tree because they were *intertwined.*

Who is Willa? Lehua saw the answer all at once. On the wall was a miniature portrait of a familiar blond girl with pale rosebud lips and even paler blue eyes. *Willamina Jacobs.* That was why the name had sounded familiar when she'd first heard Leigh say it. She'd glimpsed the portrait's golden plaque.

And that same girl was now walking toward Lehua, carrying a silver lunch tray.

Lehua raced back into her room. Quickly, she kicked Ohia's bag and clothes back under the bed, dropping the quilt over the edge as the doorknob twisted and Daisy entered her room.

"Miss Amaya said you'd be hungry," Daisy said, depositing the tray on Lehua's vanity. Her pale eyes were lowered and her back was unnaturally straight and stiff. The Daisy in Ohia's photos had been slumped in the sand, doubled over by laughter, full of eager mischief. Lehua couldn't believe this was the same girl.

"Thanks, Daisy," Lehua said with a forced smile.

Her head bowed. "Of course. I'm happy to help our guests."

"You know," Lehua began, dragging the fork against the plate, feigning interest in the food even though she'd never touch another meal prepared by the resort. "I never asked if you met Ohia while she was here."

Daisy's smile slipped, just for a moment. "I help all our workers."

Lehua's eyes narrowed. *Sure.* "Did you two ever hang out outside of the resort?"

"That wouldn't be appropriate. We're on the island to work," Daisy said. "Now, if that's all you require . . ."

Lehua's jaw tensed as Daisy turned toward the door. She had just seen footage of her twin being chased in a field. Maybe even attacked. Whatever this charade was, it needed to end now.

Lehua leaped up, pushing Ohia's phone toward Daisy. "Don't lie to me," she snapped. "This photo shows you two together."

"I don't know that worker," Daisy answered with a tight smile, and another angry surge shot through Lehua.

"You're not even looking," she growled, snatching Daisy's wrist. She shoved the phone closer, gripping it inches from Daisy's averted gaze with her other hand. As soon as her fingers closed around Daisy, a cold current coursed through Lehua's veins and the other girl's eyes flashed an unnatural silver. The room seemed to blur around them.

Lehua took a sharp breath as Daisy tried to claw her wrist free, tearing at her with her nails. Daisy's pupils were fully dilated and black like tar, reflecting the phone's light with a sheen of silver.

And Lehua knew then that the other girl was ʻeʻepa, just like the other workers.

"Willa," Lehua said. "That's your real name, right?" The girl froze.

She looked at Lehua, then the room in confusion, as if waking up from a trance. Her cheeks pinked, her eyes reverting to their normal color. "Alana? What are you doing in my room?"

My room. Lehua trembled, holding on to the ʻeʻepa girl. "Willa, I'm not Alana," she said. "I'm her sister, Lehua."

Willa's pupils turned huge. "You shouldn't be here," she said, fighting to tear her wrist free again, but Lehua held firm. Whatever was happening, it was working, and she couldn't risk Willa returning to the shell of Daisy, not when she was this close to finally getting answers. "You have to run before he takes you to the orchard—"

One moment Willa was speaking clearly, the next she was pulling her wrist away, her face glazed with terror. The two struggled, colliding with the vanity, sending the food tray to the ground. Still, Lehua wouldn't let go. "What happened to you, Willa?"

Tears brewed in Willa's eyes. "I went to get a persimmon for us . . ." Her voice trailed off as she stared at the wallpaper behind Lehua's bed, at the gems of persimmons. "And I asked him to spare you after I saw the orchard."

Spare you. Lehua's mouth turned dry. "Willa, where is Alana now?"

The girl twisted in her arms violently and that spark of recognition was extinguished, lost in her amnesiac state of horror. "No, not Alana, no." Her pale eyes grabbed on to Lehua, shiny and full of terror. "Did he kill you, too?"

Too. Lehua's stomach bottomed out as the full meaning of her words sunk into her. "What do you mean 'too'?" she whispered, gaping at Willa. Just who was Willamina Jacobs? If Ira could do this to his own flesh and blood, what could he do to Lehua? What did he do to Ohia? Tears spilled down Lehua's cheeks as Willa didn't answer. "Did he . . . kill you? Are you dead?"

Willa looked away and the world seemed to tilt under Lehua's feet as she replayed every interaction they'd had—the way Willa never seemed to sleep, how she always appeared when Lehua needed her, and the flies that had buzzed around the girl—each pointing to the terrifying truth: Willa was similar to the 'e'epa field-workers with their cold touch and silver eyes, because she was dead like them, too. Because Ira had killed her.

Lehua's grip weakened and the dead Jacobs girl pried herself free. She looked at Lehua with stunning clarity as her silver gaze slowly faded into blue, the same color as Ira's. "He took my name. He'll make me forget again if he finds me. Take the boat tonight—and run."

"The boat? No, please. You have to tell me. Where is my sister? Where's Melia? Are they together?" *Are they dead?* Fear sluiced through Lehua at the thought of finding Ohia's lifeless body in the cane fields, or Melia's dashed on the island's rocks, obscured by the surf.

"No, no, no." Willa sobbed. "Just follow the resort rules and you can escape tonight, Miss Sayer."

Lehua shook her head. What had happened after that video ended? If Willa didn't know where Ohia was, maybe that meant her sister had escaped. Her sister had been afraid, but she'd been getting away. Lehua felt a spark of hope, a fragile seedling pushing through the fear in her naʻau. No one could catch Ohia when she was running.

Lehua looked at the fruited wallpaper Willa had gaped at with terror. *Before he takes you to the orchard.* "Are they in the orchard? Is that where the workers go missing?"

"You aren't listening," Willa choked out the words as tears fled her darkening eyes, and her gaze flashed like pearls again, turning an uncanny silver. "I have to go before he finds me again."

Before Lehua could say anything more, Willa stepped back. She vanished into the wallpaper, her body wasting into thin air like smoke, leaving Lehua stumbling in shock.

TWENTY-SEVEN

Lehua stared at the spot where Willa had disappeared. All traces of the other girl's presence were lost amongst the golden persimmons and leafy branches.

Willa was gone, and Lehua was on her own.

Chicken skin crept down her bare arms. *I should run, too,* she thought, trying to breathe evenly. But she felt as if a hand was clamped over her throat, squeezing tight.

She was stranded on an island—where could she go? The resort's security system was too vigilant. There were too many cameras for her to hide. The more she thought about it, the more the pressure on her throat grew.

Swimming to Maui was out of the question. The only way to escape Kōpa'a was the boat. But Lehua couldn't just abandon Melia and Ohia, not without learning what had happened to them.

Lehua raced to her balcony and looked out at the persimmon orchard. The orchard was a stain on the island, a mess of tangled black limbs and metal fencing. She knew she had to go there to uncover the truth, despite her gnawing dread and the danger that likely awaited her. She didn't know what answers she'd find. But from Willa's sobs, she could guess.

Did he kill you, too? Lehua couldn't ignore what she'd heard, the finality of it. She only hoped Willa was wrong. That her sister and Melia weren't already dead. She had to push past that fear before it could break her, and she hurriedly got changed. It was too hot to wear her sweatshirt and dirty jeans, but she put them on. If she needed to disappear into the cane, the extra fabric would protect her arms and legs. Then she pushed Melia's bandana into her pocket, next to her sister's phone, and exited the room.

In the hallway, Lehua touched her sister's phone, rubbing Ohia's pearl charm between her thumb and forefinger. *Pearls for the girls born in June*, their grandma had sung, icing their cakes for their twelfth birthday. She had wreathed their names with pearls of white and silver fondant. Chocolate cake for Ohia, strawberry for her.

Lehua was halfway through the lobby when she saw Chiyo with her cheeks pink like she'd been running.

Chiyo exhaled deeply. "Lehua, I was coming to get you. It's Melia. We found her." Lehua thought of Melia's bandana stuffed into her pocket, darkened with blood. "No, nothing like that," Chiyo said quickly, reading her face. "She's *safe*."

"Where is she?"

"She's resting in the barracks." Chiyo offered her hand. "We can visit her now, but we have to hurry. We don't want you missing your boat tonight."

Lehua hesitated. She thought of Willa's warning to follow the resort rules until the boat arrived. What if this was a trap? But . . .

If Melia was okay, Lehua had to risk it. She had to see her.

Lehua took Chiyo's hand. They made their way down the resort's steps.

"She seems to be experiencing a temporary state of shock," Chiyo said as they reached the grand entryway. "I told her she should rest."

"Did she say what happened? Did she see who started the fire?"

"No. She doesn't remember much."

Dread filled Lehua. "Is she hurt?"

They pushed the doors open and Chiyo shook her head. "She didn't look hurt. Please keep in mind it may take her some time to fully process what happened. I know we're both worried, but the last thing we want to do is overwhelm her. She hasn't spoken much since Daisy found her wandering the town alone."

The dead girl Chiyo called Daisy had been in her room until she vanished five minutes ago, and Willa had been inconsolable. There was no way she had found Melia and told Chiyo.

Chiyo was lying to her.

That instinct to run itched at her legs. Lehua could bolt into the sugarcane and hide. She looked at Chiyo, beautiful and petite, and imagined driving her elbow into the soft column of Chiyo's throat—to make her talk. *Tell me what happened to Ohia.* Her fingers reflexively tightened. She was tempted to give in to the allure of that violence. But throwing that punch would take away whatever opportunity she had at escaping Kōpaʻa tonight. *Just follow the resort rules*, Willa had told her.

As long as she continued playing along with the manager's polite deception, there was a chance she'd return to Maui tonight like Chiyo had promised. Otherwise, the resort manager probably wouldn't bother lying.

Still, Lehua surveyed the sugarcane as they walked, wrestling with her fear. If her instinct about Chiyo was proven wrong, she would be ready to run.

Then she saw Melia through the window.

The girl was curled on a bed in the barracks, turned away from Lehua. *She's okay*, she thought with a torrent of relief, her eyes blurring with tears.

"Melia!" Lehua ran toward her, stopping short of her bed. She felt Chiyo's gaze on her back and resisted the urge to pull Melia into her arms.

Melia lay unmoving with her shoulders folded and her legs drawn up to her chest, breathing low. Only her dark hair matted with grass faced Lehua.

Her bandana's missing from her hair. Lehua's stomach sank, confirming her worst fears as her fingers closed around the bloody fabric hidden in her pocket. "Melia?" she choked out. Nothing.

Lehua reached for her, but Chiyo stopped her with an outstretched arm. "Slow, Lehua. Melia's not herself," she said.

"Clearly," Lehua snapped, whirling toward the resort manager. "What happened to her?"

Up close, Melia smelled like smoke and something bucolic, almost like soil and mowed grass. Lehua needed to rouse her and get her out of here. *Look at me*, she thought. *Say something.*

"Are you okay, Melia?" Lehua whispered, brushing past Chiyo when she tried to stop her again. "Are you hurt?"

Melia was still lying down, curved protectively over her middle. But then she turned to Lehua. For a second, her eyes seemed to glow.

"No," Melia said, smiling vacantly. She didn't clarify which question she was answering.

"I came looking for you," Lehua said. *Look at me again*, she thought, her pulse climbing. But Melia's attention was adhered to the dusty ground. "Where'd you go?"

"Melia's had quite the ordeal," Chiyo said, reaching for Lehua, who willed herself not to flinch. "And you really should pack, Lehua. I'll write down your email address—"

No. Lehua didn't know if she was too late to save Ohia, but she wasn't leaving Melia behind. "C'mon, Melia. You're coming with me." She grabbed Melia's wrist where her ti leaf bracelet had once been, brushing her skin—

The cold swam up Lehua's fingers, raising chicken skin all the way to her collarbone. Something floral and metallic, like the aftertaste of an electric shock, drowned her tongue and throat as she met Melia's eyes.

Her pupils were dark and glittering, two yawning pits that reflected the afternoon light like a nocturnal creature's.

"Lehua," Melia whispered. Her name sounded wrong, sparking terror in Lehua as her eyes filled with tears. "Did you find her? I *tried* to."

"What?" Lehua trembled, fighting a swell of raw emotion.

Suddenly Chiyo was between them. "You've pushed her too hard and upset her. She *needs* to rest," Chiyo said pointedly, dragging Lehua out, surprising Lehua with her strength.

Behind them, Melia lay utterly still, as if she hadn't moved at all. *No.* Lehua twisted, struggling to get another look. *You're supposed to come with me.* But Chiyo only released Lehua once they had left the barracks.

"Now that you've seen Melia, you should prepare to leave," Chiyo instructed in a clipped voice, guiding Lehua toward the resort. "While *I* take care of Melia. Don't worry. She will receive the best care, and will contact you as soon as she recovers. Be patient. You'll hear from her in no time."

Lehua followed Chiyo numbly. She wanted to scream at the growing distance between her and Melia. A sharp pain pulled at her chest as they walked, a fetter tightening, its chain connecting her back to Melia. *You were supposed to come with me.*

Chiyo called Melia's condition shock. But her eyes . . .

Did he kill you, too? Both Willa and Melia's eyes had glowed, lit by the same unnatural light. Only Lehua refused to accept what it meant.

Not Melia. Lehua's throat burned like it was on fire, scorching with her unshed tears. She held onto the girl's bright eyes in her mind but the image was chased away by the cold truth.

Melia was likely dead, just like Willa.

The painful realization ripped through her, slicing like a wound. Lehua knew she had to hide the terror welling inside her. Confronting Chiyo would be a death sentence. She had to play along, pretending she knew nothing, as Willa had warned—or she wouldn't escape this place.

"I am actually more concerned about you right now. Your boat arrives in two hours. Do you have a place to stay in Lāhainā until your flight back to Phoenix? Maui can be *so* expensive. If it's all right with you, I'll ask the captain to arrange some accommodations for you."

Lehua nodded along, feigning ignorance, even as Chiyo's betrayal cut into her, another painful wound. The manager had offered Lehua her help in her search for Ohia. But Chiyo had been playing a part in the cover-up and withholding information from her the entire time.

Lehua's chest cleaved in two. A guttural sob threatened to escape her lips, a desperate sound of grief and anger that she almost choked on before forcing it down so Chiyo wouldn't notice.

When they reached the resort and the estate's walls closed in, Lehua tried to maintain a calm façade, hiding her trembling hands. Her terror was a heartbeat away from consuming her as she and Chiyo trudged up the resort steps. When they stopped outside her room, Lehua smiled and promised to be ready when the boat arrived.

But when Chiyo left, Lehua locked the door and pulled Melia's bandana free. A broken sob escaped her. *Did you find her? I tried to.* Squeezing the bloodied bandana tight, Lehua cried into her hand, muffling her tears as her horror and grief set in. Melia could only have been talking about Ohia.

From her room, she could see the orchard, and a warning

clawed at her stomach, a dreadful feeling twisted her naʻau that she couldn't ignore.

Thanks to Willa, Lehua knew what to expect, and that fear gnawed at her. *Did he kill you, too*? But she had to find Ohia, no matter the cost, even in this nightmare.

The resort's famous persimmon orchard awaited.

TWENTY-EIGHT

Dusk lit the persimmon orchard ahead. The tops of the sugarcane blurred with the darkening sky, oozing together like grease. A black tarp covered the orchard's fence beyond the thick cane, the material reminding Lehua of the body bags used at the mortuary.

That, and the smell.

The air was thick with a putrid perfume, the rank taste of decaying fruit. It was the scent of the dead brought into the mortuary too late.

Lehua had a dozen chances to reconsider. She would know, wouldn't she? She'd *have* to know if Ohia was dead. *'Ōhi'a lehua. We're meant to stay together,* she thought, her chest rising and falling faster and faster. There was nothing to do but keep going.

Lehua pulled her sleeves over her hands and pushed her way through. The jagged leaves stabbed through her hoodie. The pain threatened her away, a portent of what lay ahead. Willa's words came back to her: *Did he kill you, too?*

Eventually ebony branches, heavy with golden persimmons, reached over the orchard fence like black lightning. She climbed the tarp-covered fence. A verdant canopy shadowed the orchard floor, its persimmons shining like ore. The stench of decay churned her stomach, too familiar.

She slung her leg over the rim, then dropped down. Her feet slid in something wet.

From somewhere in the dark, the persimmon branches scratched together, snapping like bones. A ripe sweetness coated the back of her throat like syrup, mingling with the undercurrent of rot filling the orchard.

The familiar scent of human decay.

She almost retched. A subtle drip plinked, splashing an unseen puddle. She took a step and stumbled. Her heel squished something *soft*. It didn't feel like fruit.

Lehua grasped for her phone and pointed her flashlight toward the ground. Her breath hitched as she hyperventilated.

The ground was tacky with old gore. Bloodstains smeared the orchard floor and her jeans up to her ankles. Her hand shook, tracing the bloodstains with her flashlight's beam, stopping short at the first corpse.

Lehua choked back a strangled sob. She'd been right: It wasn't fruit she'd stepped on.

It was a *man*.

His aloha shirt was torn, revealing his withered body, shriveled like a fruit rind. A gash split his middle. His pulpy stomach gaped open, cored like an apple. *That* was where her foot had landed.

Lehua heaved, spitting bile until there was nothing left. She took a shuddering breath and regretted it. Death was everywhere—she was swimming in it.

The man was one of the fresher corpses. The deceased filled the orchard in rows shrouded by weeds and roots, their sunken skin barely visible. There were bare bones wrapped in dirt and threadbare fabric that Lehua realized were the remnants of their uniforms, aloha shirts worn into rags after decades embedded in the soil.

Lehua sidestepped the rot and bones, the putrid smell worsening as she approached the younger persimmon trees. The bones and bodies looked like roots forced aboveground, extensions of the trees that marked their graves. She grasped the terrible truth when she saw the trees unspooling out of the fresher dead, springing from their stomachs.

Each tree *was* a body.

Her flashlight darted back to the first corpse she'd seen. A crunched sapling was broken where her foot had gone through his cored stomach. Every dead body had its abdomen cut open, tilled like soil for the persimmon trees taking root in them.

Lehua looked across the orchard, its darkness devouring her flashlight. The field of bones continued, disappearing beyond her bloom of light. She didn't want to trail the dead like an abandoned spirit. She scoured her palms with her nails, terrified she'd find Ohia. What would she discover if she kept going? But Lehua had to know.

Lehua bent to look at the bodies she passed, and cold recognition snapped around her. The three workers she'd met on the road. Their faces were ruined with rot, their bellies rent open. Lehua saw the shriveled breasts of the woman. Her straw hat stamped above her head, lying in a heap of loose hair.

Lehua trudged forward. She checked every face, fearing the worst, until she toed the fresh blood snaking the smallest trees. There, her resolve weakened.

Two more bodies lay heaped along the orchard floor ahead. One of them was blond, and the other was a Hawaiian girl.

A hole split Lehua's heart open and tears spilled down her cheeks. *No.* Two mulberry wounds trenched the girl's body, pooling blood around her and her dark hair. *No.*

Lehua's gaze traveled from the girl's cut throat, shining red like a second mouth, to the persimmon sapling planted in her cored stomach. Her naʻau. Tendrils tethered the plant to the girl like pulled sutures. Its roots spread out of her mouth and tangled in her hair, seeding the blood-soaked soil around her.

Melia's open eyes peered up at Lehua.

Lehua sank to her knees. She thought of Melia pulling her close, melting into their kiss, Melia threading between the boat's railing, leaning fearlessly into the surf with each loud reset of the waves. Brave Melia, who climbed abandoned mills after dark and swayed into white-water waves unafraid, promising to help her find Ohia. That girl now lay in the dirt, mottled purple like bruised fruit, the wound in her stomach black. Her tawny eyes empty.

"No," Lehua cried as the tether that she'd always felt to Melia broke within her. The drawing tide disappeared, the current ripping away from her. "No, please."

She reached for the girl's cold, swollen hand and shivered, remembering the warm feel of Melia's fingers in hers and her soft smile as she shared their stories. Lehua thought of the promise she'd tasted on her lips, and her chest flooded with grief and anger.

Any possibility of that future had been taken—*stolen from them.*

Melia's hair was pushed away from her face, tangled where her mauve bandana used to be. Lehua pulled the bloodied bandana from her pocket. She tied the fabric around the girl's wrist where her ti leaf bracelet had been. After Melia had given her bracelet to Lehua, she hadn't made another.

Heartbroken, she could hear her grandmother's voice, telling the legend of their names, *Lehua asked the other gods for help.*

Except Melia was gone, and there were no gods to ask. Not on this island.

She remembered how Melia's smile had spilled across her face like sunlight, how flinty her eyes had been in life—even when she'd looked so young and small against the scope of the world—and how she'd come to this island by virtue of having no other choice.

This can't be the end, Lehua thought. *That can't be what's next.*

Not for Melia. Not for Ohia. Not for her.

Mai poina, Lehua, Melia had told her. *Don't forget*, and Lehua wouldn't. She didn't yet know how her and Ohia's story would end—but she could guarantee this wouldn't be the end of Melia's.

She wasn't going to let Ira and the rest of them keep what they'd stolen.

"Mai poina," she told Melia, turning away from her and walking past Willa's corpse lying next to her. Unlike Melia, her right hand was missing—torn from her fair arm.

Another wave of nausea and horror hit Lehua as she recalled the dismembered hand in Ira's room. The delicate fingers had been floating in formalin and a treacle syrup. It'd been Willa's hand. *Did he kill you, too?*

Mingled in her grief, Lehua took solace that Ohia wasn't there, even though this was likely where she'd been headed last. Because no one could catch her sister when she was running. Not even Lehua.

Seeing the bones and the sheer number of bodies filling the orchard, Lehua remembered the island's graveyard and the shoe prints she'd seen. She had a good idea where her sister was hiding.

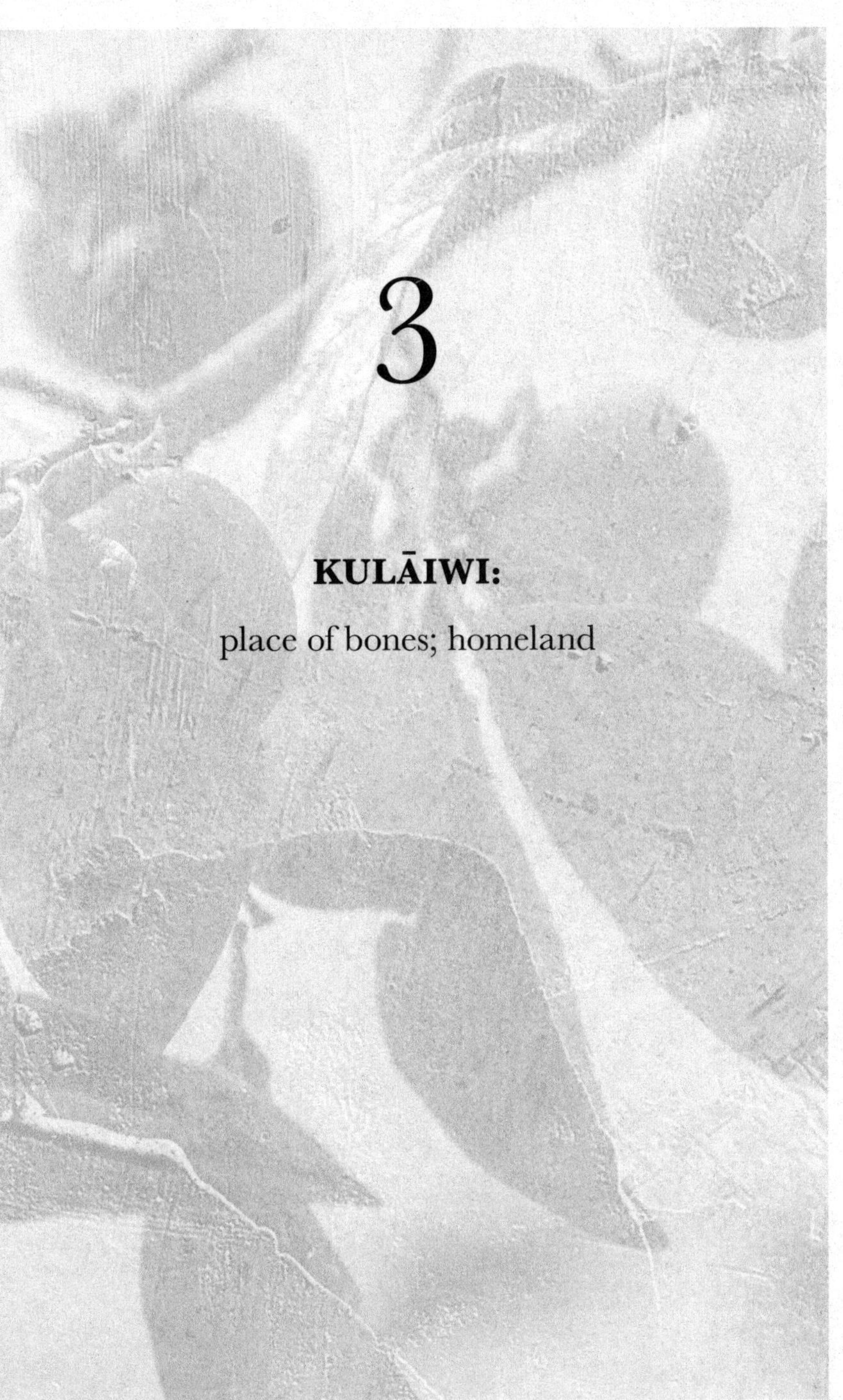

3

KULĀIWI:

place of bones; homeland

TWENTY-NINE

The family crypt towered before Lehua in the twilight. Weaving between the surrounding gravestones, Lehua felt the island wind clawing down her arms, scattering grit onto her inked skin.

A crypt was the last place Lehua would've searched for Ohia. *She doesn't do ick.* When Lehua had first told Ohia about her job at the mortuary, Ohia had shuddered. *Never touch me again.* And yet Lehua kept going. After seeing that orchard, Lehua had the feeling there were no human remains in the crypt—and Ohia would have realized it, too. *Nothing is wasted here*, Chiyo had told her, so why wouldn't the resort empty the mausoleum and use the dead inside to cultivate their fruit, too?

Undoubtedly, Ohia had seen the orchard floor, glinting with pulpy human remains and the glistening fruit trees growing from their stomachs and had come to the same conclusion. *If she got away.* The thought snaked down Lehua's spine. Her sneakers on the gravel sounded loud in the brittle quiet.

From here, she could see the thin watery light of the boat coming into town. So the captain had returned after all. She knew she was running out of time to leave this island tonight. *She's here,* Lehua thought, feeling the insistence in her naʻau, reeling her toward the crypt's ornate doors—*she's here, she's here, she's here.*

Ad vitam aeternam was carved into the bronze double doors, weathered into a ghoulish green, and below the Latin words was a scripture verse. *And the world passeth away, and the lust thereof: but he that doeth the will of God abideth for ever.*

The grille covering the door was welded into a sugarcane motif, similar to the doors in the resort. Lehua saw a tiny lock, and worried for a moment she'd have to break it open. But when she grabbed one of the door's two massive ring pulls and heaved, the door shrilled open.

Lehua nudged past the door, feeling like a wayward ghost finally slipping back into her crypt. She pushed the door shut behind her, its hinge creaking loudly as an eerie feeling crawled down her neck, and she turned back, blinking as her eyes adjusted to the darkness of the crypt.

A girl sat in the stone vestibule. Her umbra eyes gleamed with tears in the scant moonlight seeping in from the door's grille. There were notches running up and down the walls around her, empty of the caskets and the dead that should've lined the tomb.

There was only her and Ohia.

Her sister sat still on the ground, beautiful and sad like a relief sculpture.

"There you are," Ohia said, wiping the tears from her face.

Lehua ignored the pain inking down her exhausted legs, following the trail of sweat beneath her jeans from running. She collapsed on the stone floor next to her sister, overcome by sobs at the mere sight of her twin.

Ohia sagged against her for a moment. When she lifted her head to meet Lehua's eyes, there was little of her sister in her expression. Lehua was used to seeing her sister's eyes burning like molten night. Right now, those eyes were dark and dull, like ash left over from a fire.

Lehua wanted to help Ohia up, and tell her everything was going to be okay, that they would survive—one way or another. But Lehua had no idea how they were going to get off the island together.

"I didn't think I'd see you again," Ohia admitted.

"Me either. How have you stayed hidden for so long? How have you survived all this time?"

"I left one of my shoes on the beach, so they'd think I drowned trying to swim away. Other than that, protein bars." Ohia rasped out a laugh, her voice raw from disuse. "You always said I packed too many. But I guess I didn't pack enough this time. I ran out yesterday."

Lehua pulled back to look at Ohia. Despite her laugh, her face was thin, her collarbone sharp like a wire hanger, worn by hunger. Scratches gouged her cheeks and her chapped lips had split. A toe peeked out from a hole in the top of her remaining shoe—and her track jacket's arms were torn.

Lehua stared at the jacket with a wave of understanding. "You were the one in my room. You told me to leave."

"I climbed your balcony, hoping I'd find you there. I never

imagined they'd invite you to dinner and treat you like a guest. I tried to leave you a longer message, to warn you before it was too late, but I ran out of time." Her voice cracked. "Willa came in and I hid in the bathroom. After she left, I saw the mirror and remembered our messages, so I wrote a warning for you, hoping you'd know it was me."

Lehua shook her head. The message had been from Ohia after all. "Why didn't you write *I'm in the crypt*?"

Ohia swallowed. "I didn't know whether Willa would come back or not. She was . . . different than the girl I'd first met, and I couldn't risk her seeing that message and figuring out where I was," Ohia said, her eyes misting. "They have cameras everywhere, Lehua. In the resort, in the fields. Sometimes, I even saw Chiyo and that influencer following you."

Dread pooled in her stomach. She remembered how she'd seen Oliver and Leigh outside, and how Sacha had admitted she'd followed her. No wonder the planters had been sneaking around the cane. They'd been looking for Ohia. "Why didn't you run?"

"You mean swim?" Ohia laughed, staring at her lone shoe. "My plan was to sneak onto the boat Friday night and escape."

"But I showed up."

Ohia's lips lifted, a pained smile. "And I couldn't leave you."

"You should have," Lehua whispered. "I would've found a way to follow."

"I couldn't leave you. Not when you came here because of me. I didn't know what they'd do to you. Did you see the orchard?" Ohia asked, and Lehua nodded. "The resort hires their workers just to kill them, using their bones for some kind of ritual sacrifice.

And they're eating that fruit, Lehua. It's what the planters come here for."

Bones. The word prodded Lehua's memory. She dug into her pocket and pulled out the creased photographs. *Horace and His Children.* The photograph she'd found in the printing room. She'd stuffed it into her pocket when she and Melia had run.

Horace's solemn face stared up from the photograph, raising the hair on the back of Lehua's neck. *That staircase leads to the cupola and Mr. Jacobs's room*, Willa had said inside the hidden service wing. Now Lehua understood.

Ira wasn't the uncanny look-alike descendant of Horace. He *was* Horace. She'd seen him on the stairs that first night. She hadn't imagined him.

A shudder ran up Lehua's back, sharp as nails.

"The fruit keeps them young. It rejuvenates the planters using the mana from the workers' bones," Lehua said. Then she told Ohia what Melia and the old man had shared about the story of Captain Cook, and their ancestors' belief that there was mana in the bones of the deceased.

"That's why the workers haunt the island," Lehua said. She'd been right: all the island's workers had been murdered.

"I tried to free them from the fields. They told me that the ti leaf was keeping them trapped, so I started cutting it down whenever I could. When the fire started, I had hoped for a distraction, so I could reach you—" Ohia shook her head. "I never got my chance."

"You caused the fire?"

"The ghosts did." She was looking at the crypt door and its

ornate sugarcane motif. "When I first talked to them, they seemed stuck. But after I freed them, they started to remember. They told me they wanted to build a fire to burn away the rot in the fields—the sugarcane, the bones, the pineapple, and the persimmons. When they're trapped behind the ti leaf, I don't think they know they're dead. That's why some of the field-workers wander the resort, still cutting sugarcane and harvesting pineapple," Ohia said, forlorn. "I think the longer they're trapped, the more lost they become. The more they forget."

Lehua remembered the strange smiles that the workers wore, the piles of spoiled sugarcane in the mill, the way the field-workers continued cutting cane relentlessly even as they were trying to warn her, and Willa—and how she had acted before Lehua had uttered her name. Daisy had been docile and uncertain, the epitome of a happy worker, until Lehua had reminded her of the life she'd had—the life that had been stolen from her. She shuddered to think what the resort had done to make Willa forget her own name.

Ohia was biting her nails. "You need to go back." Her eyes flashed to Lehua's. "You have to get on that boat, Le."

"I'm not leaving without you—"

Ohia leaned forward, her expression serious. "You won't, I promise. I'll be right behind you, sneaking aboard as it leaves. But if you miss that boat, we're both stuck here." Her face lit up, limned with moonlight. "We leave together tonight or not at all."

Lehua nodded but paused before she moved toward the door. There was something she needed to know first—and this could be Lehua's only chance to learn the truth.

"Why did you come here, Ohia?"

Ohia winced. "Well, I didn't think I was walking into a sacrificial circle, Le."

"You know what I mean. Who's *Alana*? Why'd you lie to me? Why'd you come here pretending to be someone else?"

Ohia sucked in a sharp breath. "I guess you wouldn't remember her name."

Lehua leaned back as if Ohia had struck her. "What?"

"Mom," Ohia whispered. "Don't you remember the missing posters they put up? Alana was her middle name." Ohia looked away suddenly, running her teeth over her chapped lips. "I came here because I was ashamed. I failed the Olympic trials in Florida. My grades dropped and never recovered. In a second, I lost everything I was working toward, and I didn't know what to do or where to turn to, and you seemed . . ."

Lehua braced for the blow.

"Better off without me," Ohia said, her eyes filling with tears. "You had your job, your friends at the mortuary. You had everything figured out while I was running headfirst into a future that was going nowhere. How was I supposed to train for the next four years when I didn't even know what I wanted to study at school? I had no idea what to do. I had nowhere to turn without you."

I don't think about losing, Le. That was what Ohia had told her when they'd been on the track team together. Now her sister's voice was shaking, overrun with her own anxiety and fear.

Ohia crossed her arms, and Lehua recognized the shame and abandonment carved into her twin's stiff posture. It was how

Lehua had felt about their mom leaving, about losing their grandparents and home, about Ohia and her success in college and always coming in second to her.

She'd never thought Ohia would feel abandoned when she'd dropped out. She always assumed her sister would be *relieved* to be rid of her—just as she imagined her mom had felt when she'd left. But now, Lehua's anger cooled, a fire put out by their shared heartache.

"I'm sorry," Lehua whispered. She wanted to reach for Ohia and embrace her sister, but there was too much distance between them. A gap widened by the years they'd spent avoiding their grief. "I wasn't trying to leave you behind. I didn't belong at that school."

"I know." Ohia stared down at her folded arms. "Until the Olympic trials, I thought my place was on that track team—and you'd regret leaving, and you'd come back, wanting to be with me again. But then that night you invited me over, telling me all about the mortuary and your friends. You were so damn happy while I was struggling to keep my head above water without you—I couldn't take it.

"After our fight, I went back to my dorm, and I started thinking about her, our mom. She was our age when she'd returned to O'ahu, and Grandma said she left because she'd never felt like she belonged in Phoenix—that she'd needed to go home. You know, even when the state couldn't find her, I didn't want to think she was dead. I used to imagine she'd Google our names and find us, and she'd—" Ohia bit her lip. She took a steadying breath. "She'd come back, wanting to be our mom. When you and I stopped talking, I started to tell myself a different story. I thought, wow, she must finally be happy like Lehua. They both found what they were looking for in life, something worthwhile—a home." Ohia's shoulders hunched together. "And I wanted that feeling, too, so I decided what better place than our homeland to figure out where I belonged."

Lehua remembered all the late nights she'd spent chasing the same feeling Ohia was describing. How many times had she snuck out, trying to run away from all of those houses that had never felt like home? They'd spent their whole lives unmoored since their grandparents had died, pruning them from their family, leaving them with no safe haven to return to when life became difficult.

"I looked online to see what options were available. There weren't many jobs or places to live. None I could afford, anyway. Until I found Kōpaʻa—and when Chiyo offered Alana the job, I realized how appealing being Alana was. She wasn't a track star, she hadn't failed the Olympic trials, and she wasn't drifting through life, lost, for the next four years unsure of where to go. Hell, she had a job in Hawaiʻi, a place to go, a homeland to return to." She peered at Lehua through her tears. "I never imagined this. I'm sorry I said all those awful things to you, Le. I'm surprised you still came looking for me."

Ohia's eyes were dark, and Lehua knew she was remembering their fight, the words she'd yelled.

Lehua didn't want to talk about how much those words had wounded her. She had tried to step outside of her sister's shadow for so long that she hadn't considered what had driven Ohia to say those things. Her twin thought she'd been trying to abandon her like their mother had.

Lehua clenched her sister's hand tight. "Remember the story of our names? We're *meant* to stay together. Even if that means here."

Ohia let out a sob and hugged Lehua tight. "I'm glad you found me. But you have to head back now, Le. Before they realize you're gone."

"I don't think I can leave," Lehua finally said, wiping her tears. "Not yet."

So many have been displaced from their homes, Chiyo had told her, and Lehua remembered the brittle snap of Melia's voice when she'd asked the other girl why this job, why this resort: *It's a job. I needed it.*

How many people had the resort swept into its maelstrom over the years for the well-being of the rich—just because they had no other choice?

That's life in Hawai'i, Melia had said. Lehua's anger flared at the injustice, the loss, the cruelty of it all. All that separated their grandparents and mom from Melia, and the rest of the resort's victims, was *luck*.

Ohia had found the resort, because there'd been no other options for a girl like her or Melia in Hawai'i. Her grandparents had been priced out of paradise. But if they'd tried to stay, they easily could've been consumed by the resort. She could imagine her grandma, led here by her heartache, and her grandpa, desperate to stay in their homeland, willing to take any job to avoid that severance.

That was life in Hawai'i. You could either be priced out of paradise, your stolen homeland, or pay the price for someone else's paradise.

Lehua imagined Melia in that orchard, her eyes forever open, watching the persimmon tree growing above her while the rest of her withered—and Lehua knew she couldn't abandon Melia, not when she would never rest, not when everything had been stolen from her.

That couldn't be all there was for Melia and the resort's victims. This couldn't be their ending. She wasn't going to leave them unburied.

Lehua thought of the scorched field, and how nothing grew there, and the bones she'd seen scattered in the soil dark like mulch. Hadn't she always felt anchored to the dead? Maybe there was a way they could both leave *and* save the ghosts.

"I have to stop them from taking more," Lehua told her sister. "You know we can't rely on the authorities. If we don't do something before we leave, there's no guarantee anyone else will—and I can free those victims tonight. Then we can escape on the boat."

Ohia's chin quivered as she nodded. She leaned in to give Lehua a hug. "Make sure you come back," she whispered into Lehua's shaved undercut.

Lehua squeezed her sister's hand, then released her, stepping away slowly. Fear washed down her throat as she stared at her sister, memorizing her face in case it was the last time she saw her. She didn't want to leave Ohia behind, but they couldn't risk anyone from the resort seeing Ohia—not if they wanted to flee together.

"I'll see you on the boat." Lehua slid through the mausoleum's metal doors, careful to shut them silently.

Chiyo was leaning against a tombstone in the graveyard, waiting.

The resort manager was standing so still she looked like a marble statue.

"Lehua," Chiyo said, her voice hollow.

Lehua backed up against the crypt's doors. She was about to shout for Ohia, to tell her to run, when four other people stepped into the graveyard's moonlight.

Sacha, Oliver, Leigh, and Horace. Seeing the four of them lined up, Lehua thought of Willa and the photo shoved into her pocket. *Horace and His Children.*

It's a family thing, Sacha had told her. Sacha, who'd mocked Jennifer by reminding her of her widowed status, and Jennifer, who'd claimed Sacha had the type of pedigree they couldn't say no to. *Not on this island.*

"This was more my husband's spot," Jennifer had said. "He was the planter."

Lehua remembered the grainy photos lining the hallway outside her room, the decades of Jacobses photographed, interspersed with the resort's long history. Their shared features. Hadn't one of the paintings showed a blond woman named Margaret? And a man named Sylvan? That had been Jennifer's husband's name, and Sacha's mother's name was . . .

Marguerite Tasse.

An impossible idea rose in Lehua's mind as she stared at the *family* in front of her. The Jacobses.

"I'm so glad you found your sister." Ira—Horace—smiled, his veneers gleaming white like bone. He looked less gaunt and sickly than he had before. His face had filled in since she'd last seen him and shone with a strange ethereal beauty. Lehua wavered in front of the crypt. Had his illness been a ruse this entire time? Or had he recently fed from the orchard's persimmons? "I told Chiyo you'd lead us right to her."

"Run, Lehua!"

The door shoved open behind her, and Ohia darted out of the darkness past Lehua, brandishing a cane knife at Horace. She was fast, the fastest person Lehua knew. But Oliver sprang forward quickly, swinging something large and heavy. Lehua didn't see what it was, but she heard the slam of it hitting her sister's back, knocking her to the ground.

"No!" Lehua yelled, running toward her sister. But Oliver was already throwing her slumped body over his shoulder, lifting Ohia like she weighed nothing.

Remember the story of our names, she heard Ohia whisper in her memory, holding their hands together as they'd left their grandparents' home. *'Ōhi'a lehua.*

They were meant to stay together—even if that meant here.

Chiyo appeared next to her. Her eyes glinted in the dark.

"You should have listened, Lehua," she said, with the thinnest veil of regret.

It was the last thing Lehua heard before something struck her from behind. The pain fell over her like a mantle, and she plunged into the dark.

THIRTY

Lehua woke on the floor of a musty room. Her hands ached with the stinging sensation of pins and needles. She tried to push herself up, but her arms were bound behind her.

She rolled over and saw Ohia tied up next to her, her dark hair piled on the ground.

"Ohia?" Lehua nudged her sister. Her head lolled to the side, her eyes and face static. *Shit.* She was still unconscious.

Roots sank through the room's walls and the island's red clay stained the shelves and ceiling in shades of carmine. They were underground.

Dimmed recessed lights lit the room's shelves, which were weighed down with sacks of milled sugar, cans of syrupy pineapple, and jars of persimmons. Lehua's stomach twisted as she thought of the orchard. Each shelf was labeled with a year, counting back to the 1900s. How many harvests had there been?

"Lehua?" Ohia said suddenly, groggily. "Are you there?"

"Yes," Lehua answered, contorting her bound arms to reach for Ohia. "I'm here."

They were too old to hold hands, but Lehua grabbed Ohia's anyway, pressing their palms together, even as the rope chafed Lehua's skin.

"Where are we?" Ohia asked.

"The cellar," Chiyo said from the shadows, startling Lehua.

The resort manager came out of the darkness toward them. "You were supposed to be on a boat, heading back to Maui tonight. But you didn't listen."

"You can't keep us here," Lehua said, hating the quiver in her voice. She had to convince Chiyo that the resort couldn't make her and Ohia disappear like the others. "My boss knows where I am—"

"Avery, right?" Chiyo interrupted with a sad shake of her head. "Your email was never sent, Lehua. That was only a ruse to get access to your account. Your boss will get an email from you. Your resignation. It will say you've decided to stay in Hawai'i, living happily with your sister."

Lehua's nose flared. "If you were going to kill me this whole time, why drag it out?"

Chiyo shook her head. "That's where you're wrong. I didn't want to kill you. Why would I? I wanted to send for the boat, but Horace and his brood pushed back. They thought you knew more than you were saying, that your sister had figured something out and somehow contacted you. I convinced them they should let you leave, that . . ." Chiyo trailed off.

"That what?"

Chiyo had the decency to look ashamed. "That it'd be better if you went back to Maui, to look for your twin there, because it'd lead the trail away from the resort."

"You wanted me to think Ohia had run away, so that when I went to the police, that would be the story." Lehua scoffed.

"I was trying to save you."

"*This* is you saving me?" Lehua let out a shallow laugh. "Because it sure looks like you're helping them kill us and cover it up. Just like you helped them kill Melia. And Willa."

Chiyo's eyes turned dark. "You don't know what I've done."

"I saw the persimmon orchard," Lehua said. "I can guess."

"You didn't see the fields before I got here." Chiyo's voice cracked as she paced the cellar. "Scores of people were killed by Horace and his family every year for decades even as their crops fell. The fields were drowning with bones when I arrived."

"And then you helped them."

"No. You don't understand. For decades, I've controlled his slaughter, limiting his appetite to a handful of workers a year. Without me and my persimmons, this island would be no more than cane and bones. I have saved hundreds of lives."

"Including your own," Ohia bit out.

"Yes, and you two would benefit from some self-preservation," Chiyo said, shooting the twins a dark look. "I came here looking for honest work when I found the bones in the cane. I escaped and hid on the island while they killed the other workers to revive their spoiled sugarcane. But Horace knew he was one victim short."

Chiyo smiled grimly. "When they found me, I begged for my life. I offered Horace a change of crops. I knew persimmons would guarantee a steady harvest—once grown, their trees are hardy, drought-resistant, and less susceptible to disease—and he let me live. But you're wrong to think I was only bartering for my life. I bargained for the future, saving countless lives."

Lehua's anger surged. "You're *stealing* lives to spare your own."

"Do you think he would've stopped killing if I'd let him kill me?" Chiyo's voice rattled. "Of course not. Horace let me live then, but it was up to me to change this slaughterhouse into something new. I told him about the tourists flocking to Oʻahu after the war. He couldn't believe there were people flying to Hawaiʻi, bringing millions of dollars every year while his house fell into disrepair. He was so dependent on his sugarcane he couldn't leave the island anymore. So I made myself too valuable for him to whet his appetite on. I went to the other islands, advertising our resort, and picked which guests to bring, building up the resort's fame from nothing."

"But you could've run. Why build all of this for them?" Ohia demanded.

"Because this is my home now, and I can outlast him," Chiyo said fiercely. She turned to Lehua. Her crescent eyes burned with conviction. "He stole everything from me. But I've been patient and it's paid off. The Jacobses' greed will tear their family apart with their infighting. Leigh has wanted to expand the resort for decades, but Horace ignored his son Charles—and now I've convinced him I am the best person to manage that expansion."

Charles. The name hung in Lehua's mind, bringing her back to her first night at the resort. Chiyo had called Leigh Charles when she had been eavesdropping outside the lounge. Lehua remembered the conversation she and Melia had overheard while hiding inside the printing press room. *He has a waitlist a mile long and he brings up scripture as if this isn't a business*, Leigh had said to someone they couldn't see. It'd been Chiyo. Hadn't Sacha said the resort manager wouldn't show their waitlist to just anyone?

Lehua had no doubt Leigh would gladly partner with Chiyo if it meant finally getting a bigger piece of Kōpaʻa.

"The other Jacobses all live in fear of Horace," Chiyo went on. "But Horace is dying. You can smell the rot on him and his hunger has changed. He's insatiable now. Despite what he says, the fruit can only delay the inevitable."

Jennifer's downcast eyes as she'd stared at her husband's photograph, at his face, hollowed by cancer, flashed through Lehua's mind.

"But how many people have to die while you wait? You can help us right now." Betrayal burned through Lehua. "You told me Kōpaʻa could change under the right hand. Is this the *right hand* you had in mind?"

Chiyo turned away. "I tried to help you. I gave you shelter in our resort. You and Melia would've both been killed if I hadn't intervened. I told you to stay away from her, but you ignored my warnings. I finally had Sacha slip you a sleeping pill, hoping it'd keep you out of the way until the boat arrived. But you still got involved.

"I've been trying to save you all this time," Chiyo whispered. "You and Ohia weren't supposed to die." To Ohia, she said ruefully, "You never would've gotten through our selection process if I'd known your real name."

"Because she's a famous track runner and has a family," Lehua surmised. "Everything you said about giving your workers a second chance at life—that was bullshit. You're picking and choosing people to die, people you think no one will miss, who have no other option—people like Melia." Lehua's chest burned as Chiyo's cheeks pinked—the only answer Lehua needed to know she was right. "Who gave you the right to decide that?"

"I did," a raspy voice answered, and a whiff of decay descended the stairs as Horace stepped into view.

The cellar's light clung to his sharp face and warmed his mussed blond hair. The knot of his necktie was loosened and dirt stained the fabric of his dark coat. In his hand he held a persimmon and slit it with a paring knife, the blade peeling the fruit's flesh.

"You've done well, Chiyo," he said, without turning to look at the resort manager. The persimmon's astringent sweetness filled the room, curdling Lehua's stomach. "Grab us some more rope. I think Lehua and I are long overdue for a chat."

Lehua's gaze slashed to Chiyo's in one last plea. She didn't want to discover what Horace would do to them, what frightened Chiyo so badly that it reflected in her eyes any time he entered a room—even after all these years. But Chiyo spun away, unwilling to meet Lehua's beseeching eyes.

Lehua burned with anger watching the resort manager climb the stairs and shut the door behind her. Lehua clutched Ohia's hand tighter. *It's okay*, she lied, squeezing her fingers, trying to soothe Ohia in the shorthand they'd never been able to master, that twins like them were supposed to know. *I will keep us together.* Her hand squeezed. *Like Lehua in the legend.*

Alone with them, Horace cocked his head to the side, and a smile played over his thin lips. "Chiyo was persuasive. She tried her best to manage the situation. But after I met you, I chose to interfere, dropping hints where I could. I'm surprised she kept you in check for as long as she did, given your people's nature."

Lehua thought of the dinner, and Horace's glee when he'd told her the story about Captain Cook. How tauntingly he'd watched her. He'd wanted her to know the story, in case she found the bones in his field. She grunted, wrenching at the ropes binding her wrists.

"My father tried to change that nature through the gospel. That was his calling from the Lord, and this island is mine." He cut the persimmon in his hand into thin slices, the knife glistening with juice. "Once the provisional government took over the monarchy, I knew no one would care if I claimed the island for myself. It was a gift from God, if I was willing to put in the work. All I had to do was make sure it was vacated first."

"So you killed the families here."

"I separated the wheat from the chaff," he said without remorse. "The Kānaka here were . . . savages. Lazy. Unintelligent. *Unfit.* They barely worked the land. They didn't deserve a place on my island. And when we planted our sugarcane, I learned years later that God had blessed my family for cleansing his threshing floor. The field they were buried in yielded the sweetest of my crops.

"My workers found the bones and started a strike, so I chose to experiment. I left their bones to lie fallow, and another sweet harvest sprung." He licked his lips. "It was then that I noticed the effects. The spoils had stopped the clock on my life, offering me another of the Lord's blessings. Another reward for my hard work. But blessings come with trials. After a while, only my crops could sate my appetite—until the sugarcane field spoiled, and wasted in my mouth, tasting like ash."

If you take care of the land, it will take care of you, Lehua heard her grandma telling her—and Melia was right: Horace hadn't. His soil had eroded, and his island had become ʻeʻepa.

"So you planted pineapple instead," Lehua gritted her teeth, wrestling with the rope. "And killed again."

Horace pressed a persimmon slice into his mouth. He chewed slowly, wetting his dry lips with the juice. "Yes, but that fruit soon lost its savor as well—and the ingrates revolted, burning my fields and cannery when they realized what I was doing." He rolled his eyes. "Because of the ghosts."

"They warned them," Lehua said, thinking of the workers who'd led her into the field, to show her that graveyard of bones. *You shouldn't be here, kaikamahine.*

"The Kānaka always said the world of the living could become tangled with the world of the dead. That the afterlife was only a curtain's push away. Well, we had *quite* a tangle."

The way Horace talked about her people itched down Lehua's spine like hives. He talked like they had been wiped out, extinct. *We're still here,* she thought. Despite everything he'd done, they were still here, alive, and maybe they could've been thriving if it weren't for the leash he had kept on them and their land.

"Chiyo thinks we tainted the land. She said I needed to practice more restraint." He laughed, unable to resist gloating. "So

I learned to restrain death itself. I corralled the island's ghosts using ti leaf." He gulped another slice of persimmon greedily, then grinned. "The Kānaka method for handling spirits."

"You have enough." Lehua took stock of the full cellar around them. "You already have all of this. Let us go. Why do you need more?"

He stalked forward, stopping in front of Lehua. He grabbed her face with one hand, his fingers digging into her as he turned her toward the light. The knife glinted in his other hand. "This has nothing to do with need. God gave me a taste of His immortality. But unlike God, I acquired a certain palate. Chiyo tries to curate her selection, employing only the scraps of society." He shook his head. "You've seen what my fruit can do. Not everyone is fit to taste it."

He tilted his head toward the light, illuminating the sharp ridges of his pale and handsome face. "I mean, look at me, Sacha, Chiyo, or my sons. Chiyo's persimmons have done wonders, reversing the worst effects of aging. Unlike the other resorts my son Charles so desperately wants to emulate, our fruit provides true rejuvenation, a true resurrection."

A tremor chased through Lehua as understanding came. She saw Sacha rubbing cream onto her hands and neck before dinner, its persimmon scent veiling her body like perfume. When Lehua had tried to pull away from the influencer's kiss, Sacha's skin had felt like dried fruit.

Lehua shuddered, remembering what Jennifer had said about Sacha's mother. *She wanted her daughter to grow up.* Now she understood. Sacha looked Lehua's age, but that was the work of the island's persimmons—and the resort's victims. That was the beauty influencer's secret.

Horace smirked at her repulsed expression. "Our blessed crops shouldn't be shared with just anyone who has a dime to their name, regardless of what Charles thinks. But thanks to him—and Chiyo's insistence on discretion—it's been a while since I got to indulge in a full meal. I can survive on scraps, but—" He pulled Lehua toward his face, and inhaled against her hair. "I can't wait to see how you'll taste." He leered at Ohia. "Maybe you two will taste the same."

He pointed toward the wall of milled sugar, pineapple, and persimmon jars. "I like to keep my favorites close by. You know Willa, yes?" His eyes darkened on Ohia. "She didn't want to be a part of our legacy, so I'm keeping her hand in a jar until her fruit ripens. Now she will never be able to leave."

Ohia gasped at the mention of her friend, then started to cry. Horace's smile widened. "You know, I think I'll keep you two in the same jar."

The knife glinted in Horace's hand. He yanked Lehua's head back, hauling her off the ground with one hand, and Lehua braced for the blade. She was glad Ohia's back was turned to her. She didn't want her twin to witness this.

But Horace didn't slash at her throat. He leaned closer, showing her the single slice of persimmon resting on his knife's metal edge—then he pushed the fruit to her lips.

Lehua recoiled from the cold metal and astringent fruit, thinking of the persimmons taking root in the field-workers' stomachs. But it was no use. With his long fingers, Horace pried her jaw open, and clamped her mouth around the persimmon. All she could do was gulp it down.

The taste was sweet as honey and delicate. Lehua felt the persimmon slide down, tender like flesh, as Horace dropped her back to the floor. He force-fed Ohia next. A rush of déjà vu ran like a sharp edge down Lehua's throat. In her dreams, cold fingers had tipped open her mouth, forcing a persimmon down.

"Why?" Lehua asked with a wince, her head pounding, her skin feverish. "Why feed us if you're going to kill us?"

"A good farmer never leaves his field to go barren," Horace told her, smiling. "And I'm giving you the best fertilizer I have." His voice was almost fond. "My personal store of persimmons."

He looked down at the twins, his blue eyes lingering over their faces. "Chiyo was the one to suggest we feed the fruit to the workers before we planted them. At first, I balked at wasting such a luxury, but she was right. It ripened those we culled." He chuckled. "Their bodies waste away slower. The harvest tastes sweeter and their bones feed the orchard for far longer."

And now it was her and Ohia's turn to fertilize the land of their ancestors, to sustain Horace and his family who'd stolen it, to rejuvenate the guests who would continue to reap the land over the years.

"Mr. Jacobs?"

They both looked up at the sound of Chiyo's voice. She hovered on the stairs, standing in a half circle of darkness.

"Excellent timing, Chiyo," Horace said as Chiyo came up behind him. "I'll have Charles and Oliver carry them to the orchard." He smiled at them hungrily. "We can plant them tonight."

"Chiyo," Lehua whispered as the persimmon's sweetness stole through her veins. She tried the ropes at her wrists again and felt she might be able to slip loose. "Chiyo, please."

"Come now, Chiyo, bring me the rope," Horace said impatiently, glancing behind him.

Chiyo raised her hands. She stood behind Horace, brandishing the cane knife high. "No."

THIRTY-ONE

The cane knife struck Horace's thigh. Then Chiyo turned and sliced Lehua and Ohia's bindings with the bloodied blade, freeing them. "Run! Get out of here!"

Lehua pulled Ohia to her feet and shoved her twin ahead of her. They raced up the stairs, flinging back the door at the top of the cellar, and found Oliver waiting.

Surprise flitted across his face. He made a grab for Ohia and she ducked under his broad arms.

Lehua threw a punch, her fist glancing off Oliver's face. He barreled into her, knocking her against the wall. Her breath caught as pain radiated up her back.

Ohia froze, staring at Lehua. The hallway behind her was empty, a vacant track and all the running lanes were open. She could escape—if she left Lehua behind.

"Go, Ohia! Run!" Lehua shouted. "I'll take care of him!"

"I'm not leaving—"

If Oliver was here, that meant the others were nearby. But Lehua knew the one person who could sprint past them all.

"Run, Ohia!"

Tears welled in Lehua's eyes as Ohia nodded, then ran out of view. She could hear shouts echoing down the hallway.

Oliver took one lumbering step after her sister, and Lehua jumped onto his back, her head nearly colliding with the doorframe.

"Get off me!" he shouted as Lehua swung at his head, batting his temple and eyes. He tried to reach for her as she hung on to his shoulders. Lehua winced as his nails clawed at her skin, drawing blood. She wrapped her arms around his head like a vice, blocking his eyes. Oliver stumbled wide, swaying toward the opened cellar—and the stairs.

As he veered forward, she knocked his skull against the doorjamb. Once. Twice. The impact shuddered her palms.

Oliver's arms pinwheeled, trying to catch himself before he tripped, but he tumbled down the steps. Lehua rolled off his back before they hit the bottom, pain lancing her knees as she slid into the wooden balusters, while the film producer landed with a sickening *crunch* at the base of the stairs.

Lehua scrambled to her feet. On the cellar floor, Oliver lay in a heap, his bones twisted at odd angles, distending his skin.

In her peripheral, Lehua saw Chiyo and Horace grappling with each other. A trail of blood encircled them as they struggled.

She should run and catch up to Ohia—but Horace had pulled the cane knife free from Chiyo. He stood over Chiyo. She was crouched on the ground, holding a hand against a wide gash in her side, her aloha shirt dark with blood.

Lehua looked wildly around and saw the persimmon jars lining the stairs. She leaped down the rest of the stairs, dodging Oliver's crooked arm, his hand reaching uselessly for her.

Lehua didn't think. She grabbed a heavy jar and flung it at the back of Horace's head. Glass shattered against his shoulder blades, spraying persimmons and juice down his suit.

Horace glared at her, his eyes burrowing into her like maggots devouring a corpse.

He scoffed. "A noble Kanaka. How surprising."

Lehua snarled. "Fuck you."

She shoved the shelf nearest to her, and Horace's eyes widened as his jars toppled to the ground.

"You don't know what you're destroying," he barked.

Lehua met his gaze defiantly, and saw Melia in the orchard, her tawny eyes empty. Her heart slammed against her ribs, torn asunder. "Yes, I do."

Horace roared as she toppled another shelf, diving for the falling preserves. But he was too slow. He crashed to his knees atop the ruined fruit, the loose sugar spilling over the floor from its split sack, mingling with the cellar's shattered glass.

He dropped the cane knife and clawed at the sugar, the fruit, the shattered jars. The broken glass sliced his skin, tracking blood down his fingers.

Lehua ran. She scooped the cane knife from the ground like a fallen baton, then vaulted over him toward Chiyo.

Chiyo took Lehua's offered arm, a mixture of shame and resolve steeling her face. They climbed the stairs two at a time, and Chiyo stumbled as she held the wound in her side closed with her hand.

"You were supposed to run, Lehua," Chiyo panted, her face beaded with sweat.

Lehua opened her mouth to argue—but then she heard Horace's feet pounding after them on the stairs. "Hurry, Chiyo."

At the top of the cellar stairs, she flung her hand with the cane knife against the light switch, the blade clanging against the wall, and kicked the door shut, turning the handle's lock behind her. Lehua knew it wouldn't stop him, but it would buy them some time.

"How do we get out of here?" Lehua asked as they rushed down the hallway, entering the massive kitchen.

"Through the lounge," Chiyo whispered, her voice threaded with pain. "Or the main entrance."

Moonlight spilled in through the kitchen windows, shining on the appliances and the marble island in the center. Anyone could be waiting for them.

Boom. Horace struck the cellar door from the other side.

Lehua pulled the largest knife free from the knife block on the kitchen island. She pressed the blade into Chiyo's hands, then yanked her down as the kitchen filled with light. They crouched behind the large marble island, sliding slowly on their knees as someone entered the kitchen.

"Horace?"

Lehua saw a pedicured toe peek around the island's corner.

Crack. Lehua met Chiyo's wide eyes. The cellar door was splintering. It wouldn't hold long as Horace continued to ram it.

“Dammit!” Sacha said, running into the hallway toward the cellar.

Lehua stood up. “Time to go.”

“Leave me, Lehua.”

“Shut up,” Lehua whispered, pulling Chiyo off the floor, out of a puddle of her own blood. *Shit.*

Lehua lifted Chiyo’s arm around her own shoulder, bearing most of the injured woman’s weight. Still, Chiyo rasped in pain as they ran, half crouched, out of the kitchen and into the west wing of the resort.

She didn’t like how empty it was here. How quiet.

When Ohia had run, there’d been shouting. Where were those people now? Had they all left, chasing after her sister? Or were they waiting for an opening?

Crack.

Another shout from Sacha. Time was running out.

“Which way?” Lehua whispered.

Chiyo pointed toward the main entrance hall. “The lounge has too many windows. They’ll see exactly where we’re running—” She hissed through her teeth at the pain. “Sorry.”

They stumbled toward the lobby and Lehua risked a peek. The wall sconces barely flickered. Somehow, the lobby looked eerier than if it had been completely dark.

From the other room, they heard the sound of feet pounding across tile. Lehua didn’t think. She lifted Chiyo, hoisting her onto her back. The woman gasped, seizing in Lehua’s grip, as Lehua ran for the door.

Immediately, someone rammed into them. Lehua crashed

against the wall, holding on to Chiyo as tight as she could. Chiyo slashed at their unknown attacker with her knife, flicking blood onto the walls.

The light glinted off Leigh's face and his clenched hands, holding the bloody bridge of his nose. "Chiyo, you traitorous bitch." Blood streamed between his fingers, running over his lips.

"Run," Chiyo rasped against her ear. "Leigh probably locked the front doors, and he always has his gun."

Lehua swore. They couldn't turn back. That's where Horace and Sacha were. Their only option was up the stairs.

Lehua dodged Leigh as Chiyo brandished her knife, keeping him at a distance. As he clutched his face, he rammed a hand into his suit pocket.

Lehua broke for the stairs and her feet caught on the steps. She lurched forward, nearly throwing Chiyo off her back. Chiyo cried out in pain as Lehua fought to keep her footing. They'd gone up two steps when the staircase's sugarcane newel post exploded. The gunshot echoed through the lobby as shards of wood ricocheted around their heads.

"Charles! Don't you dare waste your bullets ruining my house!" Horace was free, and right behind them.

"You're okay," Lehua said, her ears ringing as she raced up the stairs. Chiyo's chest hitched with pain with every step they took. "Horace got his leg sliced up, and he's fine. You'll survive this."

Chiyo croaked out a humorless laugh. "Horace is different. He's been eating from this island for almost one hundred and forty years." She shook her head. "I don't know how much it would take to kill him at this point."

The words sank into Lehua. She remembered Jennifer pushing her out of her room, the way Sacha had easily restrained her in the lounge, and how Chiyo had pulled her from Melia. The island's harvest was why the planters had seemed unusually strong. "You've tried?"

"No, but others have—there were guests who wanted what he had." Chiyo's eyes flickered. "I saw what happened when they failed—and when Willa failed. She'd wanted to run."

That was not a comforting thought.

Lehua finally reached the top of the stairs. "Where to now?" she asked, panting.

Chiyo pointed her knife. "Horace's room."

Lehua sprinted past the resort's party photos and family portraits, Marguerite Tasse's painted eyes on her, followed by the much younger portraits of Leigh—*Charles*—and Oliver—*O. Orin Jacobs.* Lehua ripped the far door open, and they raced inside Horace's room, slamming the door shut behind them.

In the dim moonlight, Lehua saw the human skulls on display atop Horace's long desk, some knocked sideways on his papers, while other skulls watched from the library's ornate shelves next to his personal stash of persimmons.

"Next to the bookcase," Chiyo said in a thin voice, directing Lehua to the split in the wall, one side darker than the other. She grabbed the latch hidden in the wallpaper's seams next to Horace's books. The service wing opened, revealing corkscrew stairs that spun up to the resort's third floor. Behind the stairs, the thin hallway led into darkness.

Lehua opened her mouth to ask which way to go—then she and Chiyo froze, smelling the smoke.

Lehua flicked the curtains aside and peered into the field, looking for the telltale sign of fire or the running shape of her sister. But the night was too dark. She heard the footsteps in the hallway change direction, charge downstairs, then fade into the distance.

"It's a distraction," Lehua coughed, smoke trickling into the room now. "Ohia didn't run. She stayed."

Chiyo nodded. "Something's burning in the house, but the resort has a sprinkler system. If she'd meant it as a distraction, it won't last long." She pointed toward Horace's desk. "Quick, grab the candles in there, while I do this."

Before Lehua could stop her, Chiyo pushed herself off Lehua's back to stand on shaky legs. The woman shuddered in a breath, then peeled back the persimmon wallpaper draping Horace's room, the same wallpaper that had covered Lehua's walls, until it pooled in strips. Planks of glossy persimmon wood lined the wall with chips of bleached bone between them like mortar between bricks.

"Horace's addition when we renovated," Chiyo said as she met Lehua's queasy look. She struck the match against the wall, then took the candles from her hands and lit them, throwing the burning wicks onto the piles of peeled wallpaper.

The fire caught, devouring the paper, then spread to the carpet. Lehua offered her hand to Chiyo. But she limped forward, vanishing into the hidden hallway.

"This leads downstairs," she said, using a candle to light the spiraling staircase.

Ohia will be okay, Lehua told herself, bolting after Chiyo. *She has to be.*

"This is the only unlocked door," Chiyo said, pulling the wall open. They exited the service alcove onto the resort's ground floor, ducking under a plume of thick smoke.

Lehua recognized the long table pearled with empty candelabra sticks. The dining room. Water sprayed from the ceiling's sprinklers as a smoke alarm blared.

Lehua looked at the large glass windows that made up the back wall of the dining room. If they couldn't use any of the doors, they'd have to make their own way out. Lehua grabbed a dining chair, and hurled it at the window.

A crack snaked the glass, the noise drowned out by the booming alarm. Lehua seized the chair by its legs and batted it against the windows. Cracks spiderwebbed across the glass until the glass fell out, shattering.

Lehua bent to help Chiyo through the broken window, slicing her elbow on the shards. The pain registered dimly, feeling far away. Once they were both through, they ran for the cane field. Behind them, the dining room door opened, revealing a drenched and heaving Oliver. He ran when he saw them, his collarbone sagging from his chest, broken.

He should be dead, Lehua thought, unable to shake the image of the film producer's misshapen limbs from her mind. He sprinted, his shattered arms and legs swollen and thrashing toward them, bending impossibly under his skin.

Lehua tore through the field, slashing at the sugarcane stalks with the cane knife, tugging Chiyo along. He couldn't be far behind them. She didn't want to think about what he would do if he caught them. Unlike Horace and Leigh, Oliver hadn't looked mad. He'd been grinning.

Oliver burst from the cane to their right, narrowly dodging Lehua's knife as she swung at him. He grabbed Chiyo and shoved her out of the way. She collapsed onto the ti leaf outside the cane. Then Oliver seized Lehua by the neck and slammed her into the ground. The cane knife tumbled out of her hand and into the grass.

He rolled her over, pinning her down as he straddled her, and Lehua screamed. She raked her nails down his face. Oliver clamped his iron hands around her wrists with a practiced ease.

He leaned down and sniffed at her neck, inhaling deep. "Do you know my father's problem when it comes to running this place?" Oliver smiled. "He only sees you as cattle for the slaughter."

The cold soil chilled the damp spot Chiyo had left on Lehua's back and leached up the manager's blood. A splash of lantern light behind Oliver shone like a nimbus around his handsome and battered face.

Kaikamahine.

She remembered the workers watching from the cane, herded into the fields, trapped there by the ti leaf for centuries.

The same cane she and Oliver now lay in.

Lehua saw a cane knife rise above Oliver's head. She shut her eyes as the blow slammed into Oliver sideways. A grisly tearing noise punctuated the field's silent wall of stalks, followed by the cracking thud of something landing hard on the earth.

Oliver's grip went slack.

Lehua shuddered against the ground as a warm splatter fell onto her eyelids, wrong and viscous. Each rivulet was a wet shock against her skin. She recognized that familiar copper tang and scrubbed at the blood snaking down her face. Then her eyes opened and a choked gasp escaped her lips.

Oliver's headless body loomed over her.

Lehua scrambled, desperately pushing his corpse off her. He slid into the cane, next to a cluster of the resort's field-workers, their shining eyes piercing the dark wall. She crawled to her feet, trying not to heave as the workers dragged the body away.

Lehua could see the resort's courtyard through the rustling stalks. Chiyo lay bleeding in the grass next to her, sprawled halfway out of the dense cane wall, her face a mess of sweat and blood. She was panting, her eyes half closed, staring at the firelight consuming the upper floors of the resort, burning faster than the sprinklers could stop it.

"C'mon, grab onto me," Lehua commanded. They had to get out of there before the Jacobses found them.

But it was too late.

Hands trembling, Chiyo pointed. Horace was crawling out of the dark mouth of the burning resort, smoke billowing around him and Leigh.

Sacha screamed and tripped out behind the two men, sprawling onto the gravel outside. They were all soaked through from the sprinkler system.

Her dandelion hair was scorched, and one half of her face was shiny and red with angry welts and burns. She was crying out of one eye, leaking tears onto the burned tatters of her dress. "It's all gone," she moaned.

Next to his father, Leigh wiped both blood and water onto his pants, then straightened his cuffs. But Horace was glaring at Lehua as she tried to help Chiyo. His pale eyes flashed from her to Chiyo, and he barked out a laugh.

"See what happens when you bite the hand that feeds you, Chiyo?" he taunted, striding toward them.

"You never fed me, Horace," Chiyo panted through a smile, blood streaming from her mouth and nose. Lehua could hear the scrape of Chiyo's heaving lungs as she struggled to her feet and faced the remaining Jacobs family. She wasn't even putting pressure on the wound leaking at her side. Her hands were clutched into two dark fists. "The ʻāina fed me."

A murmur rose from the dry field behind Lehua and she took a startled step forward.

The island's workers surrounded them, leaning toward the very edge of the sugarcane. Their glowing eyes were wide and strained, staring at the Jacobses. Their whispers snaked through the stalks, building into a low wind that seemed to come from Kōpaʻa itself. The cane leaves trembled as the workers gathered, their numbers growing row by row.

Lehua tried to put herself between Chiyo and the approaching family, but Chiyo pushed past her, tearing through the ti leaf in front of them. Their leaves dyed her hands black. "*They* fed me."

Chiyo raised her fists high and let the ti leaf barrier she'd shredded from the field fall to the ground, stained red by her blood.

All at once, the workers rushed past the destroyed ti leaf barrier, breaking through the cane line. They raced across the gravel with machetes, cane knives, and sickles raised to the night sky. Without the ti leaf, they were freed from the sugarcane they'd haunted for centuries.

One of them shoved past Lehua, driving her to the ground, and she cried out as their boots trampled her hands. She could feel the firelight heating her face, see it glinting off the field-workers' thin blades, and hear the swish as they cut through both fabric and flesh.

She rolled away from the chaos, and reached for Chiyo, who'd fallen into the red clay and grass in a heap. But when Lehua's hand closed around the woman's wrist, she knew that stillness.

Chiyo was dead.

The workers were a century-long storm of anger and revenge, and Lehua saw both Leigh and Sacha fall, cut down by the knives that had reaped their family's harvest for so long.

But Horace was on his feet, sustained by decades of stolen mana. He batted at the workers, forcing an opening, then charged straight for Lehua.

She watched with a growing horror as Horace lumbered toward her, to hunt Lehua in the tall grass. Lehua pivoted on her heel and began to run through the cane, but she couldn't move fast enough. Her body was weak from carrying Chiyo and running all night, and her vision was seeping black.

"You filthy Kanaka," Horace said, spilling into the grass after her. A scythe sank wetly into his back, and a knife stabbed his suit, but he kept going. Lehua turned to face him, backing into the grass. She could see the scythe in his back, weaving after her above the cane like a shark fin, until Horace caught up to her.

He snatched her by the front of her shirt, lifting her high off the ground.

"You destroyed my home." He was panting raggedly, his hot breath exhaling over Lehua in a saccharine cloud of persimmons and rot.

Lehua met his angry eyes, wondering if his son's blood still dripped down her face.

This is what's next, Lehua thought, remembering Melia, and a grim light filled her eyes. At least Ohia seemed to have made it out alive. Maybe it was okay to be the tails side of their shared coin, face down on the table—the one no one bet on—as long as her sister was okay, and safe.

Lehua struck Horace with her hands and feet, and hissed, "You stole *ours*."

Horace scoffed. "You people didn't deserve—"

He didn't get another word out. A cane knife slammed into his face from the side, cratering his eye and orbital. He fell, dragging Lehua into the cane with him. When Lehua looked up, Ohia stood over Horace, her hands wet with his blood, carrying the same cane knife Lehua had wielded earlier.

Next to them, Horace's pulpy face stared at the sky and stars. After more than one hundred years of feasting on other people's lives and homes, he was finally dead. Who knew how many planters he'd recruited over the years, to dine with his family on the twins' homeland and people? Maybe they'd return to the island, trying to claim it and Horace's secret, now that he was gone.

Maybe.

But tonight, she and Ohia were alone.

Ohia hugged her sister and started to cry.

"You came back for me," Lehua said, gripping her.

"Of course. I always will."

A wind blew through the cane field, and Lehua resisted a shudder. The chill sank into her cuts, slicing her hands and arms like teeth. Together, she and Ohia watched as the ghosts poured back into the tall grass.

She and Ohia stayed together, holding each other in the dark, knowing they were both safe and home for the first time in almost a decade.

For now, that was enough.

Epilogue

KANU:

to bury, as a corpse; to plant, as a seed;

to cover up or hide in the earth; planting, burial

hereditary

The week after the fire died out, Lehua and Ohia learned how to put the dead to sleep.

Even with Horace gone, the ghosts didn't disappear. They watched the twins empty the house, taking stock of what remained inside, removing what the fire had spared within the persimmon walls.

In the kitchen, Lehua and Ohia found a pantry and walk-in fridge crowded with hanging meats, grains, sacks of flour and sugar, and tall decanters of oil. But when they ate the food, it roiled their stomachs—feeding them but never satisfying them. Their appetites had changed, craving the new taste they'd developed after eating the persimmons. Still, the twins ate, forcing the food down as their bodies protested.

In the security room, Lehua found most of the monitors intact, and the resort computer atop the desk. She thought about emailing Avery, but she wasn't sure what to tell her yet. She didn't know if she was ever going back to the mortuary, or Phoenix. There were too many dead here, and her sister. They all needed her.

And this was her home now, the place where Melia's bones would be laid to rest.

Ohia cleaned the workers' barracks, where she and Lehua slept in their own bunk beds. At night, her sister talked about fixing up the abandoned bungalows, with their broken windows and cracked glass.

"Maybe we could be neighbors," Ohia had joked, shooting her twin a hesitant look that Lehua had understood. The rift between them hadn't completely healed, but it was no longer so large that Lehua couldn't reach for Ohia's hand across their bunk beds.

"Maybe," Lehua had answered, giving Ohia's hand a tight squeeze.

She and Ohia had been without direction and a home for so long, but they had a plan for the island. They would build a refuge for their people, rather than the rich, offering a safe harbor for the people like their mom, their grandparents, and girls like them and Melia.

A place in their homeland. A *home.*

But first the dead had to be laid to rest.

They'd emptied the resort's lost and found, taking the smoky clothes that had belonged to past guests for their own, and carried the heavy trunks filled with the belongings of the murdered workers outside. There, the workers rubbed the old textiles between their fingers and remembered the lives that had been stolen from them.

Then they told the sisters how to put them to rest.

A Hawaiian man taught Ohia the pule to say over their bones

and repeated the words of the prayer until she no longer fumbled over it. Lehua carefully wrote down everything the ghosts told her. The ghosts called both the sisters kaikamahine. *Daughters*, Ohia translated, and Lehua cried.

The sisters found clothes to wrap the bones in, for those that asked for funeral shrouds. They gathered wood and cane grass for the fires, for those who wanted to be cremated.

Lehua spent days listening to the ghosts, writing their stories and details down on the computer. Sometimes, she got email notifications for the resort, applications from tourists who wanted to become planters, and people desperate for a chance, looking for work. She deleted them all.

She rested the computer on her lap while she sat under the resort's blackened porch. She thought she spied a mauve bandana among the ash and cane, spearing her heart with pain and hope. But that was all Lehua saw of Melia and her ghost before they began moving the bones.

In the persimmon orchard, the ghosts followed her and Ohia as they walked carefully around the bones and bodies.

Ohia spoke the words, and the ghosts gathered closer, hugging the chain-link fence as the twins removed the bones from the field. The dead stayed moored to their sides as they carried their remains to the spot each had chosen.

Our work, Avery had explained when she'd first hired her, when Lehua had been chasing a future she couldn't see or imagine, *requires precision*.

She and Ohia were careful not to make mistakes.

They followed the ghosts' requests, wrapping the bones of

those who wanted a Buddhist burial in white fabric before putting them in the fire or the ground. They prayed over the bones of the other Hawaiians, and moved them to the resting places they chose, and the island's ghosts slowly disappeared, their spirits dissipating like a plume of breath blown away.

That's what's next, Lehua thought, holding her sister's hand like it was an anchor, as each ghost left them.

Until it finally came time to bury Melia's body.

Her ghost had never gathered around them, never been drawn by the pule or the fire of the other burials—and Lehua had wanted to wait, to see Melia one last time, so she could tell her how to do this one thing for her.

But her ghost never showed.

There was a tight inhale, a squeeze in her chest, when Lehua walked to where Melia's body lay and met her open eyes. Ohia stepped aside, insisting Lehua say the pule as she wept.

Together, she and Ohia chose the spot for Melia, far away from the fields and the orchard, within view of the ocean. There, Lehua wrapped the other Hawaiian girl in dirt, covering the ugly wound in her stomach, where the persimmon sapling had been rooted.

She thought of the brave girl she had met, who brushed her lips against hers and told her stories of their homeland—and Lehua cried.

Ohia held her, not saying a word, as they knelt near the grave.

When the sky darkened, Ohia pulled Lehua to her feet. They walked the long road back to the barracks, past the abandoned resort on the hill. There, a bird trilled, the first Lehua had heard since coming to Kōpaʻa. Strong and vibrant.

She looked. A bird with inky black wings and a red and yellow bill sat in the resort's loch, watching her and Ohia with an uncanny stillness, a lehua flower held gently in its bill.

Our family's ʻaumakua is the ʻalae. Lehua remembered Melia leaning against her after midnight. Her soft voice full of pride.

The ʻalae dropped the carmine flower into the pond, then disappeared into the reeds.

Reunited with her sister beneath the abandoned resort, Lehua heard Melia's laugh, bright as birdsong.

AUTHOR'S NOTE

Mahalo nui loa for reading *That Which Feeds Us*. Colonial amnesia is a concept in postcolonial studies to describe the erasure of the history of the colonized. Despite the important role Hawaiʻi plays in American expansionism as its first overseas territory, few stories about Indigenous Hawaiians are widely available, and those that are accessible are often tarnished by colonialism's lasting, and ongoing, effects.

Fellow Kānaka ʻŌiwi may recognize the moʻolelo that inspired Lehua's story. I am sure there are those who will deplore the cultural deviations I chose to utilize; all I can say is *That Which Feeds Us* is a contemporary horror novel. It should not be mistaken for a cultural text or scholarly work.

With that said, the story was inspired by real-life events to accurately capture the modern-day horror that Native Hawaiians endure. While the island of Kōpaʻa and its plantation are constructs of fiction, the historical events mentioned in *That Which Feeds Us* are true. For readers interested in learning more, here is a list of the many books and authors whose work helped build the world of *That Which Feeds Us*.

Pau Hana: Plantation Life and Labor in Hawaii, 1835–1920 by Ronald Takaki

Unequal Freedom: How Race and Gender Shaped American Citizenship and Labor by Evelyn Nakano Glenn

Nana I Ke Kumu: Look to the Source (Volumes 1 and 2) by Mary Kawena Pukui, E. W. Haertig, and Catherine Lee

Hawaiian Blood: Colonialism and the Politics of Sovereignty and Indigeneity by J. Kēhaulani Kauanui

Hollywood's Hawaii: Race, Nation, and War by Delia Malia Caparoso Konzett

The works of Mary Kawena Pukui, Noenoe Silva, Noelani Goodyear-Ka'ōpua, and Haunani-Kay Trask were invaluable resources. Additionally, I feel it would be inaccurate and remiss to not acknowledge the slave trade of Melanesians and Polynesians in the South Pacific during the sugar plantation era. To learn more about the history of "blackbirding," I suggest reading Gerald Horne's *The White Pacific: U.S. Imperialism and Black Slavery in the South Seas after the Civil War*, and to learn more about the African Americans who worked in plantation-era Hawai'i and their contribution to the labor unions in 1946, look into "Alabama Camps."

ACKNOWLEDGMENTS

So many people supported this book's journey, and I wouldn't have made it to the end without them.

To my agent, Jennifer March Soloway, as well as the wonderful team at Andrea Brown Literary Agency and Sophia, thank you for guiding my career and this book. Thank you, Jennifer, for seeing the potential in Lehua's story and me. Your vision and tireless care allowed this book to truly flourish. More than that, your support kept me going through my grief this year. I couldn't have done it without you.

I am deeply grateful to my editor, Tiffany Liao, for going to Kōpaʻa with me. Your patient feedback and insight helped shape this sprawling story into a terrifying garden that Horace Jacobs would be proud of.

Thank you as well to Havilah Sciabbarrasi, Elizabeth Stranahan, Clare Perret, Jamie Johnson, Rebecca Vitkus, Liz Dresner, Michelle Canoni, Frances Wren, Andrea Baird, Michael Caiati, Joey Ho, Erica Trotta, and the rest of the phenomenal team at Random House Children's Books for making my dreams (and readers' nightmares) come true. Thanks also to my film agent, Mary Pender, for believing in this book.

All of my thanks (and apologies) to my early champion and reader, Katherine Locke. When I told you what waited inside the persimmon orchard, you encouraged me to keep writing. Without you, I wouldn't have been brave enough.

Thank you, Cortney Radocaj, for taking a chance on me. This journey would not have been possible without your belief and guidance. Much appreciation and gratitude to my writing friends Melody Simpson, Dr. Manuia Heinrich, Claire Winn, Kealani Netane, and Shay Kauwe; early readers Chris Kaufman, Keanan Cantrell, and Carolyn McDonald; and my many college roommates and friends, who by unfortunate proximity were subjected to my raw drafts, for seeing me through the dreaming, scheming, and writing of this book and others.

Thanks to Jess Aragon, Rukman Ragas, Charlie, A.L. Goldfuss, Arumi, and the rest of the gang at Sci-Fi Writers Placeholder Name, for reading my diary. You kept me laughing through all of my whining.

All my love to Asian Author Alliance and my Pacific Islander family here in Los Angeles and elsewhere, including the Pacific Islanders in Publishing community, the Books for Maui team, the members of PEAK Pasifika—especially Dana Ledoux Miller for providing me with crucial wisdom and encouragement—and so many others for your friendship and community. I am also grateful to and inspired by my publishing peers and fellow authors—my Twisted Tale family, Rebecca Kuss, Britt Rubiano,

Heather Knowles, Kelly Austin, Karuna Riazi, Kat Cho, Kelsea Yu, Andrew Joseph White, Jamison Shea, and Sarah Kuhn—for allowing me to learn from you and grow alongside you this year.

Thank you to my friends for being there between deadlines, with an extra special shout-out to Jake and Kathryn Wyatt, my gluten heroes.

I want to thank my mom, my aunt Susan, my brothers, and my late grandma Joyce. I miss and love you every day, always. Thanks for believing in me.

To Melemahina, my writing assistant who can't read and naps while I work: Thank you for filling our office with toys and laughter—and for the love and joy you've brought into my life. You got me through this year.

Finally, thanks most of all to Jacob for his support on this journey. I'll always remember you getting on the boat with me.

ABOUT THE AUTHOR

Keala Kendall (kay-ah-luh) is the *New York Times* and *USA Today* bestselling author of *How Far I'll Go* and *Nobody Gets Left Behind* in Disney's A Twisted Tales series, and *That Which Feeds Us: A Hawaiian Gothic.* Hapa Native Hawaiian, she is a cofounder of Pacific Islanders in Publishing, and a past organizer of the Books for Maui charity auction.

Born in Honolulu, raised on Moloka'i, she now lives as part of the Native Hawaiian diaspora in Los Angeles.

kealakendall.com
@kealakendall